MURDER FOR A WORTHY CAUSE

Neal Sanders

The Hardington Press

Murder for a Worthy Cause is a work of fiction. While certain locales and organizations are rooted in fact, the people and events described are entirely the product of the author's imagination.

Cover illustration © Lynne Schulte, www.LynneSchulte.com, Georgetown, MA.

Also by Neal Sanders

Murder Imperfect (2010)
The Garden Club Gang (2011)
The Accidental Spy (2011)

Liz Phillips and Det. John Flynn mysteries:
A Murder in the Garden Club (2012)

For Dorothy Jasiecki

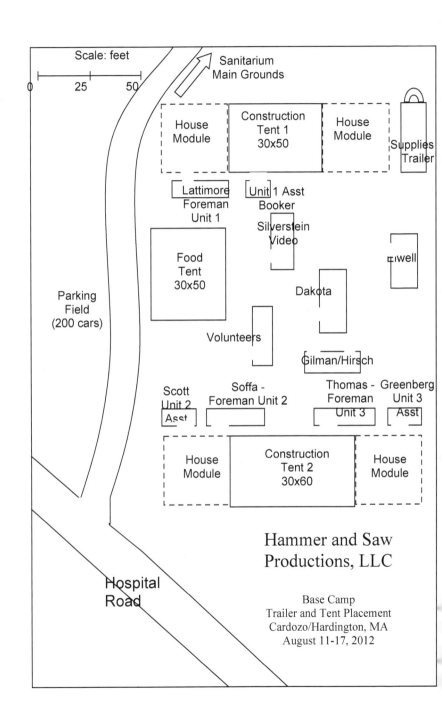

MURDER FOR A WORTHY CAUSE

1. Monday

Liz Phillips slammed her fist on the table, as much an act of frustration as to get the attention of the bland-faced man across from her, whose eyes had increasingly wandered toward the blinking, red LED of his phone.

"Do you have any idea of what 'Hardy to Zone 7' means?" she asked, pushing a four-page-long bill of lading across the table. "It means that these plants will thrive somewhere in North Carolina. It means that in Massachusetts, we'll plant them today and they'll look pretty for about a month, but they'll freeze and die this winter. A mild winter here is Zone 6. If you want things to live for a couple of years, you plant for a Zone 5."

Barry Zimmerman, the 26-year-old associate producer of *Ultimate House Makeover*, said nothing. He also appeared fearful that if he glanced at his phone again or even down at the papers that had been placed in front of him, the aggravated woman across from him, old enough to be his mother but with a demand for attention that rivaled his fifth grade teacher, would again slam her fist on the flimsy table. He had absolutely no knowledge of what she was talking about and had never heard of these 'plant zones' she was so angry about. He lived in Santa Monica in a houseplant-free apartment building.

"Let's look at it another way," Liz said, more softly, but keeping firm eye contact. "We're all here to give the Cardozo family hope. You've got five hundred people who are giving up a week of their lives to build a house for a family. Fifty of them are members of my garden club. Trees, shrubs and flowers are all part of that hope. *Living* trees and shrubs. What kind of hope are you giving them if the Cardozos walk out of their house next April and see that half the plants in their yard are dead?"

"But the plants were donated by our sponsor. The sponsor's experts picked them out," Zimmerman protested. "And the stuff is already on its way."

Liz glared at him. "Then you need to tell them they're sending the wrong 'stuff'. And tell them that their free 'stuff' is going to look pretty pathetic when the reporters come around for their follow-up story next spring."

It was a warm, humid August morning and the temperature inside the Winnebago where they sat was already uncomfortable. Who was this blonde dragon lady and why wouldn't she go away? Zimmerman looked quickly at his volunteer list, afraid of the slamming fist.

"Hardington Garden Club, right?"

Liz shook her head, incredulous that Zimmerman had no inkling of why this conversation was taking place.

"Are you saying you won't plant the stu… the bushes and trees?" he asked.

"I'm saying you have five days to correct your sponsor's mistake."

Zimmerman breathed a sigh of relief. Dragon Lady wasn't bailing on him. Like every volunteer group he had dealt with in the past year, she and her garden club biddies would do anything to get on camera. He forced a smile and turned on the sincerity, just as he had seen the senior producers do. "I think we can straighten this out before Friday. You just have your group here at…." He pulled a spreadsheet from the top of a pile. "Eight a.m. sharp on Friday. The sod will already be in place. You've got until three. That's when we start shooting the reveal. Can't disappoint the Credozas."

"Cardozo, Mr. Zimmerman," Liz said pointedly. "Their name is Cardozo."

Zimmerman looked at the vacant table next to his. Where was this Terhune guy, the volunteer coordinator? He was supposed to have been here before 7:30. Terhune had assured him last night that he would be in the office before the first volunteers arrived. To protect Zimmerman from people like this woman. Whoever she was.

Liz rose. Zimmerman instinctively did the same. "By the way," she asked. "Who is this landscaping sponsor?"

Zimmerman didn't have to look at any list for this one. "National Home Centers," he said proudly.

"And they're based in….?"

"Dallas, Texas," Zimmerman said promptly.

Liz nodded. "I'm sure they know all about New England landscaping."

"We'll make it right," Zimmerman said, using his most reassuring manner.

Liz said nothing. *Right. In two minutes you'll have forgotten this conversation ever took place. And in four days, you're going to say, 'gee, I asked them to fix it' and expect us to put in whatever shows up on the trucks. Which means I have four days to make it right.*

Once outside the motor home, Liz tried to relax. Inwardly, she still seethed at the condescension of the associate producer. *Associate producer,* her husband, David, had told her this morning. *That's the title these shows give out instead of 'junior woodchuck'. The guy you're meeting is a glorified gofer. Let him know that you know.* She had let him know. The question was whether it had done any good.

She looked around her at the sea of tents and trailers that had sprouted seemingly overnight. *Ultimate House Makeover* had come to Hardington. People in town had spoken of almost nothing else for weeks. Jenny and Mac Cardozo were going to get a new home, and on network television. Their application to the program had stressed the family's genuine need: an electrical fire had destroyed their modest home three months earlier, forcing them to live with Jenny's parents. But the true hardship was on the children, and especially on eleven-year-old Jackie, who had been diagnosed with leukemia just before the fire.

The producers of *Ultimate House Makeover* had come back with a challenge: if Hardington could supply the volunteer labor, the show would pay for a new home. It would all be done in a week. When the program's staff had come to town in July to sign up volunteers, a thousand people had crowded the high school gym to offer their time and skills – fully a tenth of the town's population.

As president of the garden club, Liz had gotten the call from Fred Terhune, the Hardington town selectman who had helped the Cardozos assemble their application and had been asked by the *Ultimate House Makeover* producer to coordinate the town's volunteer workers. "Could you get fifty able-bodied people – members, husbands, sons, daughters – all to come plant a yard in one day?" he had asked Liz.

Liz was initially dubious and had said so, but she made a few calls to club members and explained what was needed. The combination of an opportunity to do good and to be seen on a popular television show was overwhelming. She had called Terhune an hour later. "Fred, are you sure all you need is fifty?"

She had heard the audible sigh of relief on the other end of the telephone.

Now, all around her she could see the beginnings of what was to take place in the next five days. She was on the grounds of the old Hardington State Sanitarium, a Victorian relic of a Victorian idea. A century earlier, it had housed more than two thousand people. As the science of mental health progressed, the need for such facilities faded and its population dwindled. Closed for the last decade, its spacious lawns were a delight for walkers and families.

Over the weekend, three enormous tents had risen and nearly a dozen trailers had been set in a grassed area a few hundred yards from the main campus and its 150-year-old red sandstone buildings. Across the access road, a dozen cars were parked in a newly mown field. Flags and ropes indicated that, at full production, as many as 200 cars would fill the site.

There was as yet no sign of a house; it would be delivered in modules later this morning. The Cardozo's property – the old house and foundation had been razed Saturday and a new, pre-fabricated foundation dropped into place on Sunday – was a mile to the south of the staging area where Liz now stood. The modules would be prepped here at the sanitarium, then trucked to the foundation where they would be assembled on site.

There was already activity at this early hour. In one of the large tents less than 50 feet from where she stood, Liz could see three women setting out coffee and pastries. To her left and right in other tents, there was the whir of power saws as volunteers and production staff began preparing for work. Liz watched as one of the women lifted the lid of what appeared to be a large wooden crate or footlocker.

The woman immediately dropped the lid and screamed. And continued to scream, covering her face.

Liz broke into a run and quickly covered the distance. She was there in time to see a second woman whom she vaguely knew from the town's tennis courts lift the cover of what was indeed a large wooden crate labeled 'supplies'.

Inside the crate was a body that Liz recognized as Fred Terhune. His shirt was red with dried blood that appeared to emanate from a head wound. There was no question but that he was dead. The woman quickly dropped the lid.

The first woman's scream had brought half a dozen people to the tent. Only Liz, who had been the first to arrive, and the three women, had seen the body. The first woman was still sobbing, the other two appeared too shaken to move. One man, wearing a black tee shirt with an *Ultimate House Makeover* logo, started to lift the crate's lid.

Liz instinctively said, "No, don't do that. And I think we want to stay well away from this area. There's a body inside the crate –

I'm pretty sure it's Fred Terhune." At the mention of the name, the volunteers collectively gave a little gasp. "It looks like someone hit him on the head. There's a lot of blood. I think we need to call '911' and not disturb the scene."

Three cell phones came out of three purses and she heard the 'beep-boop-boop' of 911 being called. Liz marveled at her own coolness and her ability to effectively stop everyone from looking inside the crate. Then she realized that she, too, ought to be making a call. One that she knew from memory. She pulled her cell phone from her purse and punched a ten-digit number. It was answered immediately.

"John Flynn."

"John, this is Liz Phillips. In about thirty seconds, all hell is going to break loose in the police department. I'm up at the staging area for the TV show they're shooting. We've just found Fred Terhune's body in an equipment chest. It's pretty bloody."

"You're at the sanitarium?"

"The big tent closest to the volunteer parking area."

"Give me five minutes. And try to keep people away from the area."

* * * * *

Detective John Flynn of the Hardington Police Department had arrived that morning, as was his custom in the three months since he had joined the department, at seven o'clock. He had already gone through the weekend reports, looking for anything that required the services of a detective. Except for a lone domestic dispute at Washington Gardens, the low-income project in the center of town, every report had been associated with the *Ultimate House Makeover* program. More than a thousand people had been on hand to watch the Cardozo house get razed on Saturday, and their cars had jammed Hospital Road and every side street for half a mile, prompting dozens of homeowner complaints. More than just an opportunity to see a house get torn down – something that had long since lost its novelty in Hardington – it was a chance to perhaps be seen in the background as film crews recorded the event.

And more than a few of the onlookers were there to catch a glimpse of Whit Dakota in person. Whit Dakota, the carpenter turned star. Flynn vaguely remembered Dakota's antics from his stint as handyman on one of the cable quick-and-cheap-home-renovation shows. Dakota had come up in the world, either because of his ham-it-up carpentry advice or because women apparently found him irresistible. Flynn suspected the latter, noting from the police log that five Hardington residents – none over the age of twenty and all female -- had received warnings after they attempted to cross the barricades separating the crowd from the house and Whit Dakota.

The crowds had returned on Sunday when the foundation for the new home was put into place, except that now the reports showed that Hospital Road had been closed to all except local traffic. This had resulted in complaints from residents of two other neighborhoods about being parked in, and a rash of twisted ankles as everyone walked to the Cardozo home site.

There had been a party Sunday evening for the volunteers in one of the big tents set up at the sanitarium grounds. Liquor had apparently been served. There were three alcohol-induced fender-benders in the hospital parking lot and two more DUI arrests on Hospital Road. A fifteen-year-old girl last seen at the party had been reported missing, though she apparently returned home before 1 a.m.

This is what I have to look forward to this week, thought Flynn, glumly. *Traffic duty*.

Which is when his cell phone rang. And Liz Phillips said there was a body up at the sanitarium. She didn't say 'a murder' but she did say the body has been found in an equipment chest and that there was a lot of blood. The 'Terhune' name he had written down meant nothing to him.

Liz Phillips. My God, he thought.

Together, two months earlier, they had solved Hardington's first homicide in more than fifteen years. The murder of a woman who had been pushed down her basement stairs. A murder that, within five days, had triggered two more deaths. A case he knew he could not have solved on his own because he did not yet know the community, and because one detective never has the critical benefit of a second point of view.

Liz Phillips. Mid-fifties. His age, he now knew. Very attractive. The kind of woman who made you wish your life could have gone differently. He pushed the thought out of his mind. The dispatcher was yelling for him.

"Old state sanitarium. Somebody's found a body in a chest…"

"I just got the call," Flynn said. "Get two squad cars up there and tell them to start sealing off the area. Call Chief Harding at home and have him call me on my cell. I think he's going to want to know about this one."

* * * * *

Five minutes, he had said. Liz watched the crowd growing as each new arrival gravitated toward the tent. "Please stay away from the tent," she implored. "This is a crime scene."

It was then that Liz heard the sirens and saw the flashing lights of two police cars, preceded by a third car that she knew belonged to John Flynn.

John Flynn. In hindsight, those five days had been exhilarating. Afterward, she had stayed carefully and consciously away from the limelight as Hardington briefly was in the news spotlight. She declined all requests for interviews, though her name appeared in a number of articles about the murder and her photo – apparently supplied by someone in the garden club – ran in the weekly Hardington *Chronicle*. People in town had looked at her differently ever since. As people talked, which they inevitably did, her role in solving the murder became generally known and then that role grew. The cashiers at the supermarket greeted her by name; the man at the dry cleaners inexplicably gave her a handful of half-off coupons. Attendance at the July garden club meeting had doubled.

John Flynn. With the kind face but the sad eyes. And a keeper of secrets about himself she had not divined in their time together. Her efforts to draw him out had been rebuffed, politely and even apologetically, but rebuffed nonetheless. She had thought many times since of calling him, inviting him to lunch. But each time she had backed away.

And now, here he was, striding toward her, a broad smile on his face.

"Seems like old times," he said. And held out his hand.

Liz took his hand, and put her other hand over his.

Flynn quickly pulled his hand away and barked orders to the two police officers. Liz felt her face redden with embarrassment. "Let's get tape around this entire area," Flynn said to two policemen standing nearby. His arm traced a wide circle around the tent.

"So tell me what happened." His attention was back to Liz.

"I was here for a meeting with one of the associate producers at eight o'clock. About ten minutes later, I came out of that trailer and happened to see these three women setting up coffee and pastries." Liz pointed to the Volunteer trailer and motioned with her chin at the women, who were standing together. "One of them lifted the lid of this supply chest, saw the body, and started screaming. I ran over as fast as I could and was here when another woman lifted the lid. No one has touched it since, and I've tried to keep everyone away from the area."

"You said a name – Terhune."

"Fred Terhune. He's the person who is coordinating all of the volunteers."

"You're certain it's Terhune?" Flynn asked. "Do you need to take a second look? I ask because I'm going to pass that name onto Chief Harding."

"I'm certain it's him," Liz said. "I don't know him well but we've met on a dozen occasions. He's a town selectman." Liz was surprised by how calm she was. Two of the three women who had found the body were still crying.

"Town selectman – is that like a town council?"

"Close enough. I'll explain later. It looks like he was hit on the side of his head. There's a lot of blood."

"Head wounds bleed a lot. Did you check for a pulse?"

"I know a dead person when I see one."

Flynn nodded. "Liz, stay close for a while. And thanks for keeping the crowd away from the tent." He walked over to the chest, took latex gloves out of his pocket and put them on. He lifted the lid. Liz saw him spend several minutes examining the body. Then he pulled out his cell phone and made a call.

* * * * *

Several things were immediately apparent to Flynn. First, Fred Terhune had died elsewhere and been placed in the trunk. So, somewhere else in the area, there was a lot of blood. Second, Fred Terhune had been hit with an object, probably metallic given the extent of the damage to the skull. Judging from the angle, the assailant was almost certainly right handed. Death had not been instantaneous. Whoever did this had allowed Terhune to die. This ruled out an accident. Either the object was fairly heavy or it had been swung by someone with a fair degree of strength. That someone had then dragged Terhune's body to this spot and had gotten it into the chest. That someone would likely have blood on their clothes. There was a smear of blood on the side of the chest.

Looking beyond the tent, Flynn thought he discerned a path where the grass was bent as it would be if a body was dragged. The faint bent-grass path ended at the yellow tape put up by the two policemen, where a crowd now numbering more than fifty -- including a woman with a shoulder-mounted video camera – followed his every move. If the body had been dragged to the tent and if this bent grass was the trail used by the killer, then he or she had come from the little village of trailers and other tents, not from the area beyond the staging grounds.

He took out his phone and called the dispatcher. "First, I've got a tentative ID on the body as Fred Terhune. He's a town selectman. Pass that along to Chief Harding as soon as possible. Second, I need another policeman up here. Third, call the Norfolk County medical examiner's office and tell them I have a homicide. I want an ME on site within the hour. Tell them if they aren't here by nine thirty, I'm calling for support from Boston. And fourth, as much as I hate to, call the state police, fill them in and make certain they get a fingerprint and crime scene team out here."

Flynn called over the two Hardington officers. He showed them the possible trail. "See if you can trace it back. It isn't likely with all of these people, but it's worth a try. And walk every inch of the area. Somewhere around here is a pool of blood from where this guy was bludgeoned; I'd like to find it."

Flynn walked over to the three women. "This must have been a terrible shock for you." Two of the women were still wet-eyed and were being comforted by the third. Flynn brought chairs from the tent for them to sit. "What time did you get here?"

The oldest of them, easily 75 years old but clear-eyed and erect, answered for the group. "We drove together because of the road restrictions. We got here right at eight."

"What did you do when you got here?" Flynn asked.

"We started setting up for coffee and refreshments. The tables were already here, the coffee pot was in a box. We brought about five cans of coffee and enough pastries to feed a hundred people. But we didn't have the cups or the napkins. Geraldine saw the chest, which was marked 'supplies', and thought they might be in there. She lifted the lid and started screaming and pointing. Alice asked what was wrong and Geraldine said someone was in there. So Alice lifted the lid and we all saw it was Fred Terhune. That's when Liz Phillips came running. She saw Fred, too."

"You're parked in the parking lot?"

"That's Geraldine's car right there." The woman pointed at a minivan just across the roadway in a gravel parking area. He saw the familiar shape of Liz's green Jag next to it.

"Were there other cars in the parking lot?"

"Ten or twelve."

"Could you identify them?"

The woman nodded. "I'm pretty sure."

"Did any of you walk in the grass out here?" He motioned to the area between the tent and the closest of the trailers.

"I don't think so. We had everything we needed in the tent. Except the cups and the napkins."

Flynn asked the woman to write down her companions' names and addresses. "I'd like you to walk through the parking lot with one of my police officers and identify the cars that were already here. After that, I'll try not to keep you; I imagine this isn't a place you want to hang around."

The woman looked at him with surprise on her face. "We're not leaving. I mean, it's awful with Fred, but we've got work to do."

Flynn nodded. The lure of celebrity. Point a camera at someone and they wanted to perform.

Point a camera! Flynn walked over to the woman with the video camera. "Who's in charge here?"

The woman clicked off the camera. "Don Elwell. He's the executive producer."

"Is he here?"

"That's him in the black shirt." She pointed at a tall, heavy-set balding man.

He asked the woman with the camera, "Were you filming at the party last night?"

"Two cameras. Mostly for B-roll and motivation."

"Bee roll?"

"Background. The more you shoot, the more excited the volunteers get and the harder they work. *We* know that the only part of it we're going to use is about thirty seconds of Whit's 'let's do it for the family' speech, and a few seconds of the crowd applauding, but *they* don't. They assume if we shoot it, there's a good chance we'll use it. Those are the instructions: Keep the cameras rolling; it's what motivates the volunteers."

"I'll want to see your footage from last night."

"You clear it with Don and you can take home a copy with a bow on it."

Flynn walked over and introduced himself to Don Elwell. Elwell looked to be around sixty, with leathery, well-tanned skin. "We had a murder here last night," Flynn said. "A town official who is also the person who was your volunteer coordinator. Fred Terhune. He was bludgeoned and dumped in one of your storage bins."

Elwell shook his head. "I barely met him. I don't do the parties."

A little too quick for an answer. And a little too comprehensive. What are you hiding, Mr. Elwell? "I'm going to need someone from your staff to show me around and to run interference."

Elwell grimaced. "We'll do all we can, but you can't slow down our schedule; we've got to build a house by Friday at 3 p.m."

"And I've got to find a murderer, Mr. Elwell. You give me the cooperation I need and I'll do everything in my power to stay out of your way and not hinder your schedule. Can we agree on that?"

Elwell looked directly at Flynn. "You'll get cooperation. And if you hinder our production by even an hour, you'll regret it. Do we understand each other?"

Flynn ignored the threat. "I need two things immediately: the person in charge of that storage chest, and a place to look at the video you shot last night at the party."

Elwell nodded. He took a flip phone from his pocket, pushed a button, and spoke into it. "Sam, get over to the food tent right now. And tell Joel I want last night's video set up in the screening trailer in ten minutes." A voice at the other end of the phone said, "Consider it done."

"Did you have security here last night?" Flynn asked.

Elwell again nodded. "We have a million bucks worth of tools, cameras and equipment on site. Of course we have security. I'll have Sam – that's Sam Hirsch -- get you their name."

Flynn watched a third Hardington police car pull into the parking lot, and saw the familiar face of Eddie Frankel, the young African-American cop who had been instrumental in carrying out the legwork of the Sally Kahn murder.

Flynn motioned over Frankel. "I need a couple of things," Flynn said. "In about an hour the state police are going to come in and tell us to go back to handing out parking tickets. We've got to work fast. First, there are three elderly ladies over there who found the body. They said there were about a dozen cars in the parking lot when they got here at eight. Make sure they agree on the cars, and then run the names of the owners. I want to know who was here before 8 a.m."

"Second, a guy named Sam Hirsch from the TV show is going to be here in a few minutes. I want to know everything about how that chest got there; whether it belonged there; how it came to have enough room in it to contain a body; who set out the coffee equipment and the tables. I want a timeline of how everything in that tent came together."

"Third, there was some kind of security patrol here last night. Hirsch is going to give you their name. Get hold of them and let them know they'll be hearing from me this morning. Fourth, someone from the Norfolk ME's office is coming out here. I'm going to be looking at videotape. Get the ME started and then give me a call. When the clowns from the state police show up, be polite but don't tell them where I am. Make sure they get prints for the two ladies who touched the equipment chest, and try not to let their tech crews destroy too much evidence."

"Finally, get a list of the TV show people and find out when each of them left last night. Someone should have seen Terhune after the party."

Frankel grinned. "Good morning, Detective, and it's nice to see you, too. I'll give you a full report." He was already walking briskly toward the group of elderly women.

Flynn turned back to Elwell. "Can you show me the screening trailer?"

"I'll show you the whole layout," Elwell said, and started walking into the group of motor homes. "This is our fifth season and we've pretty much got it down to a science. We do one house or major renovation in a week and twenty-two projects in a year. Hardington is our eighth project of the season. We were in Rochester last week, we'll be in New Jersey next week, then we break for two weeks and everyone goes home."

"How many of you are there?" Flynn asked.

"The road staff is fifteen," Elwell said, ticking off people on his fingers. "Three associate producers, three construction supervisors and three assistants, two camera people, a sound engineer, video engineer, Whit, and myself. We travel with eleven specially outfitted Winnebagos with contract drivers plus an equipment trailer. The tents, we arrange for ahead of time. We flew in Friday night, the tents were already up; the Winnebagos were here when we came back from the demolition. We spent Saturday demolishing the old structure and Sunday putting in the foundation for the new one. The camp stays together until Friday afternoon when it goes to the next location. We shoot the 'reveal' Friday afternoon..."

"What's the 'reveal'," Flynn asked.

"The grand finale," Elwell said. "When we show the people their new home. It's the highlight of the show. Viewership goes up by as much as twenty percent during those last ten minutes. The DVR stats show people look at that segment four times on average."

"Does the staff live in the trailers?"

"Nobody lives in the Winnebagos," Elwell said. "They're outfitted with beds but they're really designed as mobile offices and editing suites. Later on in the week – when we're going eighteen hours a day – some of the staff will likely stay here just because it means an extra half hour of sleep. Each producer and construction supervisor has a different area of responsibility; the camera, sound, and video people share the production trailer, which is where we're headed."

They stopped in front of a long Winnebago. Elwell walked up the three steps and opened the door without knocking. Inside, the trailer was dark and cool, the air was dry. One wall contained racks of electronic equipment. A twenty-something man in tee shirt and jeans hurriedly stood up.

"Detective, this is Joel," Elwell said. "Joel will walk you through last night's video and copy out any segments you want to take with you. Joel, give the detective whatever he needs." And with that, Elwell left.

"My name is John Flynn," Flynn said to Joel, offering his hand. "I take it your boss isn't keen on remembering names. But he is right, and I'm with the Hardington police. Do you know why I'm here?"

Joel took Flynn's hand. "Joel Silverstein. I get sound and a live feed from any active camera we're using. Actually, I got some good close-ups of the body if you need them. Peggy got a good position to be able to see inside the equipment chest."

"Do you have last night's video?"

"I got three hours each from two cameras. You're looking for the dead guy?"

Flynn nodded.

"We keep one camera pretty much on Whit and whoever he's interacting with. That's the duty Peggy draws – she's the girl you talked to out at the tent. It's kind of an ego thing for Whit, and keeping Whit happy is high priority. The other camera circulates among the volunteers. If your guy talks to Whit, we'll switch to that stream; otherwise, we're probably best off staying with Camera 2."

Joel tapped buttons on a console. A date and time stamp ran in one corner. "We started shooting at seven o'clock. We were just getting to critical mass in the tent, maybe two hundred people."

The monitor was a flat-panel one, probably a forty-inch screen, Flynn thought, and the resolution was superb.

Joel saw Flynn's reaction to the screen. "This isn't videotape," Joel explained with obvious pride. "We're shooting digital video in high resolution. Everything goes directly into the computer's hard drive for faster editing. Everything is hi-def now, and this is our second generation of gear, maybe six months old at most. Don – Mr. Elwell – sprang for the equipment. Hardington is episode 96 of *UHM*. By the end of this season we'll be past the magic number – one hundred episodes – needed to sell the show into syndication. Syndication is where the real money is, and having everything in high-def should make the sale a lot easier."

The video opened with a long shot of the tent, seemingly already filled with people. Except for the small production team in their black tee shirts, the two hundred people were Hardington residents, dressed for a casual party on a warm summer evening. The crowd was a representative cross-section of Hardington as Flynn had come to know the town. Mostly Caucasian, a handful of African-American faces and perhaps ten percent Asian ones. Flynn saw only one couple he would identify as Hispanic.

It was a catered party, with a bar and a long table heaped with trays of food. Waiters and waitresses circulated with trays of drinks. There was sound: music, laughter, and the din of two hundred voices.

The camera operator moved slowly into the tent, the picture remaining smooth.

"Do they teach camera operators how to walk without jiggling the picture?" Flynn asked.

"I said this is digital video, and it's also being shot with a state-of-the-art smart camera. It's all computer-stabilized. No bumps, no jiggles. Let's find your guy."

The camera was panning the crowd. "There!" Flynn said, and pointed to the screen.

Joel froze the screen and zoomed in so that Terhune filled the frame. The picture was still crystal clear. "That him?"

Flynn nodded.

"Let's paint him." Joel touched a control on the console and pulled back slightly on the image. Using a touchpad, he highlighted Terhune in red. Another control filled in Terhune's outline so that there was a red cutout of a man amid the crowd. "Now comes the magic." Joel touched a few keys on the console. The video started again, but now, Terhune stayed in the center of the frame.

"I'm guessing the camera operator didn't plan this in advance."

"The camera is smarter that the eye," Joel explained. "You look at me, and your brain focuses on me, even though your eye takes in far more. Your brain throws away the information you don't need. Not so the camera. If the aperture is 150 degrees, the camera records everything in that zone. As long as your guy is within 75 degrees of where the camera is pointed, we'll stay with him."

"And if he's outside of that frame?"

"Then the video skips ahead to when he comes back into view."

"Then let's look at the party from Mr. Terhune's view."

The first hour was dull and Flynn asked Joel to fast-forward the footage. As an elected town official and the volunteer coordinator, Terhune knew virtually everyone in the room, and he was continually being greeted. For the most part, there were smiles all around. After a while, Flynn could read Terhune's body language. There were people he was genuinely pleased to see and others about whom he was neutral. A few were clearly not friends, though Terhune kept smiling through these encounters.

There were especially warm greetings from several women and, from the overt smiles and touching, Flynn concluded that Terhune was not married. Several women took his hand in both of theirs, just as Liz had done when they met earlier. Flynn winced at how he had reacted, pulling his hand away quickly to avoid the contact. Why had he done that?

And then another woman approached, and Terhune's face said this was an encounter he would rather avoid. He could only see the woman's back. She was wearing a strapless sundress, very tasteful and, Flynn assumed, very expensive. Terhune tried smiling, tried getting the attention of other people to defuse this encounter. But the woman was guiding Terhune toward the edge of the tent and into the darkness beyond.

"Slow it to normal speed," Flynn said.

The encounter took place about fifteen feet outside of the tent and the video – bless the technology – stayed with them. By now, Terhune and the woman had turned so that Flynn could see her in profile. Age, maybe late thirties. Very attractive and very well built. She put her arms around Flynn's neck and pulled him to her to kiss him... and then kneed him in the groin.

"Ow, that smarts," Joel said.

Terhune doubled over and the woman slapped him. Hard. She then turned and walked back into the tent as though nothing had happened. The time stamp showed 8:17 p.m.

"Can you mark that footage?"

"I already did."

The camera stayed with Terhune, who remained bent over. But then the camera swept elsewhere and the time stamp jumped to 8:33. Terhune was walking slowly and painfully to the bar where he asked for a drink. Whiskey, by the look. To that time, he had stayed with the white wine.

Other people continued to greet him, and slowly Terhune recovered. By nine o'clock, he was back to being himself, with only an occasional wince to give away the pain he had endured earlier.

To this time, the sound had been a jumble of noises. At 9:03, the crowd went silent as someone tapped on a microphone. Terhune sipped his whiskey and looked attentively in the same direction as everyone else.

It was the voice of Whit Dakota, and this was his motivational speech. "Excuse me, everyone. Hi, I'm Whit Dakota." There was applause and Terhune clapped politely. "I hope everyone is enjoying themselves. The drinks are on me tonight because, starting tomorrow, I'm going to ask you to work very hard for a worthy cause. Five days from right now, Jennie and Mac Cardozo are going to see their new house. And Jackie and her brother Sam are going to have a great yard to play in. And we're going to make that happen!" More applause. "In case you're wondering about the Cardozos, we've sent them to Florida for the week. We did a video conference with them yesterday afternoon when we knocked down what was left of their old house. I've got to tell you, Mac looked a little nervous. He thinks he's going to be spending the winter in a tent." Polite laughter. "But tomorrow morning, you're going to see the parts of that new house right where we're standing. And in five days – thanks to you – the Cardozo family is going to have a brand new home." Lots of applause. "I want to introduce the construction team to you and let them explain what you're going to be doing…"

"You can fast-forward through this," Flynn said. Joel dutifully tapped a key and the time clock began to scroll quickly. Fifteen minutes later, the party resumed. Joel tapped a key and the video went back to normal speed. The crowd was starting to thin out, though Terhune seemed in no hurry to leave.

At 9:35, two Hispanic appearing men approached Terhune. The look on Terhune's face was one of apprehension coupled with concern. Clearly, he knew these men, had not expected them to be here, and he made no attempt to hide his displeasure at seeing them.

"This looks interesting," Flynn said. "Mark it and slow it down." Joel nodded.

The three men began an animated discussion.

"Can you narrow the audio?"

"There are still a hundred people in the tent. Sorry."

"Pull back and let's see if anyone would have been close enough to eavesdrop," Flynn asked. The scene cut to a longer shot. Several people were within hearing range, though none appeared to be attempting to overhear the conversation.

The men's appearance stood out for its inconsistency with the party's other attendees. They were Hispanics in jeans and tee shirts in a tent full of people whom only a handful were non-white and everyone was well-dressed. The men appeared to be in their thirties, were heavily muscled and towered over Terhune, whom Flynn judged to be about five-seven. One of the men held up two fingers. The look on Terhune's face passed beyond concern to fright. After about three minutes, the conversation seemed to conclude. The man who had held up the two fingers shoved Terhune as they departed.

"Wow," Joel said. "That was serious."

"Are they part of the television program?"

Joel shook his head. "Never seen them before."

Terhune was alone now. He went for another drink and looked at his watch. At 9:50, something seemed to catch his attention on the other side of the tent. Terhune made no move to go to that side of the tent, but there was a look of worry on his face that seemed to grow with each minute.

"Show me the other camera starting at 9:50."

Joel tapped keys on the console and shook his head. "Camera 1 stopped at 9:45. Whit usually gives Peggy a high sign a little while after the speech."

"Then show me the last few minutes of what you have on that camera."

More tapping of keys. The crowd was dense at that end of the tent. Whit Dakota was surrounded by a crowd of mostly young women and he was clowning around for them, an actor with an appreciative audience. Flynn scanned the crowd: the woman in the sundress was at that end of the tent, chatting amiably with a couple. Could that have been what drew Terhune's attention? Then Whit Dakota motioned to the camera and drew a finger across his throat. The video ended.

Flynn thought for several moments. For a detective, this was a gold mine. *These are the last hours of a man's life, captured for posterity. In all likelihood, someone in that tent is a murderer.*

"Give me a print of Terhune, the woman in the sundress, the two men in jeans, and the crowd closest to Terhune when the men were threatening him."

"Piece of cake." Keys were tapped and a printer hummed. Thirty seconds later, Joel handed Flynn the prints. "Good luck, Detective."

2.

Flynn had told Liz to stay close, and she had no difficulty staying busy. A stream of volunteers wanted to know what had happened and she provided a concise explanation. She watched what she assumed was the medical examiner arrive and begin working with the body.

She felt a tap at her shoulder. It was Barry Zimmerman.

"I think I was rude to you earlier," he said, a note of contrition in his voice.

"Rude is a good starting point as a description."

"Well, I want to apologize for my behavior. You must have known Fred Terhune pretty well."

In fact, Liz thought, she had hardly known Fred at all. Their paths crossed perhaps a dozen times a year, always on town business and never socially. She could not say if he was married, had children, or where in town he lived.

"Mrs. Phillips, I couldn't help but notice that everyone here seems to know you."

Oh, now he remembers my name, she thought.

"It's a small town. This isn't Boston... or Los Angeles," Liz said.

"Well, what I mean is..." Zimmerman was looking at the ground. "...with Fred dead and everything... I need – no, the Cardozos need – someone to pick up where he left off."

"You want me to be the new volunteer coordinator?"

"Well, yeah."

"After you blew me off an hour ago with a 'don't you worry your little brainless head' routine?"

"I said I was sorry."

"How sorry are you?"

"Sorry enough to beg," Zimmerman said. "And to let you write your own ticket on whatever you want to plant."

Liz considered. The kid was pleading. "What do I have to do?"

"All you have to do is know the volunteers. That's all. I get a message that says I need 'construction crew one' at the Unit 3 site. You either call or go find the leader of construction crew one. You tell them where they need to be. It's easy, honest."

"I need Wednesday morning off for a garden club meeting."

"I can work around that," Zimmerman said.

"You must be desperate."

"When could you start?"

"Let's go back to your office and talk about it," Liz said.

An hour later, Liz was deeply into construction schedules and the choreography required to move blocks of people from place to place. Fred Terhune had, in fact, done all of the difficult work. An *Ultimate House Makeover*-designed flow chart diagrammed what activities were planned in two-hour blocks, day by day. That chart ran eight pages. To the document, Terhune had annotated names of volunteer leaders.

A four-page spreadsheet contained names, addresses, home and cell phone numbers for more than five hundred volunteers with specific skills ranging from carpentry to roofing. The goal was that volunteers never arrived until they were needed and that, once they arrived on site, those volunteers were kept busy.

Barry Zimmerman's cell phone chirped. Each *Ultimate House Makeover* staff member carried a walkie-talkie type phone that allowed one-button access to each other. "Trailer one pulling in," was the lone communication.

"That was the lead construction supervisor," he said. "The trailer with the first house module just pulled into the parking lot. Now, we need to get Team 1 in place at Tent 1. You have the team list and the team leader. Give them a call and tell them where to be."

Liz made the call. The leader of Team 1 picked up his cell phone on the first ring. "We're here and we're watching it," he said. Five more trailers bearing house modules appeared over the next thirty minutes. Each time, the volunteer team was already in place. Liz's call was superfluous.

"Barry, this is too easy," Liz said.

"There may be a few snags later on," Zimmerman said. "But you can handle them."

Liz flipped through the spreadsheet again, looking for those prospective snags. Her eye fell to a line of small type at the bottom of the first page:

FT-UHM Volunteer List Rev. 8/13/12 12:23 a.m.

She looked again; it was today's date.

She walked over to Barry Zimmerman's desk holding the spreadsheet. "Did you create this document?"

He glanced at it. "No, it was Fred's. He started working on it a couple of weeks before we got here. He was still revising it yesterday."

"Do you have a copy of it?"

Zimmerman pushed a few papers on his desk and found a copy. "Here's mine."

Liz looked at the same line of type. *Rev. 8/12/12 6:45 p.m.* She pointed to the line. "What does this mean to you?"

He squinted at the line. "It shows the time and date of the last revision of the document. He saved and printed it at 6:45 Sunday evening."

"So, if I have one dated early this morning, it means Fred was working on the document after midnight?"

"Or someone using his computer worked on it," he said.

Liz looked around the trailer. There was a silver laptop off in one corner, partially visible inside a canvas carrying bag, standing on edge. Clipped to it was a cell phone. "Is that his?" Liz asked.

Zimmerman nodded.

Liz took out her cell phone and called Flynn.

"Do you have a time of death yet for Fred Terhune?" she asked.

"I'm with the medical examiner right now. We're discussing it. Come on over. I've got some photos to show you."

* * * * *

Viewing the video of the party had taken under two hours and Flynn had a good feeling. He could see Terhune's movements until just before 10 p.m. and had viable suspects for the murder. Except for domestic disturbances, investigations seldom came with this much clarity so early on.

The two policemen who had been sent to look for the trail of Terhune's body being dragged through the grass found no visible track. To their credit, they had searched the site looking for blood, but found nothing. As soon as the state police contingent showed up, though, the two Hardington policemen had been relegated to keeping people out of an area a hundred feet around the volunteer tent.

Eddie Frankel's work had been brisk and professional. By the time Flynn returned from the video trailer, Frankel had found the names of the owners of eleven cars that were in the parking lot before 8 a.m., including Terhune's eight-year-old SUV. He had improvised a curtained area so that the ME could work with a degree of privacy. The state police had sent a two-man evidence team, already departed, that had dusted for fingerprints and made a cursory look for other physical evidence. It had apparently not occurred to them that there might be video footage of the previous evening.

Frankel, on the other hand, had everything that could be learned about the chest, having badgered two associate producers and a construction supervisor. He had constructed a timeline of when each staff member had departed the previous evening.

Frankel held out a clipboard. "Before I forget, here's a list of the contents of Terhune's pockets. Basically, it was wallet, keys, and change. The staties dusted for prints, bagged it, and took it all away. The billfold had a few bucks in it and there was a full complement of credit cards. Obviously, this isn't a robbery gone bad."

"Robbers don't usually stuff their victims inside chests. What about the chest?" Flynn asked.

"The tent is a rental job," Frankel said. "They all went up Saturday morning and will stay up until this coming Friday. Most of the production company rolled in late Friday but Sam Hirsch – he's one of the assistant producers – came out a day earlier to make certain everything was as ordered, which it was. The equipment chest came with the tent. It held ropes, pulleys, stakes; that sort of thing. Hirsch saw the tents going up and watched the chests get unloaded. When the ME took Terhune's body out of the chest, we found a couple of lengths of nylon rope; apparently left over from the tent rigging."

"The tent rental people don't take their supply chests back with them after they set up?"

"Hirsch said that most rental companies want to keep everything together. As long as it's out of the way, it's not a problem. There's a similar chest with each of the tents."

"But this chest was left in the tent. That's hardly 'out of the way'."

"This is the first morning that the food tent has any business," Frankel said. "Hirsch told me that someone would have moved it this morning as soon as anyone noticed it was in the way. If whoever did this knew what the chest was for, then they only bought themselves until about nine o'clock, which is when either one of the associate producers or a volunteer would have moved it. The ladies just opened the chest an hour earlier than would have happened otherwise. There was no way that chest was going to remained closed."

"And the coffee pot, table, and chairs?" Flynn asked.

"All by the numbers; all rentals. The coffee pots and tables all got set up last night after the party for this morning. All this would have been here by ten o'clock last night."

"Eddie, from your perspective, why put Terhune in the supply chest at all? Why not just leave him where he fell?"

Frankel pondered the question for a moment. "I can think of a couple of reasons. First, whoever killed him perhaps didn't know the chest was going to be moved first thing this morning. They might have thought they were buying themselves a day or two. Or, maybe Terhune was killed in a very inconvenient place and, if it hadn't been hidden, the body would have been found last night."

"What did you hear about the security patrol?"

"Hirsch hired them and gave them their instructions," Frankel said. He pointed to a spot beyond the video production trailer. "Over on the other side of that trailer is a 40-foot tractor-trailer with the *Ultimate House Makeover* logo on it."

"I saw the trailer on my tour," Flynn said. "Don Elwell pointed it out to me."

Frankel continued. "That's where the security patrol car was parked. The tractor-trailer is where they keep their tools, and that's mostly what the security patrol kept an eye on; that and the gear in the video trailer. Someone was always in the car. One guard did an hourly round of all the tents and trailers, and had instructions to call if they found anything or anyone."

Frankel continued. "Hirsch said he didn't get any calls last night from the guards. He also said that everybody is staying at the Hilton over in Cavendish, at least for the first night or two. Later in the week, when they're getting to crunch time on construction or when they're editing, there could be a dozen or more people staying here, and Hirsch says everyone is quick to stop anyone who doesn't belong."

"So, if Terhune were murdered on a Wednesday night, we'd have a dozen witnesses and someone would have stopped it," Flynn said. "But last night it was just Terhune, his assailant, and two guards whose main job was to keep someone from stealing power saws. That's just great."

Flynn showed Frankel the photo of the woman in the sundress and the two men who had threatened Terhune. "Any of these people look familiar?"

Frankel studied the photos. "The woman is local. I've seen her around town a lot. Drives a big Lexus. The men aren't familiar. I assume they're suspects?"

"The woman did a very unfriendly thing to Terhune. He also had words with these two guys. They might well have waited around for him."

They were interrupted by the medical examiner, an Indian woman in her late fifties.

"I'm going to take the body back to Norwood for an autopsy, but I thought you gentlemen might like a quick preview," she said. She then looked closely at Flynn. "You're the guy who thinks Norfolk County isn't good enough for you. Flynn, right? You had the Boston ME do the work on that woman who got murdered here in June?"

"I was new," Flynn said. "I worked with who I knew. The end-around wasn't of you; it was of the state police."

"Well, you didn't make any friends in Dedham, either. We do fine work."

"I trust you're going to prove it, Doctor...."

"Sajahada. Minal Sajahada. Let me tell you what I know so far." She led them into the cordoned-off area. "Mr. Terhune was hit from behind. The angle suggests the person wasn't overly tall and was right-handed. I don't see any splinters of wood or glass, so the weapon was metallic, probably with some kind of a round rim."

"Like a bar bell?"

"Not a bad thought, though I think it would be difficult to hold a bar bell as a weapon and do this kind of damage. No, think in terms of a heavy flashlight. The killer had to be able to grip it in his hand and swing it. As to the hit, it was one blow and fairly lucky – for the killer. It cracked the skull; death was the result of internal bleeding and external blood loss."

"Time of death?"

"Before 1 a.m. After midnight."

"And he was dragged here?"

"There is grass and dirt on the back of his shoes consistent with being dragged. Also some on the back of his pants. Whoever dragged him dropped him once or twice."

"Meaning the person who dragged him might not have been especially strong?"

"Or got distracted," Sajahada said.

"Any indication of a struggle beforehand?" Flynn asked.

"If you mean somebody else's blood or something under his nails, I'll check when I can do a more thorough examination. I was under the impression you wanted something quickly."

"I respect first impressions," Flynn said. "And I assume you've already told this to the state police?"

Sajahada shook her head. "They don't go by first impressions, but I think you already know that. They'll form their own opinions based on a full report." Flynn thought he heard just a touch of disdain in her voice.

Flynn's cell phone rang. He looked at the caller ID: Liz Phillips. They spoke for a moment.

"Doctor Sajahada, I leave Mr. Terhune in your capable hands." He handed her a card. "Give me a call if you find something especially interesting; otherwise, I'll look for your report."

"Should the state police know you were asking questions?" Sajahada asked.

"I wouldn't lie to them," Flynn said. "But what you volunteer to them is between you and your code of ethics. I haven't been told to stay out of the investigation but, on the other hand, I haven't made my presence known to the official investigating agency."

"I think we understand each other," Sajahada said. Flynn thought he saw the first hint of a smile before her face became opaque.

Flynn was still processing that exchange when Liz Phillips appeared.

"I've been drafted," she said. "I now have Fred Terhune's job. And I've got something to show you."

"And I've got something for you too," he said. He handed her two photos. "Anyone look familiar?"

"The two men, I don't know." She held up the second photo. "This is Mary Ann Mandeville."

"OK. And who is Mary Ann Mandeville?"

"Real estate agent. Hardington Properties," Liz said.

"Don't tell me she's a member of the garden club."

"She's a member of every organization in town, probably including the Elks. She's a real estate agent. She networks. The bylaws say she has to come to at least six meetings a year and work on a wayside garden site. She shows up for the social hour and slips out the side door before the presentation begins. She and six other professional women share watering duties at one site, and I swear they pay someone to do it. She doesn't know an aster from a geranium. She wants to know who's thinking about selling their home."

"That's probably more information than I needed, but it answers the question. She and Terhune had a kind of an argument…"

"What do you mean, a 'kind of an argument'?" Liz asked.

"She kneed him in the groin, if you must know," Flynn said.

"Does that make her a suspect?"

"It does until I know that it was just a lover's quarrel and nothing more."

Liz thought for a moment. "Mary Ann is married. Big diamond ring."

Flynn shrugged. "That doesn't stop it from being a lover's quarrel. Would you mind discreetly asking around?"

"Glad to help," Liz said.

"And you asked about the time of death. The ME says after midnight and before one."

"Then make it after 12:25. Fred was in the volunteer trailer and printed this spreadsheet." She showed him the time legend.

Flynn exhaled. "I have him on video at the party up until a few minutes before ten. We don't know what he did between ten and 12:25, but now we know he presumably spent at least the last part of that time working on the spreadsheet, which tells me he was not concerned for his safety. But between 12:25 a.m. and one o'clock, someone hit him on the head, from behind, with a rounded metal object."

Flynn held out the other photo. "These two guys had a serious altercation with him about 9:30. They were clearly threatening him, and he was definitely not pleased to see them. They're number one on my list of people to find. Terhune was also staring at something on the other side of the tent just before the camera people stopped filming, though it could have been your Mrs. Mandeville, who was over in that area."

Flynn pulled out the third photo. "These are the people who were standing near Terhune when he had his altercation with the two men. They might have overheard something. Do any of them look familiar?"

Liz studied the photo. "The couple on the left are Karen and Mike McCarthy. I know them from church. I don't know the others."

"Then do this for me, please: see if anyone in that garden club network of yours knows why Mary Ann Mandeville would want to do bodily damage to the late Mr. Terhune. I've got a lot of physical evidence still to find; it would be nice to eliminate a suspect. I'll also get you a print of these two guys. If they show up at the construction site, give me a call, quick. And Liz?"

"Yes?"

"It's nice to be working with you again."

* * * * *

Two hours later, Flynn was at the Hardington police station, bringing Chief Amos Harding up to speed.

"I had half expected to see you up at the sanitarium," Flynn said.

Harding, a tall man in his late sixties with a fringe of white hair, shook his head. "It's your investigation, assuming you're going to proceed with it. Also, I'm a little too close on this one. I knew Fred very well; in a sense, Fred was my boss. The selectmen recommend each year whether to retain appointed officials. And, while I was named chief long before Fred became a selectman, I served at his pleasure – he and the other two selectmen."

"I've also been out to see Erica – that's Fred's ex-wife," Chief Harding said. "I think that's a captain's duty in a circumstance like this. I've known her all her life; I thought she ought to hear the news from an old friend."

Harding shifted in his chair, signaling a change of subject. "You may also want to know that I've gotten half a dozen calls from the state police, going right up the chain of command. They've made it clear that this is 'their' investigation and that this time there's no possible fudge factor about this being a homicide. Of course, their real problem is that they smell publicity. Their official view is that we can't cherry-pick the services we want – a fingerprint team here or an autopsy there. Oh, and that state law is on their side."

"What did you tell them?" Flynn asked.

"I told them that they had the right to conduct an investigation but that Hardington has a homicide-savvy, first-rate detective on its staff that has shown himself to be every bit as resourceful as the best state investigators and exceptionally dedicated to getting at the truth. In short, I told them all to stuff it including, just five minutes ago, the Deputy Director himself. Actually, to be completely accurate, I told him that we would avail ourselves of those resources that made sense in the time and manner that best suited the investigation and that we would share anything we found with them in a timely manner. If they chose not to supply those resources or they chose not to reciprocate by sharing what they found, my next call would be Channel 5 and they could explain to Susan Wornick why they refused to help."

"Speaking of which, we've also got the press pounding at the door," Chief Harding added. "We've got Hospital Road blocked off from the north and south, and the TV stations are having a tantrum. I told them to go talk to the staties, 'no cameras, no statement'."

Flynn marveled at the change that a few months – and a successful investigation – had wrought. Then, Chief Harding's haste to go before the cameras and announce the solution of a murder in his placid town had wreaked havoc and brought the potential to make a laughingstock of Hardington's long-time chief – the fifteenth Harding to serve in law enforcement in the town that bore his ancestor's name. But Flynn had publicly and privately backed his chief and word of his support had apparently made it back to Harding. Ultimately, there had been an official letter of commendation, though Flynn and Chief Harding spoke of that case only obliquely.

"We don't need any reporters or camera crews screwing up the crime scene," Flynn said. "We'll give them a statement when there's something to report. You may want to call Don Elwell – he's the producer -- and tell him that. In the meantime, I need all of the background I can get on Terhune. What can you tell me?"

Harding leaned back in his chair and pressed his fingertips together. "His family came here in the twenties. I guess that makes him third-generation. His father, Tom, was a few years ahead of me in school. Ran the Exxon station back when it was Esso. Could fix anything on four wheels. Died in… 1988. Heart attack."

Flynn realized he was listening to a capsule biography of Fred Terhune's father. *Be patient. He'll get there.*

"Fred was just out of law school. UMass. Came back to town, took care of his mother, who took Tom's death pretty hard. Fred's mother's people were from Needham or Natick or someplace like that. Sold the gas station. Hung out his shingle on Main Street. Folks say he was a very good lawyer; could have gone with one of the big Boston firms. But he found a couple of partners here and did well. Had a second office over in Cavendish."

Chief Harding closed his eyes and swiveled slightly in his chair. "Married Louise and Bob Gordon's girl, Erica. That was 1990. Built a nice house out on Lake Road. He got real active in the town after that; zoning advisory committee, Parks and Rec. I think Fred ran for selectman in 2002. Things seemed to be going real well. Then, something happened between Erica and Fred. They got divorced about three years ago. It was a shame because they have two beautiful daughters."

"Fred's mother died that year. She had been in one of those assisted living places over in Cavendish, and Fred and Erica had been renting out her house. Well, they got divorced, but they both stayed in town. Erica kept the house on Lake Road, and Fred fixed up his parent's place here in town. He stayed a real good father to those two girls; out at the soccer games every Saturday and then up to Dapper Dan's for ice cream."

"Do you know what kind of legal practice Fred had?" Flynn asked.

"Oh, real estate, mostly. That's what keeps most of the lawyers here busy. He did a will for Mary and me. He also did the legal work for the Home Committee."

"The Home Committee?"

Chief Harding looked through his office window to see if anyone in the department bullpen might be listening. The room was empty. "The Home Committee is private group of local people. You mostly read about it at Christmas. We give presents to the shut-ins and the kids that otherwise wouldn't have much under the tree, and we furnish the tree, too. We kind of watch out for the less fortunate and the elderly. We solicit donations but it's mostly our own money. We bought a car for a family that needed one when theirs got totaled and they didn't have insurance.   We were trying to figure out what to do for Jenny and Mac Cardozo when Fred came up with the idea of approaching that TV show. That's the Home Committee. There are about a dozen of us; I'm the only one who is allowed to be publicly known."

"Who are the other members?"

"All you need to know is that Fred was one. Like I said, this is a private charity group."

Chief Harding drummed his fingers on the desk, composing his thoughts. After a few moments, he looked up at Flynn. "John, I want you to go full-out on this. Use whoever it takes, and don't worry about the overtime. I owe it to Erica and the girls, and I owe it to Fred's memory. I don't want some sorry-assed state trooper doing their typical lousy job and marking the case 'unsolved' after three days. I want you to find who killed Fred and make certain there's no lawyer loopholes the killer can jump through. Do we understand one another?"

Flynn nodded and they shook hands. Flynn made certain he did not break into a smile until he was well out of sight.

* * * * *

Flynn contacted the security patrol, but it was exactly as Eddie Frankel had described. Two retired policemen in a brown car marked 'Security' with a gallon of coffee and a box of donuts. The car was parked next to the equipment tractor-trailer, as specified in their contract with Hammer & Saw Productions, and the car was less than fifty feet from the video production trailer with its expensive editing gear. Per agreement, one security guard made an hourly, ten-minute walking circuit of the three tents and eleven motor homes. On the midnight round there were still 'guys with clipboards' walking around, all wearing *Ultimate House Makeover* tee shirts. They had made no effort to check IDs; the possession of one of the black tees was sufficient authority.

At one o'clock and thereafter, they had seen no movement on any of their rounds. Several cars had left in a fifteen-minute period just after midnight, one car had left just after 12:30 a.m., one car had arrived about ten minutes later.

Flynn asked about the last car to leave, and the one that arrived, but was told that it was at the far end of the parking area, that they had heard no voices, and that they knew of it only when they heard the ignition turn and saw the car pull out. Because no one had approached the tractor-trailer, they had made no effort to confront the after-hours visitors. They had made no effort to observe or record the cars' license plates or occupants. It was not part of their assignment.

Flynn suspected that other cars may have pulled in and out of the parking lot during the night, but that the security guards were fast asleep. He was too polite to say so.

* * * * *

Liz had no pressing need to get into Fred Terhune's computer, but the urge was irresistible. It was password-protected, however, and she knew too little of Terhune's personal life to be able to guess what he might have chosen as a security code. The blinking cursor tormented her.

The place to start for an answer, she concluded, was with Roland.

Roland Evans-Jones, friend, antiques dealer, and the lone male member of the Hardington Garden Club, was at his shop on Main Street. She called him.

"Do you have time for lunch today?" Liz asked.

"Liz, you are once again the talk of the town," Roland said. "I've had at least a dozen calls or people stopping in to tell me what happened this morning. You tell me where and when, I'll be there."

"Come on up to the sanitarium. They're serving lunch for the volunteers. You just became a volunteer. I'll meet you at the parking lot."

The path from the Volunteer trailer to the parking lot took her past several of the house modules, where more than a hundred people were sanding, painting, and nailing. Liz watched as construction supervisors broke down jobs so that everyone was busy doing something. The production assistants kept a steady stream of materials moving to each module. Whit Dakota, trailed by a camera and boom microphone, would stop volunteers in mid-task, ask them their name, and then offer advice on a better way to hold a paint brush or a nail gun. Despite the presence of two policemen and yellow crime scene tape marking off fifty feet around the site where Fred Terhune's body had been found, *Ultimate House Makeover* was a smoothly running machine on this, the first day of volunteer-driven construction.

She found Roland by the edge of the parking lot, scanning the crowd for her while admiring the progress. *He's looking good*, she thought. *If I look like that when I'm over seventy, I'll have done pretty well for myself.*

She guided him to a table where sandwiches and bags of chips were piled high. "Take some and let's go back to my trailer."

"You probably made these yourself," Roland said. He was dressed for summer in a blue and white seersucker suit with a bow tie. His clothes all fit impeccably, though he would always claim he had not bought a new item of clothing in decades. His owlish face was accentuated by a pair of large, tortoiseshell glasses.

"No, but I spent forty-five minutes on the phone with the caterer telling them how to get here, talking to the police department to get them past the road blocks, and then corralling ten ladies to get it all organized once the truck arrived," Liz said, ticking off tasks on her fingers. "I'm learning this as I go along. All I know is that Fred had a mind for details that I lack."

She showed him the computer and the password log-in screen. "What am I looking for? A pet name? Children's name? Wife's name?"

"Definitely not the ex-wife's name. Erica and he didn't get along after the divorce at all."

"Do you know why they got divorced?"

Roland started to speak, then paused for a moment. "I think Erica got tired of having a part-time husband. Fred seemed to be there for everyone except her."

"How do you know this?" Liz asked.

"It's a small town, Liz. Gossip is legal tender in Hardington. Twenty minutes after Geraldine Cooper opened that chest, I had a call from a friend who was up here, telling me you were maintaining order and keeping everyone from destroying evidence. They also told me that your Detective Flynn was here."

"He's not 'my' Detective Flynn," Liz said. "He's the town detective, and of course he was here. He gave me a copy of a photo." She showed him the one of the two men. "Do either of these people look familiar?"

Roland put on his glasses. "They look Latino, which explains the tight blue jeans look. No. Never seen them. Are they suspects?"

Liz settled on a variation of the truth. "They were at the party last night and they were seen talking with Fred. John said they were out of place. He asked me to keep an eye out in case they show up again."

"You're a very poor liar, Liz," Roland said. "You lack the experience. I'll let it pass for the moment, but I can't help but notice that, while he's not 'your' Detective Flynn, he is 'John'."

"For crying out loud, Roland. We're adults and we're working together. What else do I call him?"

"I'm pulling your leg. All right. Passwords…" And for ten minutes, they tried variations on children's and pet's names, to no avail.

"Let me ask you one more question," Liz said. "Mary Ann Mandeville. What do you know about her?"

"I know what everyone knows. She's the hardest working real estate agent in town. She gets all the big listings. I also know that in three years she has never once stayed for a program at the garden club, which may be a record. She comes for coffee, checks out everyone's health, marital and employment status, and then slips out the side door."

"She's married, right?"

Roland paused. "Yessssss," he said slowly. "And what do I get in return for what else I know?"

"Liz sighed. "I'll tell you before I tell anyone else. *If* I tell anyone else. Come on, Roland, please."

"Oh, all right. Where do I start? Mary Ann is hard working. Mary Ann probably makes more money than God every year because she's on one end or another of twenty or thirty house sales a year. She is also – and I will use this term in its strictest, Anglo-Saxon sense – a slut. Yes, she's married, but her husband is away probably three hundred nights a year. I think he's an investment banker or a venture capitalist, and apparently in biotechnology or one of those fields where companies are being bought or sold every week. Anyway, the Mandeville household is apparently not a happy one, because Mary Ann has probably had more affairs with more lawyers, mortgage brokers, and clients than anyone else in the Hardington phone book. And possibly the Boston phone book."

"Why don't *I* know these things?" Liz asked.

"Because you always think well of people. You take them at face value. It is one of your finest qualities."

"Could she and Fred Terhune have been lovers?"

"Well, let's see… He's a lawyer. He handles real estate transactions, wills and probates. He would be in a position to give Mary Ann a head start on getting property listings – the late Mrs. McGillicutty left her house jointly to her six children, so you know it's going on the market. He's also a selectman, and selectmen are very useful people to know if you're in property. I'd say the odds are in favor of their having something going on. Is Mary Ann a suspect?"

"I said I'd tell you *if* I was going to tell anyone else," Liz said. "And if it comes back to me that you said something, I'll never speak to you again."

Roland looked dejected. "Then I shall be the soul of discretion, even if it means losing the chance, for once, to be the first person to know anything around this town."

"Mary Ann apparently had some kind of a fight with Fred at the party. These two goons also made some threats." She pulled out the third photo. "These are Karen and Mike McCarthy. Do you recognize the other couple? They were next to Fred when the goons were there."

Roland put back on his glasses. "Pam and Kip Jones. They bought a very nice upright Federal chest from me back in May. Hardly even haggled. Made me think I had priced it too low. They have an antique up on Elm Street."

Liz took several bites of her sandwich. "Why would anyone want to kill Fred? You might not like him; you might even hate him. But kill him? It doesn't make sense."

"I'm no expert, Liz, but it seems to me that you kill someone either because that person has done something horrible, or because they're about to do something that threatens you. You kill over love; you kill over money."

"Was Fred wealthy?"

Roland swallowed a bite of sandwich. "He was living in his parents' old house and supporting Erica and the kids. He probably made a comfortable living as a lawyer, but paying for two households is very expensive. As a selectman, he controlled the town's budget. But, if you're looking to swing a piece of that budget your way, you don't kill the person. That fairly well ends your influence."

"But someone did kill him. That's a fact."

"And, *ipso facto*, you and your Detective Flynn are going to find out why," Roland said; then stopped, remembering his own words. "Liz! Fred was a lawyer. Let try some legal terms."

'Probono' opened the contents of the laptop. The results, though, were disappointing. This was Terhune's personal laptop rather than his office computer, and it held principally photos, music, and stock market information. The 'last documents opened' revealed no urgent messages.

"Well, that's an hour wasted," Roland said after they had opened various files and found nothing that would shed light on the murder.

"I'll copy off the volunteer spreadsheet onto my own computer tonight," Liz said. "From there, it goes to Detective Flynn. Maybe he can find something on it we didn't see."

* * * * *

Flynn was in the office of Hardington Properties, one of four real estate firms clustered along a two-block stretch of Main Street. For an exurban town in an era of malls, Wal-Marts, and 'lifestyle centers', the center of Hardington thrived. In addition to real estate offices, 'downtown' Hardington offered four banks, three churches, three pizza parlors, two dry cleaners, two day spas, multiple restaurants, the town library and Taylor's Department Store. The Congregational Church also anchored the town common, where cattle grazed into the nineteenth century. Realtors always took prospective out-of-town buyers on a tour of this compact town center on their first visit, and Mary Ann Mandeville promptly suggested such a walk.

Mandeville no longer sported the sundress she had worn the previous evening. Instead, she was in a pale green summer-weight skirt and blouse that accentuated both her figure and her carefully styled red hair. From the video, he had estimated her age at late thirties. In person, she could have been as young as thirty. Her skin was flawless, glowing and unlined. As Liz had pointed out, she wore a wedding ring and a large diamond ring on her left hand.

"You spoke with Fred Terhune at the reception last evening," Flynn said. "Can you tell me what you talked about?"

Mandeville found an errant piece of hair on her silk blouse near the apex of her breast. She examined it rather than look at Flynn. "I don't really remember. We probably just said 'hello'." She then carefully picked it off and let it fall to the ground.

It's always nice to start a conversation with a whopper, Flynn thought. "There were two television cameras recording the event for posterity, Mrs. Mandeville."

"Oh." She continued to walk, saying nothing for about fifteen seconds. "And what did the television cameras record, Detective Flynn?"

"They showed you and Fred Terhune having an argument. May I ask what the argument was about?" Flynn tried to place the perfume being worn by Mary Ann Mandeville. It smelled floral. And expensive.

"Are you a voyeur, Detective Flynn?"

"I'm trying to find out who killed Fred Terhune. I would imagine that murders are bad for your business."

"Well, I didn't kill him. Fred and I were good friends. We've known each other for years."

"You didn't tell me what the argument was about."

"That was a private matter, Detective Flynn. If you would like to give me a polygraph test and ask me if I killed Fred, I will be only too glad to do so. But please stay out of my personal life."

"Can you think of anyone who would benefit by his death?" Flynn asked.

"I'd start with his ex-wife. He had a million dollars in life insurance, and the children were the beneficiaries."

"Did Fred Terhune tell you that?"

"No. Someone else."

Flynn said nothing in response. He allowed the silence to hang there. People frequently rushed in to fill a conversational vacuum with words. Mary Ann Mandeville seemed to have said all she intended to say. They sat on a bench under a maple tree. There were the first stirrings of a breeze.

"Who else would want to see him dead?" Flynn asked, finally.

"Do you know what a selectman is, Detective Flynn?"

"It's like a town councilman."

"Prepare for a civics lesson, Detective. New England has the last vestiges of what we call a 'direct democracy'. Hardington has an annual town meeting in October. Every registered voter is invited to the high school gym to vote on the town warrant. The town warrant is the budget, line by line down to the penny; who's getting sewers; what's being added to the historic district; everything. If you think the assistant animal control officer is a superfluous position, you can stand up at the town meeting and demand a vote on whether to eliminate the job. If you want the town to spend twenty million dollars for a new elementary school, get together a petition and demand a special town meeting. And, if your side shows up with enough people, the school gets built."

"There's no mayor of Hardington," she continued. "There's no town council. What there are, are three selectmen. Their job is to run the town according to what got voted on at the town meeting. They have an enormous amount of latitude to do their job and, while they meet in public, a lot of what they do is in private. If you want to put up a subdivision, it has to be approved by the selectmen. The selectmen can – and do – send a developer back to the drawing board a dozen times before something gets approved – if it gets approved."

She continued. "Do you want to build a garage on your property? Do you want an exterior sign for your coffee shop? Do you want to be the new chief of police? Take it up with the selectmen. They run the town. That's the way it has been for three hundred and fifty years."

"Is this one of those 'absolute power corrupts absolutely' stories?" Flynn asked.

"Hardly," she said. "To the contrary, these are very hard-working, decent people. But they don't say 'yes' to everyone who asks for something. In fact, Fred was the kind of guy whose first instinct was to say 'no' unless you could convince him that disturbing the status quo was to the town's benefit. A lot of people wish he were more compliant."

Flynn pulled out the photo of the two men. "Are these gentlemen who might have wanted him to be more compliant?"

Mary Ann Mandeville took the photo in her hands and examined it carefully. "I remember seeing them at the party. They're not from Hardington. And no, I don't know them." She returned the photo to him.

"If you were Mr. Terhune's good friend, Mrs. Mandeville, then you'll want to see the person or persons who killed him brought to justice. Who would feel so strongly about something he had done that they would kill him for it?"

She thought for a long time. "Justin Pope and his people. He's been trying for three years to build a golf course and a dozen homes on the Dietricht Farm property. He's no closer today than he was then, and Fred was the person the other selectmen listened to on development matters. There's also MetroWest Construction. They had the sewer contract for the south side of town. Fred had them disqualified, and the work went to another firm. Building sewers isn't the most lucrative work in the area, but it's steady and you can't beat the cash flow."

"Any idea why they were disqualified?"

"I said that a lot of the work of the selectmen was done behind the scenes. They met privately with MetroWest and then announced their decision. MetroWest said they'd sue. That was about three months ago."

Flynn's cell phone rang.

"It's Dr. Minal Sajahada," said the voice at the other end of the phone. "I've got some preliminary autopsy results, and I can show you what you're looking for in a murder weapon. You interested?"

"Give me thirty minutes."

Mandeville rose from the bench and smoothed her skirt. "It sounds as though you're needed elsewhere."

"We'll pick this up at another time. I'd appreciate your writing down those names you just gave me, phone numbers, that sort of thing." He handed her a card.

"I'll email them to you. And tell me, Detective Flynn, now that you've enjoyed our town for a few months, have you considered buying a home in Hardington?"

* * * * *

Liz began to suspect she needed help.

She had copied Fred Terhune's master volunteer list onto a flash drive so that she could load it into her own computer, so at least she had a starting point in tracking volunteers as they came in, but the smooth flow of volunteers in the morning was rapidly turning into an unorganized mob. Crime scene gawkers showed up, claiming to be volunteers. People left after a few hours work and other, would-be volunteers showed up uninvited and with unknown skills. Everyone meant well, but there was no longer a coherent organization.

"I suggest runners," offered Barry Zimmerman. "Go find a couple of high school or college-age kids. Give them each a clipboard and the skills inventory sheet. Have them talk to anyone who looks like they're hanging around with nothing to do." He reached into a file folder and pulled out a sheet. "There's a Xerox machine in Chip Gilman and Sam Hirsch's Winnebago. It's the little one right behind ours. They also have office supplies like clipboards."

An hour later, Liz had organized seven teenagers into a corps of runners. She knew two of them as daughters of garden club members. The first two helped recruit the others. By 3 p.m. they had collected information sheets on more than a hundred walk-in volunteers, who were assigned to one of the construction brigades according to skills. By the end of the day, even Barry Zimmerman was satisfied. "We're on schedule," he said, looking through the block diagrams. "In the end, all that really counts is that we're on schedule."

The scope of the task of coordinating volunteers, which had seemed much easier that morning, caused Liz to realize that she had only so much time and energy. And so, her next call was to the garden club's best horticulturalist, Eva Morin. She begged Eva to go through the list of New England-hardy plants and trees for the Cardozo site. To Liz's relief, Eva said it would be an honor, and would negotiate prices with nurseries. Liz put a mental check mark next to 're-do plant list'.

3.

Flynn paid close attention as Minal Sajahada pointed out the tell-tale clues of Fred Terhune's death told by the body on the autopsy table.

"We start with the murder weapon," Sajahada said. "Based on the shape of the skull fracture, I originally suggested a heavy flashlight. That is still a possibility but, unless the flashlight's lens was a polycarbonate material, a blow like the one the victim took would have shattered the glass and we'd see shards in the scalp. But it had to be something with a round, fairly heavy metal base about six inches in diameter, almost certainly flat on the bottom, with a beveled edge tapering in about an inch. The murderer needed to be able to grip it and swing it, so it probably tapered to something narrower."

"So it's flashlight-shaped but solid metal," Flynn said.

Sajahada considered Flynn's conclusion. "The length of the weapon is open to question. Too long or too heavy and the force of the arc would have split the victim's head open. Too short and it would have injured but not killed. And as for solid metal, well, just think something that weighs a few pounds. More than a pound, less than five."

"How about an automotive part or a tool used in home building?" Flynn asked.

"The edge that struck the victim was perfectly smooth and left an indentation, which is why I can say round, six inches across, and beveled," Sajahada said. "No teeth, no gears. Also, no oil or grease. A tool? Look around the site. The weapon is probably still there."

Sajahada parted Terhune's hair at the point of the fatal injury. "This wasn't a crime of passion. It was one blow, and it killed.

The killer allowed the victim to bleed out, so it rules out an accident."

"A professional killing?" Flynn asked.

"That would be an odd choice for a murder weapon," Sajahada said. "My guess is that the weapon was one that was handy. A tire iron, for example, would have also done the job, but the same force would have split open the skull."

She held up Terhune's right hand. "He didn't put up any fight, and the fact that he was struck from behind indicates he may not have heard his attacker."

"Could he also have been fleeing his attacker?" Flynn asked. "Hit from behind by someone who didn't care if it was a fair fight?"

Sajahada nodded. "Both theories are consistent with the evidence. There are no defensive wounds of any kind. There's nothing under his nails, and no signs of bruising elsewhere on his body. One other thing, though. He was held under his arms, which is an efficient way to drag a limp body."

She held up his shoes. "The victim was dragged through the grass. I haven't found any carpet fibers indicating he spent time in the trunk of a car. From what I could see of the site, I think this means our victim was killed on the grounds of the sanitarium."

"We haven't found any blood," Flynn said.

"*You* haven't found any blood yet," Sajahada corrected. "Unless the murderer had the presence of mind to hit the victim on a blanket or a tarpaulin, the blood is there. He lost multiple pints before he died, and only a fraction of that is on his shirt or body. The rest is on the ground – somewhere."

"Am I looking for a man or a woman?" Flynn asked.

"I wouldn't rule out either gender," Sajahada said. "The object he or she used wasn't heavy, the force wasn't sufficient to split the skull, and the victim weighs about one-fifty. Any man or woman with reasonable upper body strength could have done this."

An hour later, Flynn had emailed the photo of the two men in jeans to the state police as well as to police departments in all towns surrounding Hardington, and posted an enlargement in the locker room, identifying the men as "persons of interest" in the investigation. To be on the safe side, he also posted Mary Ann Mandeville's photo, name, estimated age, description, and occupation to a New-England-wide 'seeking information on' message board used by police departments.

Chief Harding stopped by his desk as he was completing the last email.

"We got us a mess on our hands," Harding said. "The state police say you and Eddie Frankel are talking to their witnesses and they're madder than hell that the people at the sanitarium are all saying that they've already told their story to the police. I'm getting press calls from every radio and television station in Boston, plus CNN and some people I never heard of. They're screaming that we won't let them into the hospital. Meanwhile, Don Elwell is telling me to 'stay out of the way of his staff' because it's a 'distraction' to the people up there. So, please tell me there's progress to report."

Flynn took out his notebook. "Mary Ann Mandeville tells me that Fred Terhune had a million dollars of life insurance on himself, with his children as beneficiaries. She also says that a developer named Justin Pope and an outfit called MetroWest Construction had no love lost for Mr. Terhune. Do either of those names ring a bell?"

Chief Harding stood at what Flynn thought of as a 'parade rest', an odd way of collecting one's thoughts. "Mary Ann has a lot of opinions for someone who has lived in this town for about six years," Chief Harding said after several moments of contemplation. "Justin Pope is one of those Dover developers who wants to turn Hardington into another town for the rich. He bought one of the town's last farms a couple of years ago. Two hundred acres. Brought in a plan to put up a bunch of million-dollar homes on a golf course. Forty of them, I think, was the first plan. Selectmen kept sending them back. Now it's a dozen homes, but the price tag for each one is about three and a half million. Good luck finding a dozen people who'll pay that kind of money for a house out here. I think the selectmen are most concerned about the golf course and the club house. It takes a lot of water to keep a golf course green, and the town wells can only supply so much. In a dry year, we ration water, and we've had dry years the past three out of five."

"Should I be asking Mr. Pope where he was Sunday evening?" Flynn asked.

"Long shot, I'd think," Chief Harding said. "Getting Fred out of the way doesn't get that project approved."

"What about MetroWest Construction?"

"Mexicans. Or maybe they're Brazilians," Chief Harding said. "They're from up in Framingham. Got the contract to lay sewers in town ten years ago. The way I heard it, they did fine until about two years ago. Then, they kept sending in bills for 'extras' that jacked up the price by fifteen percent or more. Selectmen rejected the bills, so MetroWest started shaving corners. Wouldn't repair the roads after sewer lines went in. Selectmen put out a bid this spring for connecting in about a hundred houses. MetroWest had the low bid but the selectmen threw it out."

"It sounds like they'd have reason to go after Mr. Terhune," Flynn said.

"Maybe," Chief Harding said. "You talk to Joe Delaney. He's also a selectman and is kind of the 'go-to' guy on public works. He owns the hardware store out on the state highway. By the way, you never said why you went to Mary Ann for information."

"I watched a tape of Sunday night's party," Flynn said. "She seemed to be having an interesting conversation with Mr. Terhune. I wanted to ask her what she was talking about with him."

The answer seemed to satisfy Chief Harding, who nodded and headed back to his office. Flynn turned his attention back to his computer screen, where his message light was blinking. He clicked on the icon and found an email from Mandeville. She had, as promised, sent names and contact information for Justin Pope and MetroWest Construction. She had also attached information on four homes for sale in Hardington. The least expensive bore a "Just Reduced!" notice. The new price was $649,000. The house bore an uncanny resemblance to his home in Roslindale which he had purchased, in 1978, for $23,500.

* * * * *

It was nearing five o'clock and Liz was exhausted. She had come to the grounds of the old sanitarium this morning before 8 a.m. expecting to stay the few minutes necessary to prevent the wrong trees and shrubs from being planted at the Cardozo's new home. Less than an hour after that, she had been on hand to witness the discovery of a corpse and had been cajoled into taking the job left vacant by that person's death.

Now, eight hours later, she had learned the rudiments of the job for which Fred Terhune had volunteered. She had made more than a hundred calls and dispatched her corps of runners on half as many errands. Looking across at Barry Zimmerman, she had a vague unease that she was doing the job Zimmerman had been hired to do. He seemed to have a lot of time for what sounded like personal calls and web surfing. He had even asked her about the shortest way to get to Fenway Park.

Zimmerman's phone rang and he picked it up. The call was brief. He turned to her. "Happy hour," he said. "Boss man says everyone should come over to his trailer for a drink and the daily wrap-up."

"Then I'll see you tomorrow," Liz said.

Zimmerman shook his head. "Don says he wants you, too. He wants to meet the hard-driving woman who had this place running like a Swiss watch."

Don Elwell's trailer was a thirty-five-foot Winnebago. The part of the inside she could see had been outfitted as an office and conference room. One wall was a long whiteboard broken into six days. Days 1 and 2 had red 'X's' marked through them. Around the tightly packed table were thirteen people.

Elwell was at the whiteboard, marking pen in hand. "Construction," he said, acknowledging neither Zimmerman or Liz.

A man in his 40s in one of the black *Ultimate House Makeover* tee shirts spoke immediately. "On schedule and fully staffed. All six modules got here on time and with no transit damage. We're doing one day of prep here and we expect to trailer them down to the job site tomorrow at ten. The sub-modules are ready to ship when we call the factory, and we're looking at Wednesday noon."

Without looking back, Elwell said, "Do the other two of you agree?"

"Yes," the two men said in unison. One added, "But this is still the easy part. The big push starts tomorrow afternoon. That's when things start going off the rails."

Elwell drew a red 'X' through the word 'construction'. "Whit?"

Liz looked at Whit Dakota. His name had been unfamiliar until a few weeks ago. She had never seen his previous cable television show and had not watched *Ultimate House Makeover* until the call from Fred Terhune. On camera, he was a gregarious, confident purveyor of advice and enthusiasm. Dark wavy hair, very handsome, well-muscled, and attired in the kind of working men's clothing that showed off biceps and abs. Here, in person and after a long day, he was a different person. *Angry*, she thought. *And cynical.* He had not said a word. This was just body language.

"I'm thinking we need a football game," Dakota said.

Elwell turned from the whiteboard to look at Dakota and, for the first time, noted Liz and Zimmerman. "That's a good idea. What day do you have in mind?"

"We've got a five-hour hole tomorrow when they move the modules. I figure we'd get great visuals with Tom Snipes," Dakota said. "Full scrimmage, him throwing me a pass."

Elwell nodded. "I like it. Chip, how are we doing on talent?"

All eyes turned to a youngish man who flipped through a notebook. "Snipes is OK for the reveal. That's the only time we blocked him for."

"Get his schedule," Elwell said. "Make sure he knows it's a '100% use' opportunity. Barry, how's the 'special needs' community look?"

Zimmerman didn't need his notebook for the report. "Leukemia Society wants to send three buses including their national chairman."

"One bus," Elwell said, holding up a finger. "We don't need another circus like Ohio. How did you make out with the Red Sox?"

"They've offered Ben Cherington – he's the team's general manager. I'm thinking about going to see them tomorrow."

"If that's their attitude, tell them to pound sand," Elwell said. "They may be on the road this week but half that damn team is on the disabled list, and I bet they're not traveling with the team. I want two recognizable starters, including that hot-shot pitcher, or tell them don't bother to show up. We're already long. Volunteers?"

Zimmerman spoke with confidence. "Fully staffed and with bench strength."

Elwell smiled and looked at Liz. "And you're Liz Phillips." He looked around the room. "Everybody, this is the lady who stepped into Fred Terhune's shoes. Mrs. Phillips came here to knock some horticultural sense into young Barry's head this morning and got more than she bargained for. From what Barry tells me, she has the volunteer issue well under control." Then, looking at Liz, he said, "Thank you and welcome."

There were some appreciative murmurs.

"I understand you also know the town police pretty well," Elwell said.

"It's a small town," Liz said, and offered no elaboration.

"Is that why the state police have gotten involved?" Elwell asked. "Too big of an investigation for the locals?"

"I believe it's more of a legal thing," Liz said. "The state police automatically have jurisdiction in murder cases except in Boston. Hardington, though, has a new detective fresh from a long career in Boston."

"Well, I hope whichever police force has jurisdiction can catch whoever did this quickly," Elwell said. "I called your chief and told him that. We'll help in any way that we can, but we've got a program to produce and a house to build." He smiled.

Liz thought the smile was one of the most insincere she had ever seen.

The meeting went on another ten minutes with each department reporting, and few issues. When Elwell finally said, "OK, everybody back to work," he asked Liz to remain behind.

"I need your help," he said after the last person had left the Winnebago. "Fred Terhune was the perfect volunteer coordinator because he was also well connected into the town. Over the next few days, we're going to need a lot of help from the town, and most of that is going to fall on your shoulders."

Elwell walked a few steps to a refrigerator and took out a bucket of ice. "Drink?" he asked.

Liz shook her head. Elwell poured vodka into a glass and added ice and several olives. "I'm nervous as hell that this investigation could end up throwing us off schedule. My video guy tells me that the detective looked at last night's footage and saw a couple of likely suspects talking to Terhune. That's good, because it means your police department isn't running in circles looking for suspects."

Elwell took a long drink and rattled the ice cubes in the glass. "One of my producers, though, tells me that a couple of cops went over the place looking for blood and another one has been trying to pin down everyone's whereabouts for every minute of Sunday evening." He shook his head. "Your people are looking in the wrong places. I can vouch that no one on this crew would do anything like that. And the police have to realize that we run on an unbelievably tight deadline. You got a glimpse of that in the meeting just now. I can't have those kinds of distractions."

He refilled his glass with vodka, skipping the olives. "Liz, I want the police to find the creep who killed Terhune. I don't want to leave here on Friday with a cloud hanging over the show. We've never had anything worse than some equipment theft happen during production. If your police or the state police need additional resources – and by that I mean private resources – I can get a squad of guys in here tomorrow morning. They're ex-FBI and they work fast. They'll be here on my nickel. Is that a message you can relay to the right people, or is it better that I make that call?"

Liz said nothing for a moment, absorbing the offer and its implications. "I know the detective who was here this morning. He was apparently one of the Boston Police Department's best. He came here a few months ago after he retired, and he almost immediately solved a very complicated murder case here in town. So, there's no chance that he might be in over his head, which I think is what you're asking."

"The state police technically have jurisdiction because it's a murder, but John…" Liz paused, embarrassed at having used Flynn's first name. "…When Detective Flynn solved the murder, the state police gave credit where credit was due. I will relay the offer. I think I can do it in a way that won't make anyone mad. I'll tell him that you're prepared to pay for anything that helps speed the investigation, including additional manpower."

"Then I leave it in your hands." Elwell gave another of those insincere smiles.

Liz was walking back toward her car when she heard a greeting. "Hey! Volunteer lady!" She turned to find Whit Dakota leaning up against a trailer. "Come on in, I want to talk to you."

Liz thought to herself, *"My cat is going to starve. I'm going to fall over from exhaustion. And this guy wants to be cute."*

She followed him.

Whit Dakota's Vectra trailer was suitable for a star. Forty feet long and with push-out expansions at multiple locations, it smelled of new leather and furniture polish. On a shelf between the lounge area and the galley was a row of gleaming statuettes, behind each one was a photo of a tuxedo-clad Whit Dakota receiving the award.

"Two Emmys and three People's Choice," Dakota said, seeing her attention drawn to the shelf. "Call me lucky, or call me surrounded by very good people." He plopped himself on a leather sofa. "Speaking of which. Hey, Chip!"

A door behind the galley opened. Liz glimpsed a bedroom beyond it. The young man Liz had heard identified in the meeting as 'Chip' came out. Like Barry Zimmerman, he was young, probably no more than his early twenties. Although attired in one of the ubiquitous *Ultimate House Makeover* tees, he seemed to make it a fashion statement.

"What are you doing in there?" Dakota asked. "No, don't tell me. Hey, we've got company. Liz Phillips, this is Charles 'Chip' Gilman, my assistant, and one hell of an assistant producer."

Liz murmured a 'hello'.

"Listen, Liz, we don't want to hold you up, but we wanted to pick your brain," Dakota said, putting his work boots on the coffee table in front of him. "You apparently know a lot of people in town. I mean, Hardington is your town. You're connected, right?"

"Not like Fred was connected," Liz said, honestly.

"Do you know Tom Snipes?"

Liz thought about it. She had now met with Felicity Snipes, his wife, a half a dozen times. The Snipes' charitable foundation had given the garden club $10,000 to install a garden at the police and fire station. While no words had ever passed between them on the subject, Liz suspected that the size and the timing of the gift had little to do with a desire to see a garden built, and a great deal to do with ensuring that the family's tangential connection to the murder of Sally Kahn remained buried. Several of the planning meetings had been at the Snipes' palatial home and Tom Snipes had sat for about fifteen minutes in one of them.

"I'm getting to know his wife fairly well. We're working together on a project."

"That's what I wanted to hear," Dakota grinned. "The way to a quarterback's heart is through his wife – or his girlfriend, especially if she's a supermodel. Look, you heard what we said at the meeting a little while ago. We've got Tom Snipes booked to help take the Cardozo family through their home on Friday afternoon. Their kid – what's his name?"

"Lee," Chip said.

"Lee," Dakota snapped his fingers. "Their kid, Lee, is a huge Patriots fan. Well, Tom Snipes and I are going to take the family through their new house. And I thought putting together a game of touch football tomorrow would be, like, the icing on the cake."

"But the family is in Florida," Liz said.

The revelation momentarily stunned Dakota. He looked over at Chip.

"Bonding," Chip said.

"Bonding!" Dakota said, snapping his fingers again. "Exactly. Look, Liz, when the camera rolls on Friday, it picks up all the nuances. If I've never met Tom Snipes and Tom Snipes has never met me, it, like, shows up all over the place. It looks awkward. Worse than awkward. It looks staged. That's what the football game is all about. Gives Tom and me a chance to bond. Plus, maybe we got a little footage to show between the roofing nail sequences, if you know what I mean."

Dakota cracked his knuckles. "Anyway, Tom Snipes has some hard-ass agent who can't see what this would mean to the family. We need an end-around play. Something that gets us in front of the man so he can make his own decision instead of some agent deciding how Tom's time gets spent."

"Could you do that, Liz? Could you talk to…"

"Felicity," Chip said.

"Felicity," Dakota said. "Could you talk to Felicity? You know, give her a call tonight. Or maybe even now." Dakota paused for a moment. Liz did not volunteer. "And let her know that this would be a great thing for the family."

Liz sighed. "I'll make a call. Tonight. Not now. Right now, I'm going home and I'm going to…" She started to say 'soak in a tub' but decided it was not an image she cared to share with Whit Dakota. "…pour myself a tall, cold drink."

"Fantastic!" Dakota said. "Talk to Chip in the morning and let him know where we need to be. Aw, this is going to be great!"

Dakota started talking to Chip about some aspect of filming, and Liz felt she had been excused. She let herself out of the trailer and looked at her watch. It was nearly six o'clock.

* * * * *

Flynn was two for three. Justin Pope had answered his own phone and agreed to meet him at the real estate development company's site in Hardington. "I've got to be down there this afternoon, anyway," Pope said. "Look for a white pickup truck."

Joe Delaney, the town selectman suggested by Chief Harding, had invited him to drop by anytime before six. "I'll give you all the info you need on MetroWest," he had said.

But the call to MetroWest produced only a secretary who said everyone was out of the office and she didn't know when they would return. The call was complicated by the fact that the secretary spoke minimal English.

Justin Pope was a tall, angular man with curly black hair and a perpetual look of worry on his face. He faced his land most of the time, glancing only occasionally back at Flynn.

"Detective, I don't know what you've heard, but this project is important to the town, and it's just a matter of getting it right," Pope said. "We didn't see Fred as an obstacle. We saw him as a valuable ally."

Flynn raised his eyebrow. "He and the other selectmen kept turning the project down."

Pope shook his head. "You have to start with the basic economics. Hardington has no industry to speak of, and practically no commercial tax base. The whole load falls on the homeowner. That magnificent school system everyone is so proud of is also incredibly expensive. The town needs more tax revenue and going to twenty bucks per thousand dollars of assessed valuation isn't the answer. Everyone recognizes that. I'm offering a big part of the solution."

He picked up a handful of dirt and let it trickle through his fingers. "As farm land, this property – and I'm talking two hundred acres – doesn't pay twenty-five thousand dollars a year in taxes. Each house I put up is going to pay twice that much. But the town is also getting a country club. We expected it to be taxed for what it is – a luxury – and country clubs don't put kids in the schools. They generate a fantastic revenue stream to the town that costs the town nothing."

"Then why did the selectmen keep turning down the project?" Flynn repeated.

"They didn't turn it down," Pope said. "They sent it back with recommendations for changes. Fewer houses. Add a retention pond. Preserve these wetlands. That's what they kept doing. And we're patient people. We didn't expect this to get approved the first time out."

"I'm told this has been going on for three years," Flynn said.

"And it may go on for another three years," Pope said. "But it will get built. And it will get built in a way that benefits the town. Look, Detective, I love this town. I'm planning to build one of these houses for myself. Hell, at least you can buy groceries in Hardington, which is more than you can say about Sherborn or Weston. The town needs this project. I don't know how to say it any plainer. And that means that I'm very sad to see Fred gone. Because I know that, deep down inside, he was a believer."

"There was also a problem with water, wasn't there?" Flynn asked.

Pope shook his head. "That's a myth. Thirty years ago, golf courses drank hundreds of thousands of gallons of water a week. Today, we can build an 18-hole course that uses about as much water per day as one of the houses around it. No, Detective, that dog doesn't hunt. We've even proposed piping the effluent from the treatment plant out here, which would help replenish the ground water supply. And we'll pay the town for the privilege of doing so."

Flynn showed him the picture of the two men. Pope said they did not work for his company.

"And can you account for your whereabouts this morning between 1 a.m. and 2 a.m.?" Flynn asked.

Pope laughed for the first time. "Home in bed, Detective. My wife will vouch for me. She probably shoved her fist into my ribs two or three times to stop my snoring."

* * * * *

Joe Delaney, a wiry, balding man in his early sixties, met Flynn at the entrance to the hardware store and invited him to an office in the back. Flynn noted the store was nearly empty of people.

"This isn't Home Depot, Detective Flynn. I do half my business before 8 a.m. on weekdays and the other half on Saturday morning. The rest of the time, I may as well be fishing."

"There's a Home Depot in Overfield, isn't there?" Flynn asked.

Delaney nodded. "And two more in Norwood and Natick. And a Lowe's in Milford and Framingham. If you're trying to make the case that the town hardware store is an endangered species, you're preaching to the choir. My business dropped by half when the Overfield store opened. It has held steady since, but I've had to learn what I can sell and what I can't. But this is about MetroWest Construction, not about my hard-luck story."

"Then you've got the podium," Flynn said, and took out his notebook.

"MetroWest got the town sewer contract in 2002," Delaney said. "It's basically a family business. Four cousins from Brazil. Belo Horizonte, I believe. The Oliveiras. They have access to a wonderful pool of labor from Brazil and the Canary Islands. If you ever go up Framingham way, you see those Brazilian flags everywhere."

"I've seen them," Flynn said.

"Then you know. Hardworking. The first eight years were wonderful. MetroWest performed to spec and, if there was an early completion bonus, they got it every time. The worst complaints I ever heard were that they started earlier than people in town liked. Then, two years ago, something happened."

"What?" Flynn asked.

"If I knew the cause, I'd tell you," Delaney said. "All I know is the result. The quality of the work slipped. They started using substandard materials. They did minimal cleanup. Just as bad, we started getting overage claims."

"What's that?" Flynn asked.

"Bills for labor and materials beyond what was in the contract. Suddenly, they were claiming they needed to blast through shelf every thousand feet. We'd go out and look for the evidence and there wouldn't be any. There were a lot of harsh words on both sides. Their contract was up for renewal in May. Once again, they were the low bidder."

"But they didn't get the contract?"

"We just couldn't trust them. They were sending out crews that were consistently shorthanded and connections being made by people who didn't look like they knew what they were doing. We awarded the contract to the next lowest bidder. We were within our right to do so."

Flynn showed Delaney the photo of the two men.

"I can't be sure. It would not surprise me if they were people who were on the MetroWest payroll," Delaney said.

"Do you mean to say you've seen them before?"

"I said I'm not certain, Detective Flynn. I've ridden shotgun with Mike Kelly in Public Works to do spot inspections a number of times. I've seen men who resemble these two."

Flynn thanked him.

Now, Flynn was back at his desk trying to assemble the pieces. A quick stop at the Public Works Department had confirmed that Mike Kelly, the head of Public Works, also thought the two men looked familiar though, like Joe Delaney, he could not state with certainty that they worked for MetroWest.

He knew much more than he did that morning, but he was no closer to a solution. Clearly, Terhune's role as a selectman had earned him the enmity of many people, so there was at least potentially an ample financial motive. But what had precipitated the murder? More important, why had someone chosen that particular evening?

His cell phone rang.

"Are you still in Hardington?"

Flynn smiled. "And good afternoon to you, too, Liz. Yeah, I'm still in the office, pulling together pieces of the puzzle."

"Got time to talk?" Liz asked. "I've got a laptop for you, and an offer to convey."

"Sure," Flynn said. "Can I buy you dinner? I know for a fact that the Chinese place starts serving at six."

There was a hesitation on the other end of the line. "Give me twenty minutes," Liz said. "I need to feed my cat."

* * * * *

Feed my cat? My god, what made me say that? Liz thought. *Why don't I just say I'm crocheting a doily for my favorite teapot?* As she mentally kicked herself, Abigail, her cat, rubbed Liz's leg appreciatively.

David had left the house that morning at 6:30 a.m., bound, as he had been every Monday for the past six months, for Pittsburgh. David would call twice a day and, if nothing intervened, he would return Friday evening. Since Memorial Day there had been five weekends out of eleven when either weather or the crush of rescuing the business of which he was the interim CEO prevented his coming home as promised.

Liz needed to change clothes. For reasons she did not understand, the Winnebago assigned to the "Volunteer Coordinator" was the only one not air-conditioned and she had perspired through the day. She pulled out a fresh skirt and polo shirt. Neutral. Perfect for dinner with a detective. Her hair looked lifeless after a day of humidity and she ran a brush through it, hoping for the best.

She was almost out of the bedroom when she went back to her dresser. Hesitatingly, she reached for a bottle of perfume, sprayed a mist, and walked through it. *Enough*, she thought.

Exactly twenty minutes after her call, she walked in the door of Bamboo House, Hardington's lone Chinese restaurant and, in her experience, 'Exhibit A' of the reasons why suburban Chinese restaurants were to be avoided. Liz did not consider herself a connoisseur of oriental cuisine, but Bamboo House served, in David's words, 'lowest common denominator food'.

She saw Flynn immediately. Only three tables were occupied on a Monday evening, though the phone seemed to ring regularly with take-out orders.

Flynn outlined his day and the scant progress he had made toward finding the two men. "Nobody recognizes them for certain. Tomorrow morning, I'm going up to an outfit in Framingham where the two guys may work, but my best shot would appear to be one of the police departments in surrounding towns being able to ID these guys."

"I take it Mary Ann Mandeville isn't high on your suspect list," Liz said.

Flynn thought about it for a moment. "She basically told me nothing, except that she'd take a lie detector test to prove she didn't kill Terhune. She doesn't strike me as the kind of person who'd solve a problem by killing someone, and she sent me off in a couple of promising areas. So, maybe you can tell me something more about her."

The question had caught her off guard, and Liz looked over the Bamboo House menu before answering. *Egg Fu Yung.* Did anybody still order such things?

"I got an education this morning from Roland. He says I am not wise in the ways of the world because I was not aware that Mary Ann sleeps around."

She felt herself growing red in the face, but continued. "Mary Ann and Fred were almost certainly having an affair, although Roland couldn't state that with certainty. He just listed half a dozen reasons why a real estate agent would find it advantageous to have pillow talk time with a selectman."

She took a long drink of water, hoping to return her face to its normal color.

"Is there a Mister Mandeville?" Flynn asked.

"Yes, but he never seems to be home." *Change the subject! Change the subject!* She thought. "You said she gave you a couple of leads?"

"Yes." Flynn did not appear to have noticed either Liz's complexion or the similarity of home situations. "Justin Pope. Would-be developer of a golf course property who has spent three years getting his plan rejected by the selectmen. I talked with him this afternoon and he seems like a straight shooter. And then there are the Oliveiras, doing business as MetroWest Construction. They got bumped from the town sewer contract earlier this year. Both your public works director and one of your other selectmen, Joe Delaney, say they may have seen the two men in the photo while inspecting MetroWest work. It may, however, be one of the weakest IDs ever made. Anyway, I'm headed up to see them in the morning.   Provided I can learn Portuguese between now and tomorrow."

Liz felt better. A waiter approached and they both ordered.

Flynn looked around the restaurant. "I also have a better idea about a murder weapon. It left a pretty definite indentation in Terhune's head. The part that hit him was metal, round, maybe six inches across, and beveled inward for about an inch."

"Like a lamp base," Liz said.

Flynn stopped and thought, imagining a lamp base. "Yes, like a lamp base, although I was thinking more along the lines of an oversized flashlight. Anyway, keep an eye out for anything that meets that description. While it's likely that the perp or perps took the weapon with them, there's some chance it's still at the site. The medical examiner said it was a 'weapon of opportunity' so they might have left it behind. So, what was this offer you talked about?"

"Well," she said, "First, here with my compliments is Fred Terhune's computer."   She handed Flynn the laptop. "The password is *probono*, and don't ask me how long it took to guess it. I didn't see much on it, but then I don't know what to look for."

"I'm also relaying an offer from the producer of *Ultimate House Makeover*," Liz said. "They're willing to foot the bill for anything you need to catch whoever did this quickly. That offer includes ex-FBI-types to do legwork for you."

"That's rather kind of them," Flynn said, taking the computer. "As long as we've lapsed into Latin, what do you think is the *quid pro quo* for this kind-hearted gesture?"

"I suspect their generosity – and this is Don Elwell who made the offer – is to ensure that you don't upset their production schedule."

Flynn nodded and was quiet for a moment. "Liz, do you see any suspects there? Among the production crew?"

The question took Liz by surprise. "I hadn't thought of it."

Flynn rubbed the ends of his chopsticks together. "I've spent the afternoon talking with people who might have had a reason to kill Terhune – or at least, trying to talk to them – and I keep coming back to location and timing. Why after the party? Why there? Let's say the killers were those two guys who accosted Terhune in the party tent. They've learned that he's at this party, but there are several hundred people there. If you're going to kill him, why wait until nearly one o'clock in the morning? The party broke up a little after ten. Terhune apparently went back to the trailer and worked several hours. Whoever did it waited patiently for those hours, then killed him somewhere in the vicinity."

"They confronted him in the trailer? They waited by his car and, when he didn't show, they went looking for him," Liz offered.

"That's logical, but that's also a lot of patience," Flynn said. "If it were me, I would have waited about half an hour. If Terhune didn't show, then I would start looking for him. With two people, it wouldn't have taken more than half an hour or forty-five minutes to find him. It's just curious."

"Unless Fred wasn't alone, or the area around the trailers was crawling with people until after midnight," Liz said. "Is that why you ask about the production staff?"

"Well," Flynn said, "Elwell says no one stayed overnight. Eddie Frankel queried everyone on staff as to when they left, and everyone says they were gone by a few minutes after midnight and the private security guys – both retired cops – said they saw no one on their 1 a.m. round. If the guys in the photo don't pan out, I can always check security cameras at the crew's hotel to verify that everyone was tucked in bed when Terhune got hit. But I keep coming back to the timing. I guess I'm asking you to keep your eyes open."

Liz watched Flynn expertly pick up a fried wonton, dip it in a sauce, and eat half. "You're no amateur with chopsticks," she observed.

"My last partner on the job was Chinese," Flynn said. "She wouldn't go into an Asian restaurant with me unless I could eat properly."

Liz waited for an amplification. There was none. *You said 'she',* Liz thought. *So your last partner as a detective was a Chinese woman. Finally, a nugget of information.*

An hour later, Liz was back home, tired and in need of a shower, but with one final obligation for the evening.

Felicity Snipes, wife of New England Patriots quarterback Tom Snipes, answered on the second ring. "Good evening, Liz," she said. In their previous meetings, Felicity had made no secret of the fact that she used Caller ID to screen her phone.

"I'm not sure you're going to be taking my calls after this one," Liz said. "I'm the new volunteer coordinator for the *Ultimate House Makeover* show…"

"Hammer and Saw Productions," Felicity said. "We've got them down for Friday afternoon."

"I have a personal plea from Whit Dakota for a football scrimmage…"

"When?" Felicity asked.

"Tomorrow. Any time. They're moving the house modules…"

"Where?"

"Your choice. I'd suggest the high school football field…"

Liz heard the tapping of keys on a keyboard. "If it's any consolation, Don Elwell, the producer says it's a 'guaranteed airtime' thing," Liz said as she listened to the sound of Felicity typing on the other end of the line. "Whit said it was so that he and your husband could 'bond' before the reveal on Friday."

"Uh, huh," Felicity said. More tapping of keys. "Well, your people are in luck. O.K. Tom was going to be doing weight training at home until noon. He has to be in Foxboro at twelve-thirty sharp. I could give them forty-five minutes at the high school starting at eleven-fifteen."

"Just like that?" Liz asked.

"Not exactly," Felicity said. "You tell them this: First, they're only getting a slot because you asked me. Second, it's no-touch football only. Tom throws a couple of passes and makes chit-chat. Third -- and they'll see all this in writing – I'm holding them to the 'guaranteed use' promise. If tomorrow's scrimmage isn't used in the final cut, or if they use anything under sixty seconds of it, they pay Tom's standard personal appearance fee. I'll email you a contract this evening."

"Do I want to know how much the fee is?"

"Twenty-five thousand," Felicity said. "I have no desire to stroke Whit Dakota's ego with a free football game because he thought it would be neat to scrimmage with a Super Bowl quarterback. I'm giving him an incentive."

"Will he go for it?" Liz asked.

"Of course, he'll go for it," Felicity said. "And he'll use the footage because he's got a percentage of Hammer and Saw. I watched five weeks' worth of that show before I agreed for Tom to do it, and I can spot three or four paid product placement plugs in every show. Whit Dakota is shameless. That show isn't about building houses. It's about Whit and what a cool guy he is. Tell me, is he as big an asshole in person?"

"I just met him today, but I think it's more like he's not all that smart. I get the sense that his gofers – excuse me, his assistant producers – do all the thinking for him."

"Just asking. Hey, give me a call when you get the final sketches for the police station garden. I'm looking forward to that." And Felicity Snipes was gone.

What a woman, Liz thought. Tom Snipes, the ten-million-dollar-man for the Patriots, wakes up in the morning, and his wife hands him a schedule for the day. Like a 'honey-clean-the-gutters' chore list, except that it has personal appearances and workout routines. *Why didn't I marry a quarterback?*

4.

It was 8 p.m. Flynn had no desire to go home, nor did he want to go back to the police station. Instead, he drove to the state sanitarium grounds where the parking lot was still surprisingly full of cars. Floodlights lit each of the house modules and there was a constant movement of people among the trailers, and between the trailers and the modules.

He stayed to the shadows, eavesdropping on conversations and trying to imagine the area twenty-four hours earlier. The party had been held in Construction Tent 2. Its flanking covered wings now sheltered three house modules and some fifty people worked at various tasks. Getting from the parking lot to the party would have required that people pass by several of the Winnebagos used as construction trailers.

Flynn put himself in the position of the two men. They have confronted Terhune. Something that was said was sufficiently unsatisfying that they have gone back to the parking lot to wait for him to leave the party.

Which meant that either they knew his car and waited near it, or waited somewhere that they could observe people leaving. Flynn looked through his notes: Terhune had driven a Subaru Outback. Given Hardington's affinity for SUVs, the Subaru would have been one of at least twenty similar looking vehicles in the parking lot. Unless they knew his license plate number, the two men had not waited by Terhune's car.

There were some overgrown bushes near the food tent where Terhune was found. Flynn noted they were adjacent to the parking lot, with a view of traffic passing between the party tent and the cars. Here is where they would have waited.

Flynn used a flashlight to look for the lucky cigarette butt or other detritus that might have been left by the two men. He found a few promising items and also smelled a faint whiff of urine. There were a dozen portable toilets alongside the tent. Whoever had been here did not want to be seen.

He called the Hardington dispatcher. "See if you can get that crack evidence team from the state police back out here to the sanitarium. Tell them to look for some big bushes by the food tent. I think that's where the perps waited for Terhune. There's definitely some trash, there may also be urine. These guys waited a couple of hours and they may have left something behind other than the contents of their bladders. I'll mark the area for them."

Flynn went back to his car and got a roll of evidence tape. As he was laying it, a voice came from behind him.

"Can I help you?"

Flynn looked up to see one of the assistant producers in the black *Ultimate House Makeover* tees.

"I'm David Scott. You're the Hardington detective. I remember you from this morning." The young man held out his hand.

"I'm John Flynn," he said, shaking the younger man's hand. "I've been looking over the area. Whoever hit Terhune had to wait for him after the party. This looks like a pretty good place to wait. Were you at the party last night?"

Scott nodded and gave a slight smile. "Don said we could go to the party as long as we promised not to enjoy ourselves."

Flynn took out the photo of the two men. "Do you remember seeing these guys?" Flynn offered Scott his flashlight.

Scott looked carefully at the photo. "I saw them. They were definitely out of place," he said. "I thought they might be with the caterer. They showed up after the speech. Nine-thirty or so."

"They also had an altercation with Terhune," Flynn said. "Did you see that?"

Scott shook his head. "No, and I would have remembered something like that. Also, I don't remember them being around when the reception started winding down."

"Where do you work?" Flynn asked.

"I'm the production assistant assigned to Construction Unit 2. I work with Tony... Anthony Soffa."

"You stayed after the party?"

Scott nodded. "Most of us involved with construction were here until midnight. We had to get everything ready for the modules this morning."

"You were in your trailers?"

"No," Scott said. "We were all over. Checking equipment. Making certain the power was up. That sort of thing."

Flynn pointed to the tent where the party had been held. "And that's your tent?"

Scott nodded again. "Units 2 and 3 share the tent."

Flynn pointed to the photograph. "And if these two guys were hanging around behind these bushes, would you have seen them?"

Scott shook his head vigorously. "We're kind of single-minded. We've got a six-page, single-spaced checklist to go through. If two guys were waiting over there, they would have had to do something to announce themselves before anyone would have noticed."

"You had met Fred Terhune?"

"Sure," Scott said. "I wasn't involved with the knock-down so I spent about two hours with him Saturday morning going over skill sets we needed from volunteers and checking that he had everyone we requested."

"Did you see him after, say, ten o'clock last night?"

Scott thought for a moment. "He was still here after ten. I can say that for certain. It could even have been as late as ten-thirty. He wasn't the last person to leave the tent, but I remember seeing him when the crowd was getting pretty thin." He said sheepishly, "The production people kind of want the reception to break up early because we can't start our check list until everyone has gone. I think Terhune had a couple of drinks and said something to Don – Don Elwell. Then he went off in the direction of the trailers. That's the last time I paid any attention to him."

Don Elwell told me he wasn't at the party, Flynn thought.

"You said you left at midnight?" Flynn asked.

Scott nodded.

"Was anyone else here? Did you see anyone still here when you left?"

Scott thought for a moment. "There were still a dozen cars in the lot, so someone was here. But I didn't see anyone."

"What kind of cars?"

Scott closed his eyes. Visualizing the parking lot, Flynn thought. "A couple of SUV-type things. Two or three of the coupes we rented when we flew in, so there were at least a few of the staff still here, though we were all pretty tired."

"Did Don Elwell also drive one of those coupes?"

"No, Scott said. "He always rents something nice. He and Whit get the good wheels, the rest of us get the low-end Chevys. And no, I don't remember if Don's car was in the lot. Cars in the parking lot weren't tops on our minds."

"Who are the other assistant production assistants? I met Sam Hirsch and Joel."

"Joel Silverstein is the video engineer, not an assistant producer," Scott said. "Sam is Don's assistant. Barry Zimmerman is talent and volunteer assistant, and Chip Gilman is Whit's assistant. Lou Booker and Jeff Greenberg are the other two construction assistants."

"Would any of them have had reason to be here after midnight last night?"

"Not if we could help it," Scott said. "Last night was the last time any of us expect to get a decent night's sleep until Friday. From now until we wrap, it's pretty much twenty-four-seven. I was at our hotel by about a quarter past twelve and sound asleep ten minutes later."

Flynn felt an urge to keep looking around the grounds. He handed Scott a card. "If you think of anything, or if you hear of anyone who was here after midnight, please give me a call. I'm trying to put together the last few hours of Fred Terhune's life, and witnesses would be very useful."

There were signs on each of the trailer doors. Flynn found the one marked 'Executive Producer' and knocked. Sam Hirsch opened the door.

"I need to see your boss for just a moment," Flynn said.

"He's on a call," Hirsch said.

"I can wait." Hirsch disappeared. A moment later, Don Elwell was in the doorway.

"Liz Phillips relayed your offer," Flynn said. "I don't know if I'll need to take you up on it. But I also have two quick questions."

"Ask," Elwell said.

"One of your people told me they saw Fred Terhune tell you something just before the party broke up. First, what did he tell you and, second, why did you tell me you weren't at the party?"

"Who told you that?" Elwell asked.

"Not important, but the answers could be very important," Flynn said.

Elwell took a deep breath. "I wasn't at the party. I was here in this office from five o'clock until a little after ten. I went down to the party just long enough to round up my assistant and to tell him to get his ass back to work. As to what Fred Terhune said to me, I really don't remember. It must have been something like, 'nice party' because it didn't stick."

Flynn noted that Elwell looked him in the eye when he talked about his reason for being in the tent. After that, Elwell looked at the door jamb. Elwell was lying when he said he didn't remember Terhune talking to him.

Flynn handed them each a card. "If you can think of anyone else who might have seen Terhune after the party, and especially after midnight, please give me a call. I need to establish a timeline of the last few hours before he was killed."

Another hour of searching produced no murder weapon or anything else that was of evidentiary value. At 11 p.m., he made the drive to his home in Roslindale. He found a note on the refrigerator from his wife, Annie, reminding him she was working the late shift at Brigham and Women's this week.

Annie. They had met in 1976. He was a rookie patrolman in Boston with two wasted years at Holy Cross behind him. She was Ann McClennan, second year nursing student at St. Elizabeth's and, like him, a product of Dorchester. She had been the petite brunette with the mischievous smile and the breathtaking figure. *God, it had been wonderful.* Summer weekends at Nantasket Beach, winter nights with their friends at a bar watching the Celtics or the Bruins. There was always laughter, there was always warmth.

Annie's pregnancy had not derailed their happiness, it had only accelerated the inevitable. It was a year into their relationship and Flynn had known for months that Annie was the one. He was waiting only for her graduation to propose. In the finest Irish Catholic tradition they had wed just six weeks after setting the date. There was still a wedding photo on the television. The yellows had disappeared and the reds were fading so that the portrait now was predominantly blues and blacks. Annie didn't show, she was barely three months pregnant at the time.

Annie's parents had helped them buy this house in Roslindale and they had moved in two months before the baby was due. And then came Matthew. Flynn had handed out cigars and been the toast of the precinct house. He had proven he was a man by becoming a father, he had proven he was a decent guy because he had Done The Right Thing.

In twenty-four hours, it all came crashing down. Hydrocephalus, they call it now. 'Water on the brain', they called it in 1978. The obstetrician denied it was the forceps used in delivery, the archdiocese tried to argue it was an 'Act of God'.

Everyone prayed for Baby Matthew even as they waited for him to die. Except that he did not die. Instead, the marriage of John and Ann Flynn, just six months old, died in their son's place. Annie turned her nursing school education to the full-time care of her brain-damaged son. Flynn became a bystander in his own home.

By 1982, even Annie acknowledged that no one person could care for their son and so, with the hefty settlement from the hospital, their son went into institutional care with the Sisters of Charity in suburban Belmont. Annie's cumulative anger that she had not been able to cure her son, and resentment that her husband had argued for institutionalization from the outset, came to define their relationship. She went back to work and Flynn disappeared into his career, volunteering weekends and double shifts to keep himself away from home as much as possible.

So it had been for thirty years. It had been three decades akin to an armed truce. They communicated by notes on the refrigerator and the occasional, awkward encounter. He could not remember when they had been out for dinner or a movie. To his knowledge, they had no friends in common. They maintained separate finances to the point that Flynn had no idea of Annie's salary or her savings.

Annie celebrated holidays with her sister's family, Flynn had always volunteered for holiday duty. In those years, Flynn had slept everywhere in the house except in his own bedroom. Divorce, the logical solution in any other religion, and even for Roman Catholics in the last quarter of the twentieth century in America, was never discussed.

Flynn pulled out his clothes for the morning and set the alarm next to the sofa in the cramped living room to be certain he was out of the house before seven.

5. Tuesday

The ringing of the phone startled Liz into wakefulness. She looked groggily at the clock. Six o'clock. It would be David. She reached for the phone.

"It's a good thing you called," she said. "Otherwise I'd probably still be asleep at nine." She proceeded to outline the events of the past day and her new role as volunteer coordinator for *Ultimate House Makeover*. She left out dinner with Flynn.

"That's awful about Fred," David said. "At least you didn't find the body this time. Are you helping with the investigation?" Liz thought she heard a note of sarcasm, but it could have been her grogginess.

"I've just been asked to keep an eye out for two guys who accosted Fred during the party. They're the lead suspects, I guess." Liz decided to downplay any other role Flynn might have asked her to play.

"Well, on this end, it's a busy week," David said. "Three due diligence teams in house and six million dollars of product to ship. Liz, it's finally getting close. You can feel it in the air. I really believe this will be over by the last week of September. You can start thinking about October someplace nice."

"I'll believe it when I see it," Liz said. An exchanged, "I love you," and the line was dead. Three minutes of conversation to last through the day.

Six more weeks, Liz thought. *It was supposed to be over with at the end of June.*

David Phillips, peripatetic chairman of Phillips Management, LLC. Interim Chief Executive Officer for hire, short-term rates available. Rescuer of distressed companies; liquidator of those that could not be put right. The banks and the creditors loved him. The courts showed him respect. Shareholders were given hope, even if, as was usually the case, they would get little or nothing in the end. Employees, even if they did not love him, did not fear him because he was always the antidote to the buffoons who had gotten the company into trouble. Everyone liked David because David was always there. Twenty-four-seven for the company for as long as it took to either make it right or get it sold. Which meant zero time for Liz.

There would be respites. An assignment would end and there would be a tantalizing month in the Caribbean or France. And for those few weeks Liz and David would draw closer, the painful memories of the long absences allowed to heal under the sun in St. Bart's or a hotel suite in Paris.

But long before the end of the month, the phone would ring and offers would begin to arrive. On a balcony overlooking the Tuileries, or a patio beside the sea or the mountains in a far-off beautiful land, David would listen to the horror story and begin his research via computer and phone calls, vetting the corporation in distress to determine that it was salvageable.

And then there would be the negotiation. Contingency payments, carve-outs and success fees. By the last week of their stay in whatever idyllic locale, David would be on the telephone in one continuous conference call with investor groups. Liz would be left to explore on her own, or simply to read. A few days after they arrived back in Boston, David would be on a plane to his next distressed company.

The first such assignment took him to a struggling textile firm in Atlanta. His five months of work had fattened the Phillips brokerage account by more than half a million dollars and had resulted in three months of harmony between them afterwards. They had gone to Tahiti and watched sunsets together from a bungalow on a private bay. Seven assignments later, their net worth had soared to a once-unimaginable level but their harmony was a distant memory. 'October in someplace nice' realistically meant three weeks at a Jumby Bay-type resort with high-speed,

Skype-quality internet service ranking as high as the resort's reputation for cuisine as a requirement for their stay.

On that long-ago first assignment, David's prolonged absence had been a novelty for Liz. She had taken art classes at the Museum of Fine Arts and gone on spur-of-the-moment trips with friends. She had flown to Atlanta several times and they had gotten to know the city together. Now, after five years and into his eighth 'save the company' assignment, it was clear that it was really David who relished these extended absences. Liz had never been to Pittsburgh and David had made it clear that her presence would be an unwelcome distraction.

Liz noted with irony that he had yet to accept work on behalf of a company in New England. He would complete an assignment then, true to his word, they would go away for a few weeks. Then, without as much as a few days together in their own home and their own bed, David was gone. Put at its simplest, David *wanted* to be gone.

She put on a pot of tea, fed Abigail, and walked out to the end of the long driveway to get the newspaper. Her perennial beds were in their August funk, the glorious flowers of June and July long past, but the plant foliage needing to remain in place to put nutrients in the soil.

To a casual observer, the flowers still appeared prolific and colorful. To Liz's trained eye, the beds were tired and in serious need of attention; the color supplied by just a handful of cultivars, many of them self-sown interlopers. The autumn-blooming perennials were only now heading up, and were two to three weeks away from displaying color. The hostas, at least, were in their full glory. And everywhere, there were weeds that needed to be pulled. *Not this week*, she thought.

By a quarter after seven, she had eaten, showered, dressed, and was checking email. One was from Felicity Snipes, containing a PDF of a contract between the Snipes Family Foundation and Hammer and Saw Productions. That one, she printed off. *Tell*

Dakota he needs to give me an answer before 8 a.m. He can call me on my office line,' Felicity had written. There were eleven other emails, including a long one from her daughter, Sarabeth.

'Hi, mom,' it began. *'Things are hectic out here, but I've got a couple of hours between meetings and wanted to write a note…'*

Then why didn't you call? Liz thought, irritation creeping into her thoughts. When had she taken to writing emails? Until recently, there had been long, wonderful phone calls several times a week from her daughter, now twenty-six, married, and living in Seattle. Those calls had been part of Liz's defense against the loneliness of being by herself for months on end. During the conversations, Liz felt she was coming to know her daughter as an adult. After the calls, Liz always felt better, and more ready to cope with days that sometimes seemed to stretch with their emptiness.

'The apartment is OK for now, but we're still looking for something with a better view. Todd thinks we can swing an old Victorian if interest rates come down just a little more…'

Liz sighed. She would read the rest of the letter later on this morning. She copied the Fred Terhune's volunteer list from the thumb drive onto her computer. She placed the computer in its travel bag; she was ready to go to work to a job that, a day earlier, she had no idea existed.

Fifteen minutes later, she was at Whit Dakota's massive Vectra trailer. She knocked and Chip Gilman stuck his head out of the door.

"Tom Snipes," Liz said. "Football at eleven fifteen at the high school. Here's the contract. You better read it."

"Contract," Chip said, warily.

"I remember Elwell saying he would guarantee that the footage would get used in the program," Liz said. "I think the Snipeses are going to hold you to your word."

Chip read down the first page of the contract. "Twenty-five thousand."

"That's if it's just a football game. Put it on the air, and its free," Liz said, far more brightly than the situation called for. "Oh, and I'm supposed to tell you that the only reason why Tom is willing to make time in his schedule for you is that I was the one who asked."

"And I thought people in LA were vultures," Chip said.

"We country bumpkins learn fast. I'm sure you guys can amuse yourselves other ways at noon." Liz gave him Felicity's number. "She needs an answer before eight or the deal is off."

The Volunteer trailer door was open, the interior muggy and warm, and Barry Zimmerman already at his desk, hunched over his phone. Liz opened the back windows and left the door open, hoping a cross breeze might cool things off.

"Barry, I've got to ask one question. Why is it that every other trailer here has air conditioning and this one doesn't?"

Zimmerman looked up from his computer. "It conked out last week in Rochester. The first time we can get it serviced will be after Princeton when we take the September break."

Liz looked at the stack of requests on her desk. She began thumbing through them. Some had come from Barry, others had been scribbled by the construction assistants. Most were urgent needs for specialty skills. Six additional people with roofing experience for 3 p.m. Four grading equipment operators at 1 p.m. Fairly routine stuff. Then she saw a sheaf of volunteer applications clipped together with the cover note, 'NEED PIX'.

She held up the papers. "What's this?"

Zimmerman looked over and squinted. "That's Chip and Whit. They're starting to look for on-camera subjects for Thursday and Friday when the house gets decorated. They've flagged some interesting profiles and want to see that the people are photogenic."

Liz flipped through the applications. All women. All college-age. "And I'm supposed to go find them and take their picture so that they can pick out the cute ones to show on camera?"

"I'd send out one of your runners with a digital camera," Zimmerman said, pointedly not answering Liz's question.

"You missed the irony, Barry. Whit Dakota only wants to feature cute cheerleader types when it comes to decorating the house. Anyone over twenty-five need not apply. Should I also get bra sizes?"

Zimmerman looked slightly embarrassed. "Look, I don't make the rules. Whit is the talent. He's got a sixth sense about this stuff. He knows what Don likes and he knows what the network likes. Pretty girls in the decorating sequence increases the audience. He's got numbers to prove it."

"And I suppose he'll interview the finalists himself." Liz found herself getting angry.

Zimmerman shrugged. "Please, Liz, just get the photos."

* * * * *

At 7:00 a.m., Flynn was at the Framingham office of MetroWest Construction. It was two acres of cyclone fence enclosing a dozen dump trucks, all of which looked like they needed a serious cleaning. He had dropped off copies of the photo at the Framingham Police Department and gotten a promise that, if anyone on duty recognized the two men, Flynn would be called.

Now, he watched as workmen walked in, eyeing him. Their common language seemed to be Portuguese, or at least what Flynn surmised was Portuguese. The Boston area had a large émigré population from Brazil and the Canary Islands, though they settled mostly in Cambridge and Framingham rather than in Boston.

Two men approached. They looked more prosperous than those who had gone into the truck yard.

"Mr. Oliveira?" Flynn asked.

They stopped and looked him over. Flynn, in a sports jacket and tie, obviously wasn't looking for work.

"You the cop from Hardington that keeps calling?" one asked.

"Detective John Flynn. May I speak with you for a few minutes?"

They looked at one another and spoke rapidly in Portuguese.

"Come on in," one said.

The interior of MetroWest Construction was a single, large room perhaps thirty feet on a side. Filing cabinets seemed to define the perimeter of offices and file folders were on every surface. *This is not an efficiently run organization*, Flynn thought.

Two chairs were brought and placed in front of a table covered with file folders. One of the men sat behind the desk. Flynn and the other man sat in front.

"I am Jorge Oliveira," said the man behind the desk. He did not offer a hand. "This is Miguel Oliveira. You ask your questions."

Flynn pulled out the photo of the two men. "I am told that these two men work for you. I need to speak to them in connection with the death of Fred Terhune."

The two men studied the photo far longer than was necessary. "We have never seen them," Jorge Oliveira said. "They do not work for us."

It was the answer Flynn expected. "You held the sewer contract in Hardington until last May. What happened?"

The two men looked at one another and then spoke rapidly in Portuguese. "We built Hardington's sewers for ten years," Jorge Oliveira said. "For ten years, we gave your town the highest quality work at the lowest price. Then, your town bosses took the contract away and gave it to their friends. Friends who charged more."

"I don't live in Hardington, Mr. Oliveira. I couldn't afford to live there. I just work at the police department. So, please don't call it 'my' town. I'm just an employee. And two people with no reason to lie told me that, for eight years, everything you say was true. Then, two years ago, your work began to have problems."

"That is a lie," Miguel Oliveira said.

"I only know what people told me. And they told me that taking away the contract was Fred Terhune's idea. Therefore, you might have had reason to want to see harm come to Mr. Terhune."

"*Mentiras*," Miguel Oliveira said.

"Then tell me what happened," Flynn said.

There was more rapid Portuguese spoken.

"*Pagamento sob a tabela*," Jorge Oliveira said. "You understand that? Your selectmen... excuse me, the Hardington selectmen wanted money from us to keep the contract. You look around here." He gestured with his hand to the rag-tag office. "Where are we going to get money for an envelope? We told them we would not pay."

Flynn absorbed what he was being told, trying hard not to judge. "I was told that in the last two years, the quality of your work went downhill."

"For two years, they pressured us to pay," Miguel Oliveira said.

"I was told you were submitting bills for work that was not performed. Like blasting."

"*Mentiras*," Miguel Oliveira repeated. "They wanted payments. They wanted envelopes of money."

"And you are certain you've never seen these two men?" Flynn again placed the photo on the desk.

"*Nunca*," Miguel Oliveira said. "We never saw them."

Lies, Flynn thought as he walked back to his car. Someone was lying. Did Hardington selectmen demand bribes? It seemed ludicrous on its face. He had one ace up his sleeve or, to be more precise, in his pocket. He unlocked his car door, got inside, reached into his jacket pocket and pulled out the pocket recorder. At least he would soon know what they had said among themselves.

Flynn drove to the Hilton in Cavendish where the crew of *Ultimate House Makeover* stayed, passing the massive, one-time General Motors assembly plant that had employed thousands. Now it was an auto auction distribution facility, sending used cars deemed unsalable in Boston to locations where high odometer readings or accident histories mattered less. No one made cars in New England any more. He remembered that his father would only consider a car that was assembled at GM Framingham.

At the Hilton, he asked for the general manager and explained that this was a murder investigation and that he needed to see the hotel's security video for Sunday evening between 10 p.m. and 2 a.m. in order to verify that everyone who said they had left the Hardington Sanitarium had in fact been at the hotel at the time of the murder.

The general manager looked embarrassed. "We have six cameras," he said, "but they're all just live feeds. We don't record anything. The head of security keeps an eye on the screens and reacts only if he sees suspicious activity. Coming into the hotel lobby at 1 a.m. isn't anything out of the ordinary."

"Then what about card keys?" Flynn asked. "Just tell me when fifteen guests activated the locks in their rooms."

The general manager looked exasperated. "This isn't Boston," he said. "This is a suburban hotel with 200 rooms. I can tell you what time a card key was created, but not when it was used. That kind of system costs money I don't have."

Flynn left in frustration.

* * * * *

Janey Matthews, Liz's most reliable runner and possessor of a tiny, twelve- megapixel camera brought for the explicit purpose of getting candid shots of Whit Dakota that she could post to Facebook, had undertaken the assignment of getting photos of the eighteen women requested by Chip Gilman. She now sprawled in the chair next to Liz, fanning herself. Janey was thin, her body too busy adding height to be able to add balancing muscle or fat. Fair complexioned, her brunette hair was pulled back in a pony tail.

"Everybody, like, asked why I was taking the photos, and I didn't know what to say," Janey said, a stream of consciousness at work on a hot August morning. "Then they all wanted to see the other photos. Was it OK to show them? We must have clicked through them a dozen times, but I didn't erase any. I put numbers next to the names so you'll know which person is which. So why was I taking these photos?"

Liz gave her most reassuring smile. "Janey, I just get requests. Tomorrow, I'll probably have you counting water bottles. There's no rhyme or reason. The question is, are you having fun?"

Janey continued to fan herself. "I am. It's like, totally cool to watch the house pieces get built. I think Elaine and Bobbie are still psyched. Tara said it's too hot, so she's dropping out. I don't know what's going on with Michelle. She was really up on the weekend and we were going to work together all week, but when I called her Monday morning, her mom said she was grounded for the week because she stayed so late at the party. But you can count on us, Mrs. Phillips. We'll be here every day."

"How old are you, Janey?"

"Fifteen."

God, they grow up quickly, Liz thought. She had read most of Sarabeth's email, which had been long and chatty, but which spoke of a different world. It was one that Liz could relate to only by first acknowledging that Sarabeth's world was one in which her daughter found personal and professional fulfillment in an environment that in no way relied on her mother.

She could still envision Sarabeth at fifteen on another August morning, sitting in the rattan chairs on the porch of their old house, striking the same pose as Janey did this morning. Sarabeth, too, had been fair-skinned and too thin, growing an inch every few months. Still a child, still needing her mother. Once, Liz could have confidently named all of Sarabeth's close friends. Liz knew where they lived and had met their families. Now, even the names of her daughter's friends were alien. *We had dinner with Marisa and Li Cheng at a new Japanese-French fusion restaurant...*'

There was another written message on her desk. This one from Joel, the video engineer. *Need to ID grip & grins. Stop by trailer.'* Liz took the camera, thanked Janey, and gave her a sheaf of messages to take back to the various construction foremen and assistants.

Liz walked the fifty feet to the Winnebago that served as the video production center. She knocked.

An exasperated Joel Silverstein came to the door. "First rule of camp," he said, motioning her in. "Please don't knock, at least not on my door. If I'm here, chances are I'm editing or giving directions to the camera crew, and I can better use the thirty seconds that it takes to put everything on hold while I get up and play proper host. If I'm not here, the door is locked. So, from now on, the rule is, if you need to see me, just come in and don't think I'm being rude by not getting up. Understand?"

Liz nodded. "Whatever you say." She explained the assignment to photograph co-ed volunteers for possible on-camera duty and gave him Janey's camera.

Joel took the camera. "The photos are no big deal," he said. "Whit does this in every locale." He extracted its memory chip and plugged it into a computer console. Eighteen photos appeared on the flat-screen television.

"Taken by a fifteen-year-old," Liz said. "Not exactly Annie Liebowitz territory."

Joel tapped keys and enlarged several the photos. "Actually, they're not bad. Let's tag them," he said. Liz read names from a list Janey had prepared which Joel added to the photos. Three of the women were strikingly attractive. Liz had a good idea of who was going to be asked to be on camera come Thursday.

Joel pushed his chair down the console to another keyboard. "Let me show you what else I need," he said. "I pulled about two hundred frames from Sunday night of Whit talking with people at the party. We like to print them up and give them as 'thank yous'. What I need is for you to identify the people in the photos."

He tapped a few keys and Whit had his arm around a man and a woman. "For example, do you know these people?"

Liz nodded. "Dorrie and Ed Duck."

"That's exactly what I need," Joel said. "I'm going to print you up some contact sheets. You just write the names wherever you find room." A few more keys and pages began coming out of a printer. In under a minute, Joel had handed her 25 pages of contact sheets, each page containing up to ten photos. "If I can get these by Thursday morning, I can have Whit sign them for Friday afternoon."

"And Liz," Joel said. "I'm sorry for the lecture. You're new, you don't know us yet. It's obvious that you know what you're doing and it's great that you've picked up where Fred left off, because we really need you. Just remember: we're all busy. So forget the niceties and come on in next time."

"I'll remember," Liz said. She left the luxury of the cool trailer. *And I wondered what I was going to do with my lunch time…*

* * * * *

Flynn sat in the living room of Karen and Mike McCarthy. A coffee cup balanced on his knee, occupying one hand, a pen in his other hand in the faint hope there was a reason to make notes.

Karen McCarthy, whom Liz had recognized as one of the people standing near Fred Terhune when the two men accosted him Sunday evening, placed an imaginary Fred Terhune about four feet from her.

"I remember the two men because I kept thinking that they were so out of place," she said. "And they walked right up to Fred. They were both much taller, probably over six feet, and they spoke with Spanish accents."

"Do you remember anything about what they said?" Flynn asked.

"Well, there was a lot of profanity," she said. "Every third word started with 'f'. But from what I could tell, they were angry that Fred hadn't done something, and he – Fred – was 'going to pay'. At the end, one said, 'two weeks'. That's when Fred said something like, 'you have to give me time'. One man said something very low and shoved Fred. Then they walked off. It was only a few minutes."

"Do you think your husband could add any details?"

Karen McCarthy shook her head. "Mike never listens to these things. I asked him about it on our way home and he said, 'what guys?' He's even worse in restaurants…"

Flynn excused himself after politely listening to a litany of Mike McCarthy's shortcomings. What he had learned, though, fit the theory of the two men as the most likely suspects in Fred Terhune's murder.

Now, he needed to find the two men.

There were no Portuguese speaking officers on the Hardington force, but a quick call to Public Works said that the operator of the bulldozer at the transfer station was a native of the Canary Islands.

Fifteen minutes later, Flynn was at the transfer station with Pedro De Sales's ear cocked to listen to the words coming out of the recorder:

"You the cop from Hardington that keeps calling?" Flynn now knew this was Jorge Oliveira.

"Detective John Flynn. May I speak with you for a few minutes?"

"Shit. He's trouble. I can tell just by looking at him that he's a problem," De Sales translated.

"Well, he wouldn't be here if he already had the answers."

"What do we tell him?"

"I'll do the talking."

"Come on in," Jorge Oliveira said.

Flynn advanced the tape.

"You held the sewer contract in Hardington until last May. What happened?" Flynn heard himself asking.

"Don't trust him, Jorge," De Sales translated.

"Of course I don't trust him. He's police."

"Get rid of him."

"I'll do better than that. Listen and learn."

"We built Hardington's sewers for ten years…" Jorge Oliveira said.

Flynn again advanced the tape. "…You might have had reason to want to see harm come to Mr. Terhune," he heard himself say on the tape.

"*Mentiras*," Miguel Oliveira said.

"Lies," De Sales translated.

"Then tell me what happened."

"*What does he know, Jorge?*" De Sales translated.

"*I can keep him running in circles for weeks. Watch this.*"

"*Pagamento sob a tabela*," Jorge Oliveira said.

"Payment under the table," De Sales translated.

Flynn, relieved, allowed the tape to the point where he stood up to leave. He started to turn off the recorder.

"Wait, there's more," De Sales said.

Flynn backed up the tape. The Oliveira cousins were talking to one another as Flynn went to the door.

"*You find Marco and Jorge. Find out what they did. And then you get them out of the..*" De Sales shook his head. "That's all I can hear. It gets too faint.

* * * * *

Flynn felt it was time for an update for the chief of police. He showed Chief Harding the photo of the two men. "Not iron clad," Flynn said. "Not by any stretch. But, what I have is MetroWest concocting a story about selectmen demanding kickbacks. Meanwhile, as they're talking among themselves in Portuguese, they're making up the story as they go along. The Oliveiras said they never saw these two guys before, yet one cousin is telling the other to find 'Marco and Jorge' and get them out of town."

What about Justin Pope?" Chief Harding asked.

Flynn shook his head. "I buy the story. I'll check it out, but Pope seemed to be a straight shooter."

"What about the people from the TV show?"

"That's the screwy part," Flynn said. "Elwell seems to lie – no – stretch the truth just out of habit. He said he wasn't at the party. Turns out he was there at the end though, he says, just long enough to pull some people away. Why not tell me the truth straight out? He wants to give me assistance in the form of private investigators. As long as there's a chance in hell that someone from the show is involved, that would give whoever was doing the investigating divided loyalties. And besides, I don't like rent-a-cops."

Flynn shifted his stance. "But I'm also left with the timing thing. Twelve-thirty in the morning. Supposedly, the grounds were deserted. We know Terhune was still there, working in his trailer on a spreadsheet. Mundane stuff. More importantly, why murder him there? Why not wait for him at home?"

"That's why you're the detective," Chief Harding said. "And what about the real estate lady?"

"She wants to sell me a house," Flynn said. "I'm going to keep her on the back burner."

"Well, turn up the heat somewhere else," Chief Harding said. "I'm still getting calls both from the media and from the state police. They all want answers. Let's not drag this out."

* * * * *

"Hey, Volunteer Lady!"

Liz looked up from her attempts to put names to the photos on the contact sheet. There in the doorway was Whit Dakota.

"Let's go play some football," Dakota said. "You've got to show us where this football field is. You, too, Zimmerman."

Liz gritted her teeth and gathered up her contact sheets. Ten minutes later, a caravan of three cars containing six assistant producers, two of the three construction supervisors and sound and video operators, pulled into the athletic field at Hardington High School. At exactly 11:15, they were joined by a pickup truck, from which emerged a smiling, waving Tom Snipes. He retrieved an equipment bag full of footballs and began shaking hands all around, after first noting that the camera was rolling.

A moment later, Felicity Snipes stepped out of the driver's side of the truck and gave Liz a wave.

"Does he need an escort?" Liz asked, as Tom Snipes made Dakota run an intricate pass pattern.

"No, just a time reminder," Felicity said, holding up her arm and tapping a watch. "Tom can get carried away at these things. I guess I'm also here to make certain he doesn't break the rules. You'd be amazed at what the Patriots won't allow him to do. No basketball, no handball, no hockey. No trampolines, no zip lines, no skiing."

"Not much chance of that today," Liz said.

"True, but there's also no contact football, not even touch football. If he gets injured and he was 'engaged in an enumerated prohibited activity', the Patriots don't have to pay him. And, believe me, they'd go digging for evidence. They hate paying injured players, even starters." Felicity looked at the sheaf of contact sheets in Liz's hands. "What's that?"

Liz gave an exasperated look. "Souvenirs. Literally." She pointed at Peggy shooting video. "That young lady apparently spent Sunday evening with that video camera pointed at Whit. Every time he shook somebody's hand or clapped an arm around a shoulder, it got recorded for posterity. Their video engineer gave me these this morning. My job is to ID the people in the frame. I have no doubt but that my next job is going to be writing, 'With thanks to Joe and Mary for their hard work, Whit Dakota' on the eight by tens."

Felicity laughed and leafed through the contact sheets. "It looks like you'll be writing a fair number of, 'Cindy, thanks for letting me cop a quick feel' notes. Mr. Dakota seems to like them young and well built."

"Don't get me started," Liz said. A cheer went up as Dakota caught a thirty-yard pass in a crowd. "This morning, I had the displeasure of assigning one of my assistants to photograph every female volunteer between eighteen and twenty-two. They're going to be the on-camera talent when the house gets decorated."

"With Whit Dakota personally interviewing those with an engaging smile and curves in the right places, no doubt." Felicity shook her head. "Pro teams hold cheerleading tryouts every year. They all get photographed and interviewed and, accepted or not, they go into a face book. The book goes to all the single players – or at least that's what Tom tells me – and they all get a rating, including one for 'availability and willingness'. Welcome to feminism in the second decade of the twenty-first century. Now I know why I got all those degrees in clinical psychology – in order to understand the mind of professional football players – society's perpetual adolescents."

"You have degrees in psychology?" Liz asked.

"BS, MS, PhD, with a specialty in adolescent psychology" Felicity said. "I try not to use the 'doctor' part unless I'm at the clinic. Usually 'Snipes' is enough to get a same-day restaurant reservation."

"I never knew that. I'm really impressed," Liz said.

"Because you think, 'football wives', and higher education isn't the first thing that comes to mind," Felicity said. "Believe me, the stereotype is dead-on accurate. But Tom pushed me to get the advanced degrees, except that if I had it all to do over again, I'd have gotten the degrees in marketing instead."

"Don't sell your skills short," Liz said. "One of their producers looked at the contract you sent over and immediately pronounced you a 'vulture'. I think it was a compliment."

"You have to understand," Felicity said. "Tom has an agent, an accountant, a marketing rep and a PR firm. Their job is – at least ostensibly – to look out for Tom's interests. Tom's job is to play football. My job – my *real* job, in addition to fifteen hours a week doing crisis counseling, raising our son, and running the foundation – is to make certain that all those other people on the family payroll are doing *their* job."

Felicity pointed at Dakota, who was doing a mock touchdown dance in the end zone. "Whit Dakota has a one-third stake in Hammer and Saw Productions. From everything I read, he is an egotistical, narcissistic asshole; and I use 'asshole' in its finest psychological sense. Building houses for a worthy family is simply a means to a very lucrative financial end. Does he care that he is being perceived as doing good? Only to the extent that it gets him what he wants. He's your ultimate 'live-in-the-now' kind of guy."

"On Monday, he couldn't remember the name of the family he's building the house for," Liz said, recalling her first meeting with him in his trailer.

Felicity nodded. "That's who he is. My job is to ask the question, 'why should we do business with this asshole?' Tom gets dozens of offers like this every month and, after the show airs, that volume will double. Tom's agent would just sort them by dollar value. I look at them for what they can do to help or hurt Tom's image."

"Tom gets paid for that walk-through on Friday?" Liz asked.

Felicity smiled. "Guild minimum. Three hundred dollars, I think, and the check gets paid directly to leukemia research. Effectively, he's doing it for free except that I made him get a SAG card. Doing this show is part of Tom's image. I'm thinking of what Tom will be doing in five or ten years. The agent, the accountant, the PR guys and the marketing crowd aren't thinking beyond this season and, when some rogue linebacker ends Tom's career with just the right hit to his knees , those guys will just move on to the next client. Like I said, planning Tom's post-football career is my job."

They watched the progress of the game, enjoying an easy camaraderie that Liz had not expected. At 11:52, Felicity held up her watch and caught her husband's eye. He dutifully began his goodbyes as he collected footballs. Felicity jogged over and, from her pocket, took out a marking pen. Tom Snipes began signing footballs and tossing them to the production assistants. At 11:59,

Felicity walked over, gave Liz a hug, and said, "This has been fun. Thanks." At exactly noon, and as specified in the executed contract, the Snipeses departed.

* * * * *

The third call to the Framingham Police Department finally got the attention of that city's chief of detectives, Vince Galanti, who deigned to call Flynn to find out why a small, wealthy and out-of-the-way town like Hardington was attempting to monopolize Framingham's finite law enforcement resources.

"We don't have time to track down your rich runaway brats," Galanti said. "Buy a street atlas and come find them yourself."

"This isn't about runaways," Flynn said. "It's about a murder. A town selectman. I've got two guys on video threatening the selectman a couple of hours before he died. The two guys almost certainly work for MetroWest Construction, and they're from Brazil. Is that enough to get your attention?"

There was a momentary silence on the other end of the line. "Do the two mopes have names?"

"Just first names, but I can give you pictures you can blow up to poster size."

"What do you mean, they 'almost certainly work' for MetroWest, which by the way is probably one unscheduled oil change away from going out of business." Flynn sensed Galanti was warming up.

"It means I was out to see the Oliveiras this morning. While they're swearing to me in English that they never saw these guys before in their lives, one's telling the other in Portuguese to find these guys and get them out of town. Called them Jorge and Marco."

"You're a man of many talents, Officer…"

"Detective John Flynn. If it's any consolation, I had my shield in Boston for twenty-four years."

More silence. "How do I get photos of these mopes?"

"There's one in your desk sergeant's in-box. I put it there with a note this morning before seven."

"Hold on."

Flynn heard footsteps on wooden floor and echoing voices. A minute later, the phone picked up again. "My apology, Detective Flynn. We had a shift change after you left the photo. I don't recognize these two, and 'Jorge and Marco' are very common names, but I'll show the photo around this afternoon. If these guys have a habit of threatening people, they'll be known to someone on the squad."

I guess twenty-four years in Boston still buys a little respect, Flynn thought. He thanked Galanti and hung up.

Flynn opened his email and his eye immediately fell on one with the subject line, "Re: Looking for information on Mary Ann Mandeville."

"Jesus Christ," he said aloud.

Re your query 'Mary Ann Mandeville'. Subject known to us 2001 investigation into death by stabbing of husband. Prior name Rundle. Person of interest with lingering suspicion. Suggest you call for more detail. Jared Millman, Stamford PD.

Flynn spent the first ten minutes of the call playing the 'you must know' game with Detective Jared Millman of the Stamford, Connecticut, Police Department. It was a standard exercise that established mutual credentials. From Millman's extensive knowledge of individual detectives within the Boston PD, including many now retired, Flynn concluded Detective Millman must be over sixty and very senior in the department.

"I worked the Kevin Rundle murder for six months," Millman said. "I liked Mary Ann right from the start. Four knife wounds, in the back, at three in the morning. The first one killed him. The other three were for satisfaction."

"What was Mr. Rundle doing out at that hour?" Flynn asked.

"Poker game," Millman said. "Kevin Rundle was a lawyer in the City – he had just made partner in his firm. The kind of clients you'd expect. He had a standing poker game every Wednesday night with buddies from Yale Law. Not a lot of money changed hands and, in any event, his buddies said he left with less than a hundred dollars in his wallet. The game was at a house on Shippan Point – down by the water – and the Rundles lived north of the Merritt – about ten miles away."

"Is that important?" Flynn asked.

"Fairly. Kevin Rundle left when the game broke up. Two other people remember another car pulling away at the same time and in the same direction as Rundle. But it was dark and they were headed in different directions so they paid it no mind. Rundle got about seven miles – to north of downtown Stamford. He had pulled over to the side of the road, his engine was still running, and someone had knifed him. He was outside of his car and caught it in the back. Four times. Given where he was, it made no sense for him to be outside of the car unless it was either someone he knew or some kind of an authority figure – like he had been pulled over by a police car."

"I take it you ruled that out quickly," Flynn said.

"There's no history of that MO in Stamford before or since," Millman said. "The time of death was just after three. It wasn't reported until about four. His wallet was gone, but the car – a big BMW – wasn't taken. But there was blood everywhere. Whoever did it would have been spattered but good."

"And I take it the credit cards were never used," Flynn said.

"Exactly. The wallet had to be a diversion."

"So, where was the wife?"

"At home, naturally," Millman said. "Except her car was still cooling off. After a lot of beating around the bush, Mrs. Rundle acknowledged that, while Mr. Rundle was playing low-stakes Texas Hold-em, she had a little something going, too. A guy she had sold a house to over in Darien. The timeline was perfect. She left her lover's place at two-thirty and could have been in Shippan Point well before three. She could have followed her husband until they reach the first deserted traffic light. Then, she pulls up alongside and waves, he pulls over and gets out of the car. Out comes the knife."

"Sounds circumstantial, but a jury might buy it," Flynn said.

"Except there wasn't a shred of physical evidence," Millman said. "No blood in her car, no blood on her. No knife. And she had a damn good lawyer through the whole thing who kept everything in bounds. In the absence of probable cause, there were a lot of places we couldn't look. And so we waited for a break."

"And?" Flynn asked.

"Nothing," Millman said. "No comparable crime was committed that would show Rundle's death to be part of some third party's pattern. To her credit, she was a cool one. No unusual movements on her part. We monitored everything she did for six months. She played the perfect, grieving widow."

"What happened to the guy in Darien?"

"She dumped him. I don't even think she saw him after the murder. Anyway, after six months, she sold her house, pocketed a wad of life insurance cash, and moved."

"To Hardington?" Flynn asked.

"To Newton," Millman said. "We watched her get her Massachusetts real estate license and re-establish herself. She started dating – she was twenty-nine at the time of the murder – and began living what the rest of the world calls a normal life. She got married six years ago and moved to Hardington. Except that she's moved half a dozen times since she got to your little town, which is fairly odd. As far as we can tell, she never slipped up. Never confided in anyone. Eventually, my boss said to give it up. Which I did, at least officially."

"You obviously have a theory of the crime," Flynn said.

"She had been planning it for a year, and maybe more," Millman said. "She was a very attractive woman who had been married for four years to a boring corporate lawyer. That poker night hadn't varied for four years. When he made partner, he was worth a lot of money. I think she found a pigeon living just the right distance away and rehearsed the crime a couple of times. When the right night came, she had everything ready – gloves, disposable raincoat, and a knife she had bought long enough ago that no one remembered it. I think she worked alone, flagged him over, got him out of the car, and knifed him. I think she had her timing down to the minute. I think everything she used got double bagged and put in a dumpster with an early morning pickup."

"Did she ever cooperate with the police? Point them in a useful direction?" Flynn asked.

"Through her lawyer," Millman said. "He suggested that Burton Cohen – that's the law firm where Rundle had made partner – had more layers than showed in the glossy brochure. He suggested that several of Rundle's clients may have had ample reason to want to see their attorney silenced. Mind you, there was no evidence offered. Just an accusation that the law firm had crooked clients with a low tolerance for whistle-blowing counsel. We investigated. We found nothing."

Flynn described the murder, the scene involving Terhune and Mary Ann on the video and his conversation with her of the previous afternoon.

"I wish I had something like that to show to the grand jury in 2001," Millman said. "I had adultery, but nothing else. And, in the minds of a Fairfield County jury, adultery is a Class C misdemeanor. Mrs. Rundle never showed any anger at being a suspect, which was one of the things that kept me suspecting her. She just kept breaking down and crying. A videotape of her delivering a swift kick to the nuts might have gotten me an indictment."

"Any advice?" Flynn asked.

"If she did it, she planned it," Millman said. And, if she planned it, there's evidence. She waited until she knew they were alone. She made certain she wouldn't get any blood on her. If you haven't found the crime scene yet, it's even possible she maneuvered your guy to a particular spot. Remember, she's killed once before, even though it has been eleven years."

Flynn spent the next half hour reviewing his notes and thinking about available resources.

Mary Ann Mandeville, he thought. What's *your game, and what's your next move?*

6.

Mary Ann Mandeville stood in the doorway of the volunteer trailer and knocked. Liz, who had been hunched over the table with a magnifying glass identifying Hardington residents, looked up, startled.

"I signed up to be a volunteer," Mary Ann said, cheerfully. "What can I do?"

Liz said nothing, her mind racing. *She's a suspect. I'm not supposed to know that. She was having an affair with Fred Terhune. I'm not supposed to know that, either.*

"You can help me identify these people in the photos," Liz said, finally. "They're moving the house modules down Hospital Road, and until they're at the site, it's kind of quiet."

"I know about the moving," Mary Ann said. "The streets are closed off everywhere. I had to go all the way around to River Road to get here." She sat down and picked up a contact sheet. "Oh, these are easy. David and Rosalie McCollum. They live over on the Post Road. It's a small Cape without a lot of room for expansion. They've got two kids and I've been trying to get Rosalie to look at something bigger. "

Liz picked up Fred Terhune's volunteer sheet and looked through it. "Mary Ann, you may be a volunteer, but you're not on the list. Are you part of one of the construction brigades?"

"No, Fred was looking for the right spot for me," Mary Ann said. "He said he had some ideas about how to get me, well, closer to the action than one of the painting squadrons. I know, that sounds petty. We're all volunteers and we're all trying to do well for Jenny and Mac. Oh, look, this is Barbara and Milton Kolodkin. They've only been in town about a year. I showed them several houses, but they went with a broker from Prudential Properties. Very nice people, though."

Mary Ann studied other contact sheets and made suggestions.

"I guess things are a little slow at the office today," Liz said.

"It's my day off," Mary Ann said. "Tomorrow is broker open house day and I'll be swamped. This is my 'good deeds' day."

A few minutes went by. Mary Ann added perhaps twenty more IDs to the contact sheets.

"Liz, I'll be honest. I'm not just here to help."

Liz waited for an elaboration.

Mary Ann looked momentarily flustered, then her composure returned. "I think everyone in town knows that you worked closely with the police when Sally Kahn was killed, and that you were there… at the end." Mary Ann did not elaborate, but was silent for a moment.

"I also heard that you were here yesterday morning when Fred's body was found, and that you and the detective had dinner last night at Bamboo House."

It was Liz's turn to be surprised.

Mary Ann shook her head. "It's a small town, Liz. Anyway, I assume you're working with the police again. You were there when the body was found, you've taken Fred's place with the volunteers. And you had dinner with Detective Flynn."

"All I've been asked to do is to keep an eye out for two characters who harassed Fred at the reception," Liz said. "I wasn't even there that night."

"But if Detective Flynn is talking to you, then he's going to tell you things. Things about me. And I'd rather you heard them from me rather than from the gossip mill. I was having a… what's the right word? I was having a fling with Fred. It wasn't serious, it had only been going on for a few months. I think we had both gotten tired of it."

Mary Ann paused a moment. "Anyway, when Fred had taken on the volunteer coordinator job, he had promised me an opportunity to be on camera – I mean really on camera, not just a face in the crowd. That was last month. Then things cooled down between us. On Friday, I saw him in town and asked if his offer was still good. He just kind of smiled and said something very nasty that put me in my place. I stewed about that over the weekend, and then I came to the party here Sunday night. I saw Fred and something snapped inside me. I did something…"

"You kneed Fred but good," Liz said with a smile.

Mary Ann nodded. "Yeah, I kneed him but good. Call me a sore loser. And it got caught on some stupid camera. And, as a result, the Hardington Police are going to put me under a microscope. And, when they do, they're going to find out something about me. Something I thought was completely behind me."

Mary Ann looked Liz in the eye. "Has Detective Flynn already filled you in on this, too?"

Liz shook her head. "Apparently, not."

Mary Ann nodded slightly. "He will." She paused again. "I used to live in Connecticut. I was married once before. Eleven years ago, my husband was murdered. The police suspected me. And for six months, they made my life hell. I finally gave up and moved. They're probably still following me."

"Your husband's murderer was never caught?"

"No," Mary Ann said. "And I told them who did it. My husband was a lawyer in New York. He was with one of these firms that ostensibly did tax law, except that a lot of his clients were thinly disguised fronts for organized crime."

"I think I've seen this movie," Liz said. "Your husband was Tom Cruise and he worked for 'The Firm'?"

Mary Ann smiled. "Not quite. Think more like labor unions. Extremely vicious labor unions that didn't like anyone getting too deeply into their affairs – even the lawyers they were paying to keep them out of trouble. Kevin always thought he had it under control. He apparently didn't. I tried to tell the police all of that, but they just brushed it aside. They had their suspect – me – and nothing else mattered."

"Why didn't you tell this to the police here?" Liz asked.

"Because, when I first spoke with Detective Flynn, I thought I could convince him that I had no part in Fred's murder. I said I'd take a polygraph. I thought that would settle it. Twenty-four hours later, it's apparent to me that whoever did kill Fred isn't going to be caught quickly, and that I'm a leading candidate in Detective Flynn's mind."

It was Liz's turn to smile. "Actually, he said you didn't seem like the type."

Mary Ann shook her head. "There's a detective in Stamford who wouldn't let go. It was creepy. Inevitably, he's going to read about this case and…" She stopped. "You're right. I need to tell my story to Detective Flynn."

She turned back to Liz. "You probably think very poorly of me, Liz. I am now going to be known as a confessed adulteress."

"Isn't that your business?" Liz asked.

"Except that this is a small town and 'my business' is everyone's prurient interest," Mary Ann said. "Tom and I have been married six years and in those six years I don't think we have spent two consecutive nights together since our honeymoon. I can go weeks without seeing him. And, when he is home, he's buried in deals. The master venture capitalist, with million-mile privileges on three airlines." Mary Ann's gaze came to rest directly into Liz's eyes.

"I get lonely, Liz. I don't live real estate the way he lives venture capital. However, I meet a lot of interesting people who make it clear that they find me attractive. And I guess I crave that attention. Including, sometimes, the physical attention."

"I said it really isn't anyone's business," Liz said, trying to keep the discomfort she was feeling from out of her voice.

"But you and I are a lot alike," Mary Ann said. "Your husband seems to always be on the road. You're an attractive woman. You don't need that affirmation?"

"I guess not," Liz said.

"You have children, though."

"A daughter."

"I didn't have kids," Mary Ann said, shaking her head. "Maybe it would have been different if I had two or three children. I didn't have them with Kevin because I think I knew after a year that the marriage was doomed, except that I thought it would eventually end in divorce. And I never considered becoming a single mother. Call me old-fashioned." Mary Ann smiled, weakly. "Then along came Tom and I thought everything was going to be fine. Except that his career exploded and he went over to the VC side. And they seduced him."

Does he know about your... flings?" Liz asked.

"No," Mary Ann said firmly. "Of course, I can go days without hearing from him. But you don't need to hear that, or any of this for that matter. I've spent the past day regretting the past six years of my life. When I look at any woman in Hardington, I can read them in a few minutes. Happy or headed for divorce. Immersed in motherhood or barely hanging onto her sanity. Lots of fulfilling outside interests or spends her afternoons with a well-chilled bottle of flavored vodka at the ready. I look at you and I see someone who I think is happy, but who also has a husband who travels three hundred days a year. And I wonder, 'what's the secret?' And you can't tell me because you don't know."

"I wish I could," Liz said.

Mary Ann stood up. "I feel like I've imposed on you. I had no right to."

"You also identified a bunch of people who I don't know," Liz smiled.

"Realtors," Mary Ann said. "At least they're good for something."

There was a quick embrace and Mary Ann was out of the trailer. Five minutes later, Liz was distracted by something moving outside of the back side of the trailer. She looked out the

Winnebago's window and saw Mary Ann walking toward the parking lot. She was carrying a large black plastic trash bag.

Another knock at the door. Liz turned away from the back window to find Janey Matthews, her principal runner, standing in the doorway.

"It's awfully quiet, Mrs. Phillips," Janey said.

"They're moving the modules," Liz said. "I'm surprised you're not down at the Cardozos with everyone else."

Janey shook her head. "I was there for a while. There must be five hundred people there. I rode my bike back."

"Could you help me identify the rest of these people?" Liz indicated the contact sheets.

Janey sat down, her arms and legs akimbo as she studied photographs. Liz looked at Janey and again felt the pang of loneliness, the younger version of her daughter triggering the casual bombshells imbedded at the end of the otherwise cheery email from this morning. *'Todd and I are thinking about Cabo for Christmas…'* her daughter had written. Mexico, not New England.

"This is Susan Dowd," Janey said pointing at a photo showing Whit Dakota's arm across the shoulders of an older teenager. "She's a senior this year and thinks she owns the world."

"Write her name in the margin," Liz said. "And remember, spelling and neatness count."

She wrote the name and flipped a page. "This is my friend, Michelle. Michelle Spencer. That's a good picture."

Liz glanced at the photo. Whit Dakota's arm was low around the waist of a buxom and attractive looking teenager. What was it Felicity had said? *'It looks like you'll be writing a fair number of, 'thanks for the quick feel' notes. Mr. Dakota seems to like them young and well built.'*

"How old is Michelle? Liz asked.

"We're both fifteen. I'm two months older, though."

"She looks a lot older."

Janey looked embarrassed. "She started developing sooner…"

Liz thought back to those awkward years that started about the time that Sarabeth turned sixteen. The rebellious years. The times when it seemed that every ground rule laid down was there to be evaded. And David had missed most of it, returning home from work at 10 p.m. or later, or on a plane to yet another management meeting in London or San Francisco. The high school years had been one long horror show. Then Sarabeth had gone off to college and, seemingly overnight, the daughter that had raged against everything at seventeen had become the reasonable, nineteen-year-old adult….

"…But she isn't answering text messages, which is really weird for her because she, like, lives by IM. I guess it's because she's grounded."

"I'm sorry, Janey. My mind was somewhere else. Who were you talking about?"

"Michelle. The girl in the photo. She's acting weird."

"She's your friend," Liz said. "You should go see her when you leave here. Not just send her a message."

Together, they pieced together names of the teenagers at the party. By 4 p.m., Liz was down to half a dozen unidentified faces. Not bad, she thought, considering she had started with two hundred.

Liz spent much of the next hour on the phone, getting ready for what the construction supervisors had called 'the big push'. Barry Zimmerman came in just before five.

"You've got to go by the house on your way home. It's beautiful. Are we all set for tonight?" he asked.

"You've got a full house, Barry. Two hundred volunteers ready to swing hammers, and three hundred fresh replacements tomorrow morning, plus people to serve food, hand out sodas, and bandage smashed fingers. If you can't build a house with that crew, it can't be done."

At the 5 p.m. daily meeting, the *Ultimate House Makeover* crew was in an upbeat mood. The modules had come together without a hitch. Everything that was supposed to show up made it to the site. Barry Zimmerman confidently predicted a full house for the evening and the following day.

Perhaps it was because Liz did not speak and was not otherwise acknowledged, but the Whit Dakota report cast the noontime football scrimmage in a different light than she remembered. "We got the hotshot quarterback in for some action footage," Dakota said. "Snipes is really anxious to be part of this thing. He skipped part of training camp just to throw some passes to me because he knew we'd use it in the final product. Nice guy."

Don Elwell nodded, "Nice work," and moved onto the next topic.

* * * * *

Flynn sat with Eddie Frankel, the one uniformed officer on the Hardington Police Department in whom Flynn had complete confidence, and outlined the progress of the investigation.

"I've got to find two guys in Framingham and I'm completely dependent on the police up there to identify them and probably to pick them up," Flynn said. "Now, from out of left field, the lady in the Lexus turns out to have a past that at least one cop down in Connecticut thinks includes murder. I'm going to pay her a second visit, plus I still need to sit down with Terhune's ex-wife. Which leaves me still short a crime scene and a murder weapon. I looked around last night, but can you go back with Luminol and sweep the area? As far as I know, the staties investigators did a cursory daytime search and then lost interest."

To Flynn's relief, Frankel readily agreed. "If you didn't command me to do this, I'd be pulling a second shift of traffic duty on Hospital Road," Frankel said. "You've got to see that place to believe it."

Curious about the house being built, an hour later Flynn made his way up Hospital Road. The parking lot of an elementary school had been turned into a second staging area with shuttle buses to take volunteers to the construction site. A long line of cars containing angry commuters and homeowners were waiting to show proof that they belonged beyond the cordon. Flynn was quickly waved around the roadblock and he drove the mile to the new Cardozo home.

The six o'clock work shift did not begin for fifteen minutes, but more than two hundred people were already on hand, anxious to start work. What had happened in a day was breathtaking. The six modules, plus three other house segments that did not need to be prepped, had been assembled into a two-story Colonial home. A garage wing swept off to one side of the home, a stack of lumber indicated where a large deck would mirror it on the other. A second lumber stack bore a sign, "sun porch only". Pallets of roofing shingles and other construction material were placed in orderly piles around the property, each with large signs indicating its use.

This happens all the time in Hardington, Flynn thought to himself. *People tear down old houses and put up fancy new ones. But this time, it's for charity. There are good people in this world.*

The work required on the exterior was clear. Siding had to be joined, chimneys needed to be built, completing the roof, deck and porch would require substantial labor.

A caravan of cars came from the north, led by an open Jeep bearing a waving Whit Dakota. Behind him, the woman with the camera recorded Whit's entry to the site. Fifty feet away from him and already in place, a second camera documented the procession from a stationary position. As Dakota descended from the Jeep, a crowd pressed in.

You may be nothing but a showman, Flynn thought as he watched the cheering and adulation, *but at least you're accomplishing something for this deserving family.*

Dakota switched on a wireless microphone and his amplified voice blared from speakers in the Jeep.

"Thank you for coming!" Dakota said. "We've got a lot of work to do, and not a lot of time to do it!"

Cheers erupted.

"In three days, the Cardozo family is going to walk up this street and into this house. Let's make it the happiest day of their life, and the proudest day of yours!"

More cheers.

Dakota swiftly segued into the role of construction boss, pointing to locations where construction assistants now held up signs. "Roofers over *there*. Deck crew over *there*…"

As the crowd divided into its constituent labor units and the street emptied, Flynn was surprised to see one person remaining: Liz. She had been less than a hundred feet away, yet he had not spotted her earlier.

Flynn waved and walked over to her. "I haven't seen you since this time yesterday," he said.

He was rewarded with a smile from her. "I realized I had never been to the site," Liz said. "I don't think 'stunning' is too strong a word to use.

The first hammers started pounding.

"Mary Ann Mandeville came to see me this afternoon," she continued. "Brace yourself for a surprise. Her first husband…"

"Was murdered," Flynn completed the sentence. "I had a long call with a Detective Millman down in Stamford. He's convinced she did it and got away with it."

"And she says the police wouldn't let go of her as a suspect and refused to follow any other leads," Liz said.

"I'm going to have another talk with her this evening," Flynn said. "It's interesting that she went to you with the story and never mentioned it to me."

"What she said to me was that she thought it was all behind her. It was eleven years ago. Plus, it's not the proudest moment of her life. But she thinks this detective has kept tabs on her."

Flynn watched as men picked up stacks of lumber. "She's right. Which is a sign of a detective who is obsessed by an unclosed case. I've had a couple of those in my time. The question is whether the obsession is warranted. I'll try to sort that out." Flynn took out his notebook and riffed through several pages. "Do you know Erica Terhune?"

"Vaguely," Liz said.

"She's not garden club? I'm finally going to meet someone in this town who isn't a member of the garden club?" He smiled.

"Not everyone is interested in gardening," Liz said. "Also, I think she has a couple of young kids. And she probably works, which rules out being able to get to daytime meetings. So, no, she's not a garden club member."

"So this is one time when you can't help me out with background," Flynn said.

"Sorry to disappoint," Liz said. "But I can ask around."

"That's helpful," Flynn said, "but I'm more interested in your perceptions. That's what I value most. You seem to have an intuitive understanding of people that goes beyond facts."

"I'll take that as a compliment," Liz said.

"Believe me, it is one."

There was an awkward silence.

"I guess I'd better go see Mrs. Terhune," Flynn said, finally. "She's the opening act for my talk with Mary Ann." And with that, he gave a wave goodbye and walked back to his car.

Stupid! He kept thinking to himself as he drove away. *Can't you carry on a conversation that isn't about business?* He slapped his hand on the steering wheel in frustration.

* * * * *

Erica Terhune welcomed Flynn into her Lake Road home and offered him coffee.

Three months into his tenure as Hardington's detective, Flynn was learning the pecking order of real estate in the town. At the pinnacle were a handful of trophy houses such as the one occupied by Tom Snipes. It was in such house, two months earlier, that Tom's wife, Felicity, had attempted to simultaneously impress and intimidate Flynn. A step down were the houses of the merely well-to-do. Liz Phillips' home, with its two acres of perennial gardens and Great Room the size of his house in Roslindale, fell into that category. The next step down were the homes that, until he had come to Hardington, Flynn would have thought of as belonging to the privileged. They had two-car garages, many were less than twenty years old, and they were certainly spacious.

But Flynn had come to understand that, at least in this town, these houses were merely 'step-up' homes and not an end in and of themselves. If you moved into one, it was presumed that, in a few years, either a transfer would take you to the next corporate way-station in North Carolina or Texas, or you would commission and build that four-or-five-thousand-square-foot Hardington home on multiple acres.

Chief Harding had said Fred and Erica Terhune built this house around 1999. They had divorced in 2008. By Hardington standards, thirteen years was a long time to have stayed in one home, and Fred Terhune had been a prosperous lawyer. Moreover, how did Erica afford the house now? And how did the million-dollar insurance policy Mary Ann Mandeville spoke of enter into the equation?

There was also the issue of what he should and should not say to the widow of a slain man. In dozens of investigations in Boston, he had interviewed grieving widows, taken their statements, and told them nothing of the status of the investigation or the identity of suspects. Here, his immediate superior, Chief Harding, had already been out to see the widow and had identified her as a friend. Flynn had made up his mind that he would listen carefully and show her the photos of the two Brazilian men, but would go no further in discussing other suspects or their motives.

Erica Terhune looked to be between forty and forty-five. She carried a few extra pounds around her middle and her face bore the age lines of someone who did not spend her afternoons at day spas or perusing the displays of years-erasing creams at department stores. Expressed at its simplest, she looked her age. *Divorced mom,*

Flynn thought. *Not looking for a husband; just trying to focus on raising her daughters.* Flynn thought of all of these things in the few moments it took for Terhune to bring coffee out of the kitchen.

They sat in the living room, rather than the family room. She clearly wanted to keep this formal. The cushions of the sofa were stiff, a product of having been used little in the years since the house was built. There was an unnatural quiet for a house with two children.

"Your daughters must be taking their father's loss very hard," Flynn said.

"I'm not sure they've accepted it," Erica said. "I had never heard of a 'grief counselor' except at schools when other children died. Now, I'm glad they're available."

"Where are they this evening?" Flynn asked.

"Next door," Erica said. "I thought it best that we talk privately."

Flynn nodded. "I know Chief Harding was out to see you yesterday morning. I wanted to bring you up to date on the investigation and get your perspective."

"That's very kind."

"Mrs. Terhune, your husband was murdered, but you already know that. We can now pinpoint the time of death as between twelve-thirty and one on Monday morning. He was struck from behind. One blow."

"Amos said he likely bled to death. You don't need to sugar-coat it, Detective."

"I was giving you the facts, Mrs. Terhune. We're looking for two men whom we'd like to bring in for questioning. We believe they work for MetroWest Construction."

"They have the town sewer contract," Erica said. "Fred used to talk about them."

"They had the contract until last May, yes," Flynn said. "MetroWest had the contract taken away from them." He pulled out the photo from his jacket pocket. "These are the two men.

They came to the party at the sanitarium on Sunday night, and apparently threatened your ex-husband. While we have no proof as of yet, it's possible that they waited around until the party was over, found Mr. Terhune, who had been working on coordinating volunteers after the reception ended, and killed him. Do the two men look familiar?"

Erica shook her head. "I'm sorry. I've had very little to do with my husband's work since the divorce."

"But you did see him with some frequency?"

Erica again shook her head. "He was here for Tricia and Bethany. I said hello and goodbye."

"It wasn't an amicable divorce?"

Erica's gaze went out the living room window. "He has... had two children, Detective Flynn. Any way you try to pretty it up, he walked out on them when he walked out on me. 'Amicable' is not a word I could use."

Flynn let the statement hang in the air, hoping there would be more.

She turned back to Flynn. "He was a 'good provider' – whatever that means," she continued. "But he wasn't here. He was a partner in his own law practice yet he worked himself like an associate. I told him he had to hire more people, slow down, or find some other way to have the time to be a father and a husband. His response was to run for selectman. I finally said he had to choose between his practice and his family. Well, he chose."

"I assume he had insurance," Flynn said, mentally holding his breath.

"Thank God," Erica said. "Yes, Detective, my ex-husband left his former family well provided for. Tricia and Bethany are the beneficiaries. I'm getting a crash course in how that will translate into everyday practice. I have a lot to learn."

The only answer that could keep you off of the suspect list, Flynn thought.

"Who else might have wanted to see your ex-husband dead?" Flynn asked.

"I told you I've had nothing to do with Fred's work since the divorce."

"But you hear things. You still know the same people."

Erica shook her head. "I couldn't even have told you about MetroWest losing that contract. Once he moved out of the house, we stopped talking about everything except Tricia and Bethany. I know he was seeing Mary Ann Mandeville. Or at least he's the latest notch on her bedpost. She's with Hardington Properties."

Flynn was alert. He had decided not to mention Mary Ann. Now, Terhune had been the one to open that avenue of inquiry. "She might have had reason to want to see harm come to him?"

"Mary Ann is married, Detective Flynn, although it appears to be the most peculiar marriage I've ever seen." Erica took a sip of coffee from her cup. "She is, to put it impolitely, a whore. I apologize that I don't have a more delicate vocabulary."

"If she was still seeing him, why would she want to see harm come to him?"

"Friends of friends told me." Erica poured herself another cup of coffee and drank half a cup. "Let me put it another way. I've been told recently that Fred dumped Mary Ann. He didn't want to see her anymore. It is well known that Mary Ann has a temper and that she can lose control of it in spectacular fashion."

"Lose control of her temper how?"

Erica placed her coffee cup on the table beside her. "A friend who also works for Hardington Properties told me that a few months ago – while she was still seeing Fred – she lost a listing for one of the big houses up on the north side of town. The kind where three percent of the sales price is fifty thousand dollars. Mary Ann gets ten listings like that a year but she lost this one to some junior agent at ReMax. I was told she found the other Realtor's car, took a screwdriver, and carved 'bitch' on the driver's side door in foot-high letters."

"I was on the Hardington police force a few months ago, Ms. Terhune," Flynn said. "I think I would have heard about something like that."

Erica shook her head. "Mary Ann did what she always does. She wrote a check to pay for the damage plus the inconvenience, and a very nice letter of apology.'

"May I ask the source of your information?"

Erica paused for a moment. "Supermarket gossip, Detective Flynn. You roll your cart down the aisle and you bump into a friend. You talk for a few minutes and the talk inevitably turns to infidelities. People take for granted I am happy to hear about my ex-husband breaking up with his girlfriend,　　　or that his new girlfriend is psychotic. They assume it will cheer me up to hear that he can't maintain a relationship after me or can only relate to psychopaths. The sad part is that it does cheer me up. That doesn't say very much about me as a person."

"Then I won't bother you further," Flynn said. "And either I or Chief Harding will keep you posted on the investigation."

Erica saw him to the door. All the way back to his car and on the drive to Mary Ann Mandeville's home, Flynn processed the conversation. *Mary Ann has a temper and she can lose control of it in spectacular fashion. She kneed Fred in the groin. Would she have taken it a step further?*

* * * * *

The sun was low in the northwest when Flynn turned onto Spring Hill Drive. If Erica Terhune seemed destined to permanently inhabit that 'move-up' house, Mary Ann Mandeville lived in that penultimate class of Hardington home. The house – an enormously large three-story Colonial – was perched on a granite ledge, with a steep driveway up from the street. The street itself was new, lacking that final coat of asphalt, with several homes on it still at various stages of construction. No house he passed appeared to have fewer than a dozen rooms, none seemed to be more than a year old. The Stamford detective, Millman, had said she kept moving and wondered why she did so.

Mary Ann greeted him warmly at the door and ushered him into the Great Room. The house smelled new. She wore jeans and a sweater, a *Desperate Housewives* kind of evening-at-home wear, he thought.

"I take it you moved in only recently," Flynn said.

"Three months," she said. "And, in another three months, I'll probably move again."

"May I ask why?"

Mary Ann gave Flynn a quizzical look. "I can tell by looking at you, Detective Flynn, that you have been married for a very long time and have probably lived in the same house for all that time. Is that right?"

You could also get that information off of the internet in about fifteen minutes, he thought. "That's right."

"Well, there are a lot of people who cannot envision a finished house while it is still under construction," she said. "There are people who, if you walk them through studding, think that the studding is all there will ever be. They cannot envision painting the walls or choosing a carpet, much less working with a contractor to design a kitchen."

She continued. "There's another class of people who can't envision a furnished house unless they see it in move-in condition. Not just the furnished builder show house in some Toll Brothers development, but a house like this one, ready to call your own. The kind of person I'm talking about is probably in his or her twenties and has just gotten a performance bonus from their hedge fund or they've signed with the Patriots and they want that big, new house. Now."

Without asking if he wanted anything to drink, Mary Ann poured two glasses of well-chilled white wine and handed one to Flynn. "I am the answer to those people's dreams, Detective. I can deliver them that expensive, luxurious house, with every detail already taken care of. The rooms are tastefully painted, the landscaping is just right. The kitchen is to die for and the master suite, well, the master suite is everything they ever dreamed. And they will not flinch at the fact that they are paying a couple of hundred thousand more than they would have paid if they bought it from the builder and then went shopping at Jordan's. They're getting a decision-free house available on thirty days' notice."

"Sounds lucrative," Flynn said. He held the glass and swirled the wine, mentally calculating whether it would have a better effect to drink or not to drink.

"It's also fun. I've decorated eight houses in six years. Five of the houses were sold fully furnished." Mary Ann walked into the kitchen and took a tray from a warming oven. "This is to keep you away from that horrible Chinese restaurant, Detective." She set the tray on the granite countertop.

Flynn felt a degree of control slip from him. He looked at and smelled the food on the tray. Miniature lobster pizzas. Mary Ann offered him a napkin.

"You've probably had a very long day, Detective. This is the least I can do."

He took a sip of the wine. He picked up warm food.

"I've had a call from Detective Jared Millman in Stamford," Flynn said.

"Which answers the question of whether Detective Millman is still alive," Mary Ann said. "Do you want my side of the story, or doesn't the detective fraternity entertain non-conforming theories?"

"I'm here because I want to hear the truth."

She smiled. "I was hoping you were here because you enjoyed my company as well, but we'll save that for another occasion." She took her wine and a plate of food to a massive chair set in front of an equally oversized stone fireplace. She kicked off her shoes and tucked her feet under her legs. The effect was somehow erotic and familiar.

"My first husband was killed eleven years ago. He was an up-and-coming lawyer in a small but rising firm in New York, but the firm had as its principal clients a number of labor unions with particularly unsavory reputations. He was also a dull man and, for someone who had passed the New York State bar exam on the first try – which I assure you is something very few people can truthfully claim – not a very smart person. My husband always said he could separate his clients from his practice of the law. He could not. All he could do was try to put a good face on a poor career move."

She took a long drink of her wine. "What I am certain happened, Detective, is that my husband got too close to the extortionists and shake-down artists that he represented, and that one of them decided that Kevin knew too much. Or, maybe they just didn't like his jokes or his brand of cologne. And, because his routine never varied, tracking him down was something a gerbil could accomplish. I'm just glad they didn't decide that our furnace should blow up, because then I would have likely been a victim, too."

"Millman noted that you and your husband were having some marital problems," Flynn said. He made it a statement rather than a question.

"Did you see *The Ice Storm*, Detective? The story takes place in New Canaan, which is next door to Stamford. It wasn't a movie; it was a documentary, or it could have been. Let's just say that the commandment about coveting thy neighbor's wife isn't taken very seriously in Fairfield County. So, yes, every Thursday night when my husband was engaged in his poker game, I was enjoying being young. I was twenty-nine and I enjoyed sex. Kevin was thirty going on sixty, and his idea of sex was four minutes of grunting after getting steamed up watching Monday Night Football."

"I married the wrong man, Detective." Mary Ann refilled her glass and took another drink. "If he hadn't been killed, we would have gotten divorced. That was something Detective Millman couldn't get through that thick skull of his …"

"Detective Millman said you stopped your other liaison immediately after your husband's death," Flynn said.

"I wasn't indifferent to my husband's death, Detective. I cared about Kevin. The idea that I was in bed with another man an hour before the man to whom I was married got knifed to death was rather a sobering experience. And I also had Detective Millman's obsession with me. He would be parked outside my house in the morning. He would show up at open houses. It was creepy, and I didn't relish the idea of coming out of someone's home at two in the morning to find him taking notes. Or taking pictures." Mary Ann shuddered.

"He found it telling that you left Connecticut after six months," Flynn said.

"Did I have a choice? Ultimately, I moved because of him. Otherwise, I was never going to get on with my life. I think you can understand that."

Flynn had been watching for the telltale sign of lies. He wasn't seeing any. Mandeville was agitated and emphatic, but she was telling the truth, or at least one version of the truth. Then again, she had eleven years of practice with her story, and her profession rewarded those who sounded convincing as they were selling.

"I've also been hearing reports about your…. temper," Flynn said.

Mary Ann suppressed a laugh. "My maiden name was Macdonald," she said. She pointed to her hair. "The name, the red hair and the temper are all part and parcel of that famed Scottish temperament. I am high strung. You saw it on that video. I release energy. Usually quite safely, as on a tennis court. Sometimes my temper gets the best of me. But I told you I did not kill Fred and I am still quite willing to take that polygraph."

"May I ask where you were Sunday night following the party at the sanitarium?"

Mary Ann did not pause before answering, which Flynn took as a bad sign. "I left the party at ten. I came home. I did work until midnight. I had a nine o'clock showing on Monday morning."

"And after midnight?"

"I was in bed, Detective. Alone."

"Did you make phone calls? Were you on the Internet?"

"People do not appreciate hearing from me late on a Sunday evening. It makes them cranky and therefore less prone to following my advice when it comes to spending large sums of money. And I was not surfing the web. I was doing that most old fashioned of things, reading the *Globe's* real estate section, looking at properties in surrounding towns."

"Isn't that something you do on the web these days?" Flynn asked.

"I want to see how a house is described, Detective. I want to see what words an agent chooses when she has twenty words to get across a feeling of a house."

"One last question, and then I'll not bother you again this evening." Flynn looked again for changes in body language. He sensed an unconscious tensing. "When we spoke yesterday, you mentioned that Fred Terhune carried a million dollars in life insurance, and you were aware that his children were the beneficiaries. How did you come to have that information?"

He saw Mary Ann's eyes drift over to the fireplace. She took a sip of her drink. Perhaps ten seconds passed without a word.

"I think I must have heard it from Joe Hunt," Mary Ann said. "He was Fred's law partner. Although I honestly can't remember the circumstances."

"He lives here in Hardington?"

"On Old Schoolhouse Road."

That's where Liz lives, Flynn thought.

"The mind does strange things, Detective," Mary Ann said, finishing her wine; her eyes returning to his face. "I was just thinking that Liz Phillips also lives on Old Schoolhouse Road. Perhaps you ought to drop by and see her this evening."

* * * * *

Liz, depressed, realized she had just finished her third gin and tonic. The good news was that she wasn't drinking alone.

Roland Evans-Jones heard the clink of ice against an otherwise empty glass. "Maybe it's time to switch to a pot of tea."

"Too hot," Liz said. "Besides, I have to be going. I'm supposed to be at the sanitarium at seven-thirty." She glanced at her watch. Just ten o'clock.

"You need to get it off of your chest," Roland said. "You need to talk it out. Is it the girl? Or is it something else?"

"It starts with the girl, and the girl has a name, Janey Matthews. She reminds me so much of Sarabeth at that age. She looks like Sarabeth did, and she talks and acts like her. I guess I haven't been around teenagers in a long time and seeing Janey – so innocent and so open – it got to me. And Sarabeth's email… she emails me now, instead of calling – did I say that? And she just lets it drop that she's probably going to Mexico for Christmas. We've always been together for Christmas. She's never gone anywhere else. Even when David and I were living in Hong Kong and Sarabeth was in college, we were together for Christmas. We made a point of it. It was important to us."

"Sarabeth has her own life to live," Roland said. "She's got to start her own traditions, and maybe going to Mexico for Christmas is going to be one of those traditions. Perhaps she emails you because it gives her a chance to tell you something you'd react badly to over the telephone. This way, you read it and you absorb it. By the time you and she talk, you've had a day or two to think. Yes, Christmas is important, but there are 364 other days of the year. Maybe you can celebrate Christmas a little earlier. Or a little later."

Liz listened, not wanting to concede that Roland might be right. "It's just that Janey is at the last age when Sarabeth was my little girl. When she turned sixteen, Sarabeth became this… changeling who hated her parents," Liz explained, searching for words. "By the time I got her back, she was in college, and then she was home *only* for holidays – like Thanksgiving and Christmas. And then she was working and then she was married. But she still came home. And now she's going to Cabo San Lucas, assuming that's the 'Cabo' in her letter. It isn't fair."

"It isn't fair that you're alone?"

"It isn't fair that David is always gone," Liz said, exasperated. "And I don't like Mary Ann Mandeville saying that she and I are alike. Which is her way of saying that I ought to be sleeping around like her."

"Did we just change subjects?"

"No. It's the same subject. I'm alone for months on end, and I'm getting tired of it. My cell phone is going to ring in a few minutes, and it's going to be David. And what I want to say to David is, 'get yourself home' except that what I *will* say is 'how did things go today?' I will be very sweet and very supportive. Which will let him off the hook for another twenty-four hours."

"You want him home because you're attracted to Detective Flynn," Roland said.

"No!" Liz had been laying back in one of Roland's comfortable, overstuffed sofas. Now she sat upright and put down her glass, her voice agitated. "No. I am not Mary Ann Mandeville. I do not jump in the sack with men because they're nice to me or I want their approval or whatever sick reason she has. I do not want to have an affair with Detective Flynn or with anyone else. I just want my husband back and I want to see my daughter. I want to have a family again. And I'm sick and tired of waking up to a huge, empty house every morning. I want to have a normal life with a husband who comes home at night and helps me with the garden on weekends. That's what I want."

Which was almost the truth.

7. Wednesday

Flynn's cell phone rang at 2:37 a.m. It took a moment for him to connect the sound with the object making it and, for a moment, he feared the noise would awaken Annie. But then he remembered his wife was working an overnight shift at her hospital. There was no one to awaken.

"It's Eddie Frankel. I've found the blood."

"Give me half an hour."

It was eleven miles to Hardington from Roslindale, a community within Boston's city limits of small, neat homes on postage-stamp-sized lots. On an average morning Flynn made the drive, against the tide of traffic flowing into the city, in about twenty minutes. This morning, with no one on the road but himself, the ride took eleven minutes.

Eddie Frankel met him in the parking lot and guided him into the thicket of production trailers. The Luminol's glow, which faded after less than a minute, was now a series of digital images on a video camera and white flags, all surrounded by yellow tape. Frankel's flashlight played over each important area as he talked Flynn through the progression of frames on his camera.

The origin of the trail was against a Winnebago. Even on close inspection the flashlight revealed nothing of interest. But where the Luminol had been applied, the camera captured a spray of iridescent blue blood on the motor home surface which someone had tried to wash away. Below that spray was a pool of blood in the grass below, visible as a dark red.

"Someone put boxes over the blood pool and a tarp over the boxes," Frankel explained. "I spotted the blood on the Winnie first."

Flags marked drops of blood leading toward a second trailer, where there was a second, smaller pool. "There was a box over that blood pool," Frankel said.

A wisp of blood led in the direction of the food tent where the body had been discovered, disappearing after approximately fifteen feet. "I don't see bloody shoeprints," Flynn said, looking at the camera images.

"We didn't get lucky," Frankel said, shaking his head. "Plus, hundreds of people have walked this area since yesterday morning."

Flynn took in the scene. Terhune had been attacked on the back side of a trailer. He walked around to see which of the trailers it was and found a 'VOLUNTEERS' sign on the other side. So, Terhune had either come out of the trailer or been lured out, gone around to the back side and had been clubbed. After several minutes, judging from the size of the first pool of blood, Terhune had been dragged a distance of about sixty feet. There he had died. He had then been dragged off and his body placed in the chest in the tent next to the parking lot.

Four of the motor homes would have had a clear view of the attack site, had they been occupied. Barry Zimmerman had told Frankel he had left before 10:30, so no one else was inside the Volunteer trailer, though the back window of the mobile home would have afforded an excellent view. Twenty-five feet away from the attack site was a large motor home with the name, 'Whit Dakota' on the door. According to Frankel, Dakota reported he had left before midnight. Almost as close was a much smaller Winnebago with 'Gilman/Hirsch'. Thirty feet in the other direction was a trailer he recognized as housing the video editing facility where he had first viewed footage of the party.

David Scott, the production assistant with whom Flynn has spoken the previous evening, had said he left at midnight, at least half an hour before the attack, and that everyone else either had already left or was leaving with him.

Flynn moved to the place where Terhune had been struck. He put himself in the place of the two Brazilian men. To have committed the murder, they would have waited in the bushes until after midnight and the production crew left, then gone looking for Terhune. They found him in his trailer and forced him outside. Or, they spotted him inside the trailer and made a noise that lured Terhune outside. Probably the latter.

So Terhune was hit from behind, Flynn thought. *He's on the ground, bleeding profusely. Why not just leave him there, cover him with the tarp so the security patrol doesn't see him, run for their car, and get the hell out of Hardington? Why move him at all? Was murder the original plan or was it a beating gone wrong? The M.E. said one blow. A killing blow or one administered by someone who didn't know their strength? Had he not died, had their original plan been to take Terhune to a hospital?*

Flynn walked to the location where Terhune apparently died. It was the back side of one of the construction foreman's trailers. What could be seen from this spot? There were several trailers close at hand, including the Volunteer trailer from which Terhune had been lured.   Other trailers visible housed construction managers and their assistants. The food tent was clearly visible, though not the tractor-trailer that contained the production company's construction equipment.   There had been a security detail parked alongside the equipment truck on Sunday night. Had Terhune's killer or killers first made certain that no one was in these trailers? Were they looking for a place to hide the body?

The explanation formed in Flynn's mind. *The attack site, here and the food tent are the security blind spots. Two sedentary policemen in a car, with a gallon of coffee to keep them awake for the night; probably with the radio on. The guards understand their 'real' job is to make certain no one breaks into the equipment trailer right beside them. They also have a clear view of the video production trailer with its wealth of equipment. Whatever else happened in the area, especially that night before the housing modules arrive, is immaterial to their assignment.*

Once an hour, one of the guards walks the grounds, per instructions, which takes perhaps ten minutes – including, probably, time to relieve himself. All the killer or killers needed to do was stay out of the line of sight of the security car on the off chance that one of the guards was actually looking out the window.

It took no special knowledge of the site or of the operation. Just a few minutes' observation. This was a crime that could have been committed by anyone with a motive.

Flynn walked back to the attack site, confirming that it was out of view of the security car, had anyone been of a mind to keep a true lookout. Was that by design or luck?

He now put himself in the place of Mary Ann Mandeville. She makes a noise from outside of the trailer that attracts Terhune's attention. He comes out to investigate. She hits him.

What's the motive? Flynn thought. *What possible gain is there to killing Terhune? The knee to the groin was revenge for whatever had gone wrong between them. But why come back and kill him? And why try to hide the body, or disguise the murder scene?*

Mary Ann was certainly fit enough to have dragged Terhune's body. Flynn had seen the athletic physique and the bodily coordination. But the motive was more elusive. The insurance? It was in the name of Terhune's children.

Frankel had also marked up a diagram of what Hammer & Saw Productions called its 'base camp', showing where the attack had taken place, where Terhune had died, and where the body had been hidden. Flynn looked at the map and added the location of the security car.

Now, he understood why the body had been moved, and even why it had ended up in the equipment box. *Once Terhune was on the ground, bleeding, he was as good as dead. Whoever killed him was just waiting for the opportunity to hide the body and looking for the best place to do so without being seen. This was a murder, no question about it.*

"Make a couple of copies and be sure to get ones over to both the crime scenes people and the medical examiner," he told

Frankel. "I'll request that they get a fingerprint team out here to see if they can pull anything off of the tarps or boxes."

It was nearly 4 a.m. Flynn wavered between going home and going to the police station.

Frankel saw the indecision. "They've got bunks next door at the fire station. They cook a pretty good breakfast, too."

Flynn grinned. "Officer Frankel, you're going to make one hell of detective."

* * * * *

Liz watched as the clock radio beside her bed changed to 5:45. Her head hurt and her mouth felt full of cotton. *Why did I have three drinks? Why did I drink at all?* She thought. She dragged herself out of bed, mentally calculating if she could be in and out of the shower before David's call.

She was drying off when the phone rang.

David sounded upbeat and energetic. Negotiations with potential buyers had gone well and, based on those negotiations, a recalcitrant customer had placed a large order which, in turn, would lend prospective buyers of the company greater assurance that demand for the company's products would survive the bankruptcy. Listening to her husband's good mood, Liz sensed that the time was not right to raise the issues she had talked about with Roland just a few hours earlier.

"So, how goes the murder investigation?" David asked.

"I'm not really part of it," Liz said. "The police have a couple of Brazilian suspects and I can't really offer a lot of help." She was careful to say, 'the police' rather than 'Detective Flynn', and certainly not, 'John'. And, what she said was mostly true. While John Flynn had sought out her thoughts and insights, she wasn't really part of the investigation. Unless a couple of tall, tough-looking, Portuguese-speaking men walked onto the construction site, she was a bystander.

Liz was at the sanitarium by 7:30, well ahead of any of the other volunteers. With Roland's help, she had identified all of the remaining people in the video stills the previous evening, and so her first stop was the video production trailer. She could turn over the set of proofs to Joel Silverstein, though she suspected that she would be forging Whit Dakota's signature before the week was out.

She heard the sound of laughter from within the Winnebago and, mindful of Joel's lecture of the previous afternoon, she opened the door of the trailer without knocking. Joel and Whit Dakota both turned toward her as the opened door let in the light from outdoors. On the large plasma television screen behind them was an image of a woman in her late teens or early twenties, nude and standing beside a bed, Whit Dakota standing behind her, his hands on her breasts. An instant later, the image was gone, the screen blank. The woman had looked familiar.

"Hey, Liz, how can we help you?" It was Whit Dakota, that ingratiating smile on his face.

"Joel asked me to ID the people from the party. It's all done." Liz kept her voice neutral and held up the file folder with the contact sheets. She wondered if they could discern her reddened face in the dark of the room.

"Fantastic!" Dakota said, and took the folder from her. He promptly handed it to Joel and said, "I guess you can print these up this morning. Volunteer Lady came through with flying colors."

When Joel went to put the folder down on the console, Liz caught sight of a DVD case. It was hand-lettered, '*Whit's Greatest Hits – Hardington*'.

She was out the door a moment later and felt the door close firmly behind her. From behind the door, she heard Whit's voice.

"Jesus Christ, Joel. Don't you know enough to lock the door?"

A stack of requests awaited her in the Volunteer office. For the next two hours, she kept an eye on her watch while she located volunteers with specific expertise and cajoled them into being at the Cardozo home at specific times.

Janey Matthews knocked at the door at 9:30, ready to run errands.

"Janey," Liz asked, "do you still have your camera?"

Janey nodded and reached into her shoulder bag.

"Do you still have the photos of the girls you took yesterday afternoon?"

Janey pushed buttons on the camera. A few moments later, she said, "Yes."

"Let's look at them," Liz said.

Janey displayed each photo on the camera's small screen. At number six, Liz felt herself go numb. Number six was the young woman she had glimpsed on the video screen in the trailer. Whit and Barry Zimmerman had used Liz, and Liz had used Janey, to troll for Whit's evening entertainment. And Whit and Joel had a video of the event.

"Do you remember her name?" Liz asked, indicating the image on the camera screen.

Janey reached back into her shoulder bag and brought out a sheet of paper. "Ummmm. Linda Harper. Is she going to be on the program?"

"We'll see," Liz said. "There are some things I can't tell you." Liz gave Janey a list of errands and explained she would be out for several hours at her garden club. "I'll try to be back at noon. But don't lose those photos or that list, and don't show it to anyone. OK?"

Janey nodded, pleased that her work was being recognized as important. "Can I tell you about Michelle?"

"When I get back," Liz said. "I promise."

* * * * *

Flynn sat at his desk, the ebb and flow of someone's life in front of him. The 'someone' was Fred Terhune, the ebb and flow, Terhune's bank and telephone records and the contents of his laptop computer. It was Flynn's least favorite part of any investigation, the part Flynn had always gladly turned over to his partner. His last partner in Boston, Vicky Lee, had considered such records as the lone repository of unfettered truth, and she reveled in their examination. People could lie in interrogation, they could invent alibis and shadowy figures in depositions. They could demand that all questions be routed through their attorney – or phalanx of attorneys – or be posed in writing. But in the hard records of financial transactions, telephone calls, and incoming bills, there was no evasion.

And there was no getting around the fact that Fred Terhune was a man in trouble.

He was an attorney with an established practice and, as a selectman, was one of three people that the town entrusted with its ongoing business. Yet his checking balance at Bank of America hovered near zero, his savings were negligible, and he was paying off less than half of his monthly credit card bills, where he now had an accumulated balance of more than $25,000. He had written two checks that had been bounced because they were above his overdraft limit. His parents' home, which he had inherited mortgage-free, was now encumbered with a $200,000 home equity line upon which he had drawn the full amount. Fred Terhune was effectively broke.

Part of the answer, clearly, was a $10,000 monthly payment to Erica Terhune, which was automatically debited from his account as soon as his partnership paycheck was deposited. But he was also writing out large checks to a Boston law firm and, based on the monthly deposits into the account, his income had been only about $100,000 per year for the past two years. An attorney in his early forties ought to be at the peak of his earning power, yet $100,000 per year put Terhune in the bottom fifth of attorneys in private practice in Massachusetts.

His charge receipts showed no hidden vices, and his telephone calls showed no explorations into the world of '900' numbers. He dined at good restaurants, bought suits and ties befitting his profession, and made charitable contributions to the usual, upstanding organizations. Had his income been, say, $250,000 per year, he would have been seen to be living the perfectly normal life of a successful, 42-year-old suburban lawyer. Except that his income was less than half of that amount and he was writing all those checks for the upkeep of a second household. Either Fred Terhune expected his fortunes to change dramatically, or else he had no concept that he was slowly drowning in debt.

Flynn flipped through his notes of his conversation the previous evening with Mary Ann Mandeville. *Joe Hunt – law partner of T. Old Schoolhouse Rd. Knew of $1M policy.* He opened the Hardington phone directory, found the number for Hunt, Terhune and Gardner, and made an appointment.

* * * * *

Half an hour later, he was in the comfortable, homey office of Joseph Hunt. Hunt, Terhune and Gardner, in turn, took up the second floor of a cavernous, meticulously restored Victorian house on Main Street at the western edge of what was considered 'downtown' Hardington. The ground floor was occupied by a financial planner and an architect.

"I assumed you would be coming to see me sooner or later," Hunt said. He was a man in his late 40s, with a stomach going flabby from good living and the beginning of jowls between his chin and neck. A credenza behind him showed stacks of legal-sized file folders. Cases in process. "Fred's death was a tragedy."

"I want to talk to you about several things, but I need to understand Fred Terhune's income and expenses," Flynn said. "I'm trying to find his murderer, and his finances aren't right."

"What do you mean, 'not right'?"

"Terhune showed deposits from the law firm of about $8000 per month," Flynn said. "That's not a partner's salary. That's barely even a fourth-year associate's salary."

Hunt nodded and grimaced. "By the time Fred paid his share of the office overhead, that's what he had left and, believe me, we cut his contribution 'way below what it should have been."

"His income should have been more than twice that amount," Flynn said.

"It *was* three times that amount," Hunt said. "Fred was a workhorse and had an active client list that was the envy of every lawyer in town. But that was before *Naylor v. Great Barrington Ski Resort.*"

"You'd better explain," Flynn said.

"Two years ago, a guy in crutches hobbles in the door," Hunt said, leaning back in his chair. "George Naylor. Guy in his mid-30s with his left leg in a cast. He had been skiing out in the Berkshires. Fell off a chair lift and busted hell out of his leg. He wanted us to sue the resort. Fred had just finished up some work and he said he'd take on the assignment. Had the guy walked in a day earlier, it would probably have been me that volunteered."

Hunt swiveled in his chair and opened a file drawer. He withdrew half a dozen file folders aggregating a foot-thick volume. "In a case like this, we call the resort, explain to the resort's counsel that a guest has retained us, and we work out a settlement. In this particular instance, the witnesses – and there were several – said Naylor had been horsing around on the chair lift and jumped off in an unsafe manner. Still, the resort was prepared to pay Naylor's medical expenses and give him $5000 in return for a full release. For that, we would have collected a fee of about a thousand dollars." Hunt shrugged.

"Any normal person would have looked at that settlement and said, 'do it.'" Hunt said. "But George Naylor was anything except normal. He told us, 'This accident is worth half a million dollars.' Fred suggested – and I was at the meeting – that Naylor seek representation elsewhere. That was the beginning of the client from hell. A few weeks later, we got served with a notice that Naylor was suing Fred for malpractice, failure to exercise duty of loyalty and a dozen other things. Essentially, Naylor charged that, by agreeing to a preliminary deal with Great Barrington for a couple of thousand dollars rather than the half million Naylor wanted, Fred had 'poisoned the well' for Naylor. Fred had prevented Naylor from seeking 'fair and just compensation' for his injury. "

Hunt gestured at the pile of papers. "You are looking at the result – so far – of Naylor's revenge. Fred's reputation was at stake – as well as his future ability to practice law. His practice got sidetracked by preparing his own defense. Plus, he had Ropes and Gray in Boston working on briefs and motions that have already run up a fifty-thousand-dollar tab or something close to that figure."

"Aren't there review boards that can short-circuit these sorts of things?" Flynn asked.

"I wish there were," Hunt said. "But in Massachusetts, there have been just enough cases of attorneys with their fingers in cookie jars and indifferent representation that the rules tilt in favor of pursuing claims. This is the land of justice for the little guy."

"Couldn't Terhune have gone after Naylor?"

"And take what?" Hunt asked. "Naylor's 1998 Toyota Tercel? Naylor's a nut case. He got injured and he decided that the accident was his permanent meal ticket. When we told him his claim was worth a few thousand dollars, he decided to go after the next deepest pocket, which was Fred's. The only thing Fred ever did wrong was agreeing to see Naylor in the first place, and it was hardly one of those things anyone could have foreseen."

"Was the lawsuit wrapping up?"

"It depends on your perspective," Hunt said. Naylor was never going to win and he is – or was – on his third attorney, all working on contingency. All he could do was keep wearing Fred down by piling on fresh allegations and demanding yet another deposition. But from Naylor's perspective, it was like going double or nothing at a casino when you're down a hundred grand and you can't possibly pay. All it takes is one right guess and you're even, so you roll the dice again. But I hear that after his last attorney quit the case, he couldn't find anyone to pick up the standard. So, maybe there was finally an end in sight."

"In looking through Terhune's finances, I couldn't help notice that the loss of income didn't affect his spending patterns," Flynn said.

"That's beyond my expertise," Hunt said, waving his hand dismissively. "Fred's life outside of the office was his own business."

"Yet you knew about his life insurance arrangements," Flynn said.

Hunt paused. "Well, yes, but I don't remember this conversation including anything about life insurance."

"Another person with whom I spoke said they had learned – from you – the size of Fred Terhune's life insurance as well as who were the named beneficiaries."

"It does happen to be information I possess, but only because Fred and I talked about it when he took out the policy and again when he and Erica were going through the divorce," Hunt said, carefully. "I cannot imagine ever divulging that information to a third party. In fact, I can state categorically that I've never discussed Fred's insurance with anyone other than Fred."

Fascinating, Flynn thought. *Mary Ann Mandeville, you are a work of art*.

"Then the inevitable question is, should I be looking more closely at George Naylor as a suspect?" Flynn asked.

Hunt considered his answer before saying anything. "Detective Flynn, every time I see one of these briefs come in through the door, I think to myself, 'there but for the grace of God go I'. I think George Naylor is a disturbed individual, although he seemed perfectly normal when I first met him. After two years, I believe he is capable of most anything. And, if he concluded that his lawsuit was going down the sewer, physical harm is one of the ways he might take out his anger."

"Can you think of anyone else who might have wanted to see harm come to Mr. Terhune?" Flynn asked.

This time, Hunt answered immediately. "He was a selectman, and I assume selectmen make enemies. But this is a suburban law practice, Detective Flynn. Our bread and butter is real estate, wills, and trusts. With the exception of George Naylor, I can't think of the last time that a client went away from here unhappy. So, no, I can't think of anyone connected with his law practice other than George Naylor who might have had reason to kill Fred."

"Then I need an address for Mr. Naylor."

* * * * *

August meetings of the Hardington Garden Club were generally laid-back affairs. By tradition, instead of being held at the Congregational Church's Fellowship Hall, members convened at someone's home, usually in their garden. An attendance of twenty-five – less than a third of the club's membership – was considered a good turnout. There was never a speaker at August meetings. The business meeting would be dispensed within a few minutes. Then, plants would be exchanged, lemonade and cake consumed, and those without access to summer retreats in cooler and less humid locales would tell one another that the maintaining of a second home on Cape Cod or Lake Sunapee was 'simply too much bother'.

It was a sociological oddity of the suburban garden club. People ostensibly joined because they liked to garden and chose to be club members because of the opportunity to learn and exchange ideas. Yet, at the peak of summer and the height of the growing season, attendance wilted and homes were vacant. Even those members who were not away could be attracted only by the promise of a tour of someone's private garden and the opportunity to secretly criticize it afterwards.

This morning's meeting, however, spilled into every available inch of lawn at the member's house at which it was held. Liz could identify at least two dozen attendees who maintained summer homes in Falmouth, Chatham, or Lenox. They had returned to

Hardington for the week, interrupting their August idyll, braving hours-long backups on the Mass Pike or the Bourne Bridge.

They were here because of the presence in Hardington of *Ultimate House Makeover.* There were only two important topics of conversation this morning: would the crew be filming their planting activities on Friday? And, were the police close to arresting anyone for the murder of Fred Terhune? Liz was presumed to have the answers to both questions, and everyone wanted to hear the answers first-hand.

"They film everything," Liz said, honestly. "But they record far more than they can use. Remember: this is a one-hour program; forty minutes, really, because of commercials. That said, I can assure you that, at some point during the day, you're going to be on camera, and either Whit Dakota or someone from the production company will ask you about yourself. But I think the odds of your interview making it on the air are fairly slim. I am working fairly closely with the camera people, and I'm going to make certain there's a group shot when we put in some of the trees and hang the baskets."

"We did avert a crisis, thanks to Eva Morin," Liz told the group. "Hammer and Saw Productions, the people behind *Ultimate House Makeover,* are based in California, and they went to a home center chain based in Texas to design the planting for a New England house, with predictable results. Eva re-did the planting scheme to use shrubs that will actually survive a Zone 5 winter, and got nurseries to donate a good part of what we'll use. Hammer and Saw has agreed to foot the rest of the bill. So, be sure to thank Eva because, without her, you'd be planting expensive firewood."

"As to Fred Terhune, I'm really not involved," Liz said. "The police seem to have this one under control and they don't need my help."

* * * * *

Where's Liz Phillips when you need her? Flynn thought to himself. He needed to triangulate George Naylor. He needed someone else to ask questions while he watched for the shifts in body language. He needed intuition and he needed someone off whom he could bounce ideas. Liz Phillips had served that purpose wonderfully when he investigated the death of Sally Kahn two months earlier. Now, he felt adrift with an infinitely more complex case.

George Naylor sat across from Flynn in the tiny dinette set in Naylor's apartment in Hardington Meadows. From the information provided by Joseph Hunt, Flynn knew that Naylor was in his mid-thirties although his thinning hair and pallid face gave him the look of someone who might be ten or more years older. He was a slightly built man, the kind of person who would have avoided athletics as a child and exercised little as an adult. Horn-rimmed glasses gave Naylor an intelligent look, and that perception of intelligence and earnestness was probably what kept enticing lawyers to sign onto Naylor's never-ending legal quest.

Hardington Meadows was a 1960s-era apartment complex, converted to condominiums long before the real estate boom. The buildings were each two stories with spacious, well-kept walkways and flower beds. *If it were being built today*, Flynn thought, *it would have quadruple the density.* Empty tennis courts and play areas attested to its mostly elderly population, and Flynn wondered if Naylor might have inherited the apartment from his parents. In his orientation to the town, Flynn had been told that this was a 'zero crime' neighborhood. He remembered the patrolman saying, "We only get calls when someone hasn't been seen for a day or two. It usually means either someone fell or they died in their sleep."

Flynn had started with the gentle questions, but encountered defensiveness from the outset.

"I'm investigating the death of Fred Terhune Sunday evening, Mr. Naylor, and your name came up in connection with a lawsuit you had filed against him."

"You need to talk to my lawyer," Naylor said.

"I'd much prefer to keep this unofficial," Flynn said. "I just need to ask you a couple of questions."

That was the easy part of the conversation.

The living room, kitchen, and dining area of Naylor's apartment formed one room. A window air-conditioner rattled Venetian blinds badly in need of dusting. The sofa was covered in newspapers and boxes, a coffee table groaned under stacks of papers and file folders. *This was a man who lived alone and who seldom had visitors*, Flynn thought.

"May I ask what you do for a living that allows you to be home on a Wednesday morning, Mr. Naylor?" Flynn asked.

"I write software manuals," Naylor answered.

Flynn waited for an elaboration.

"Like when a new video game gets developed," Naylor said. "People want to know how to play the game better. The software developer ships me an advanced copy of the software. I figure out the shortcuts. I did *Dark Castle III* and *Grand Larceny – Las Vegas*."

"You tell people how to cheat?"

"I tell people how to get the most out of the game," Naylor said, brusquely. "Where to find ammunition, who to avoid. The game manufacturer pays me."

"This is like *Grand Theft Auto*?" Flynn asked, naming the only video game he could think of.

"That's a really old title but it's the same idea," Naylor said. "What I work on is more like *Mass Effect 3* or *Resident Evil*. Those sell huge."

"What are you working on now?"

"*Siege of Stalingrad*," Naylor said. He was now slightly less guarded. "Do you play?"

Flynn shook his head. "After my time. The technology has kind of passed me by."

"Lots of guys your age go in for games," Naylor said. "There are some good Vietnam titles out there. Try *Call of Duty: Black Ops*."

"I'll pass, but thanks for the tip." Flynn shifted position in his chair. *My parents had a dinette set like this one*, he thought. "Mr.

Naylor, I need to know if you were at the party up at the sanitarium grounds on Sunday night."

Naylor gave an exaggerated shake of his head. "*X-Men: First Class*," he said. "No party would be worth missing that movie. It was on Cinemax. Jennifer Lawrence, just before she made *The Hunger Games*. She has got to be the hottest actress, ever." Naylor went on to describe the film in a level of detail that told Flynn that this was a well-rehearsed alibi. Naylor could doubtlessly also recount the top half dozen items on the eleven o'clock news, all of which could be culled from a DVR.

Flynn got up from his chair. "Well, Mr. Naylor, I promised you I wouldn't ask any questions about your lawsuit, but I would like to contact your attorney on the subject. Do you have his card?"

Caught off-guard, Naylor stammered for a moment. "I'm interviewing new counsel right now. Can I give you that information as soon as I've retained them?"

"That will be fine."

Flynn sat in his car, writing in his notebook, his mind racing. *This guy is prime*, he thought. *Naylor makes his living by being in a fantasy world.*

The Best Buy store in Overfield carried *Grand Larceny – Las Vegas*. A salesman who intuitively sensed that Flynn was not interested in buying the game gave a blunt assessment. "It's a second-rate knockoff with PlayStation II-level graphics and a lousy story line," he said.

"What about the playing guide?" Flynn asked.

The salesman walked a few feet down the aisle and thumbed through titles. "We carry it," and handed Flynn a copy. *Grand Larceny – Las Vegas: Official Strategy Guide* and the author *George Naylor*. Flynn turned over the book and found a photo of Naylor on the back.

"Ever sold any of these?"

The salesman snickered derisively. "You have to want to own the game first."

"But people buy these 'strategy guides'?"

"Oh, sure," the salesman said. "The *Grand Theft* series sells a ton of guides. So does *L.A. Noire, Mortal Kombat, Call of Duty*, those sorts of games."

"What about *Dark Castle III*?"

"You mean 'Dork Castle'. Same problems as *Grand Larceny*. The plot is junior high, the graphics are jumpy."

To the salesman's amazement, Flynn bought the strategy guide. "You don't want the game?" the salesman asked.

"This is fine," Flynn said.

An author who writes books that don't sell, Flynn thought, as he walked out to his car. He called Joseph Hunt.

"Mr. Hunt, can I assume that either Fred Terhune or your firm did a background check on George Naylor when he filed his suit against Mr. Terhune?" Flynn asked.

"Of course we did," Hunt said.

"Would you be comfortable sharing any of it?"

There was a momentary pause. "I couldn't give you a copy, but I could tell you highlights."

Flynn noted that Hunt did not ask why he wanted the background check. There was the sound of a drawer opening and a rustling of papers in the background.

"George Naylor, age 36, BA in English from Alfred University. Worked for a couple of high tech firms as a technical writer, but he's been 'self-employed' for the past three years. Parents both deceased. Never married, no previous lawsuits. He inherited some money from his parents and he took out a mortgage on the condo. Is that enough?"

"It gets me started," Flynn said.

Flynn drove to the Hardington sanitarium grounds and knocked on the door of the video production trailer. Joel Silverstein opened the door.

"I'm looking for a guy who may have been at the party Sunday night," Flynn said. "Can we look at the last half hour on both cameras?"

Joel nodded. "I'm doing rough-cut edits, but I'll show you how to operate the console. If you spot the guy, let me know." Joel typed in a series of instructions and the Camera 2 video of the Sunday evening party appeared. Another set of instructions and the time code of 9:30 p.m. came on the screen. "Here's how you zoom and pan. Here's how you pause and rewind."

Flynn went though the Camera 2 footage without seeing Naylor, so he hadn't attempted to approach Terhune during the party. He switched to the Camera 1 footage, which focused on Whit Dakota.

At the 9:41 time code, Flynn's patience paid off. In a corner of the tent, staying away from the crowd and seeming to observe it from a distance, was George Naylor. For the remaining four minutes that the camera recorded, Naylor stayed in one place, between light and shadow, neither talking to anyone nor acknowledging the activities around him. He did not attempt to hide, only to blend in as part of the background. The overall effect, Flynn thought, was downright creepy.

"I want to print this frame, then I'll leave you alone," Flynn said.

Flynn, his first evidence linking Naylor to the death of Fred Terhune in his hand, walked by the volunteer trailer on his way back to his car, but saw no one inside.

Maybe later, he thought.

* * * * *

For Liz, the intricacies of scheduling three hundred volunteer carpenters and painters paled beside the task of sorting fifty garden club members and spouses into three work details. Everything had to be planted, watered, and mulched by 3 p.m. The earliest anyone could be expected to arrive was 7:30 a.m.

Members who were seventy years old and using canes, and who had husbands who were seventy-five, were volunteering to spend all day planting. The youngest members had to work around day care, and Liz wondered if spouses with full-time jobs would remember to show up. She settled on a 7:30 a.m. to noon shift for the strongest volunteers to handle tree planting and hole-digging, and a noon-to-three group that would handle the somewhat lighter, but still physical duties of planting annuals and perennials, and adding mulch. A third group – the least mobile – would focus on hanging baskets, flower arrangements, and watering. When she first took on the assignment, fifty people seemed an extravagant number. Now, she wondered if it were enough.

She drove from the garden club meeting to the sanitarium via Hospital Road and, recognized by the policeman on duty, was waved through the roadblock at the elementary school. At the construction site, a bus had disgorged sixty people wearing blue 'Leukemia Society' tee shirts. The group marched toward the house with an enormous banner.

The previous afternoon, Barry Zimmerman had spent twenty minutes on the phone negotiating this appearance. Three buses had been forced to become one though it appeared to Liz that Barry had failed to specify that everyone on the bus had to be seated. But Whit Dakota was a gracious host and, with two cameras recording every move, he accepted one of their tee shirts and handed hammers and saws to the first dozen people in the group. As Barry had noted, there was nothing for the group to do except to get themselves on camera and then get out of the way before they broke something of value.

"Every week, it's something different," he had said. "Muscular Dystrophy, breast cancer, spina bifida. And they all want to be on the show. And they all get to Don Elwell and he says 'OK'. And I have to make it happen. It's all on my shoulders."

By now, Liz was weary of that last part. So far this week, Barry had spent an afternoon at Fenway Park and a morning at Gillette

Stadium. And, somewhere in New Jersey, someone very much like Fred Terhune or herself was entering hundreds of names into a computer to create a master volunteer list for the program's next building project. In Liz's opinion, Barry Zimmerman had one of the easier jobs in television.

Her reverie was broken by a tapping on her car window. It was Janey Matthews.

"Are you going back to the trailer?" Janey asked. "Can I get a ride? My bike is up at the sanitarium and the bus isn't going for half an hour."

For three hours, Liz had put out of her head the thought of Linda Harper and Whit Dakota's use of the volunteers to troll for an evening's entertainment. Now, with Janey in the car, Liz's anger came again to the forefront.

Am I being some kind of prude? Liz thought. *Or is it even any of my business? If Whit Dakota invites someone into his trailer and they end up in bed with him, that's their business. Not mine. It's their choice.*

But then she thought of the videos. *What are the chances that Linda Harper knew she was being recorded for Whit Dakota's 'greatest hits'?*

And, is that legal?

"Janey, I need your help." Liz said as she drove back to the sanitarium.

"Isn't that what I'm supposed to be doing?" Janey asked.

"Are you good with computers?"

"I guess," Janey said. It was a noncommittal answer.

"Can you make copies of DVDs at home on your computer?"

"Oh, sure." This time, Janey smiled.

"When we get back to the sanitarium, I'm going to ask you to do something very important," Liz said. "I need to do something in the video trailer. I need to be alone. Have you met Joel Silverstein?"

Janey nodded.

"I need you to get Joel out of the trailer for a few minutes. Can you do that?"

"What if I tell him you're looking for him?"

Liz thought for a moment. "That might work. But you have to get him away from the trailer. He can't see me go in."

"Are you going to take a DVD from the trailer?"

"I can't tell you that," Liz said.

"Well, if that's what you were going to do, I'd say, why not just copy it right there?"

"Because I don't know how," Liz said. And then added, "If I were going to copy a DVD. And I didn't say I was going to." *Did that sound as lame to Janey as it does to me?* she thought.

"Can we go to my house first?" Janey asked.

Ten minutes later, they arrived at the sanitarium. Janey held her laptop computer and a blank DVD in a jewel case. Five minutes after that, Liz had discovered how easy it was to insert a DVD into the laptop, activate a program that copied the footage into the laptop's memory, and then insert the blank DVD into the same drive. "You don't even have to do the last step in the trailer," Janey said. "Just load in the DVD, put it on the computer's memory, then take out the DVD and put it back where you found it."

The area around the trailers was relatively quiet with most of the day's activity shifted to the construction site. The sound of power saws came from the tents, though, and Liz suggested that Janey take Joel over to first one, and then the other.

Liz watched from the window of the volunteer trailer as Janey walked toward the adjacent video production trailer, disappeared, and then re-appeared a few moments later, headed in the direction of one of the construction tents, urging Joel to follow. Liz waited thirty seconds, and made her move.

The video trailer door was not locked, Liz went quickly inside and scanned the counter. DVDs were scattered on many surfaces. She looked at titles, not seeing the one she wanted. She opened a drawer. There were two: *'Whit's Greatest Hits – Hardington'* and *'Whit's Greatest Hits – Hardington – Vol. II'.*

Which one?

She took the first one, put it in the computer's disk drive, and pushed 'copy'.

Six minutes later, she was back at her desk, sorting through a stack of messages, her head deliberately facing away from the door. Janey knocked and Liz looked up to see Joel Silverstein behind her.

"Where have you been?" Liz said, crossly. "I told you I was coming back to the trailer."

"I'm sorry, Mrs. Phillips," Janey said. She also winked. "I thought you said you'd be at the tent…"

"Never mind," Liz said. "Joel, I've just found out that one of the people helping me may have mis-indentified some of the people in the photos with Whit. Have they already been signed?"

Joel stepped up to the trailer door. "To be honest, I haven't even had time to print the photos," he said. "I was sort of hoping you might be able to help us if we get into a time crunch."

"I don't know how to print photos off of a computer," Liz said.

"I was thinking more along the lines of signing them," Joel said sheepishly.

"Well, let me know soon," Liz said, adding a tone of weariness she did not feel.

As soon as Joel was out of sight, Liz completed the process of 'burning' the DVD under Janey's tutelage. For the next three hours, she took care of a stack of requests from the construction managers or their assistants. The job was turning into a routine, though one that Liz found enjoyable. The construction managers identified the need for people with specific skills and quantified the number of man-hours a job would take and the time frame for accomplishing the task. Liz located those people and then cajoled them into dropping what they were doing to help out for anywhere from a few hours to a full day. Success required establishing a quick rapport and reminding them of the importance of their contribution.

Liz's next call was one that took some mental rehearsal.

Diane Terwilliger was a Hardington attorney. When Liz and David had returned to Hardington from their three years in Hong Kong six years earlier, Terwilliger had handled the purchase of their Old Schoolhouse Road home and David had intimated that he would need the services of an attorney for other work as he established his management business. But he had instead called on 'downtown' law firms for that work, and Liz had long felt that her husband had at least implied promises that were not kept.

Two months earlier, however, when Liz needed Terwilliger's help in obtaining crucial information that solved the murder of Sally Kahn, that help had been offered freely. Moreover, Terwilliger, perhaps a decade older than Liz, brought a needed maturity of viewpoint in addition to a solid grasp of the law. She was the right person to approach.

"I need some legal advice," Liz said.

"Is this about Fred?" Terwilliger said. "I heard you found the body."

"Not true this time," Liz said. "I came along about a minute later. And, fortunately, it's not about Fred. I think I've found something going on with one of the *Ultimate House Makeover* people, and I need to know how many laws I'm breaking."

"Can it wait until morning?" Terwilliger asked.

"If it has to," Liz said.

"I'm going to be in a deposition for the rest of the day and I have a brief to finish tonight," Terwilliger said. "How about eight o'clock at the Silver Spoon?"

"Seven o'clock at my house would be better," Liz said. "This is not a conversation for anyone to overhear."

"For seven o'clock, you'd better have broken some really interesting laws," Terwilliger said. "See you then."

8.

Flynn's dossier on George Naylor was depressingly thin. Naylor had no fingerprints on record and he had never been arrested or even received a traffic citation. His father had died ten years earlier of a heart attack, his mother, two years later, of cancer. Naylor had a sister, three years younger than himself, living in Nashua, New Hampshire. It took more than an hour to track her down, time during which the 'no report found' responses continued to pile up on Naylor.

From the sound of her voice and the incessant crying of an infant in the background, Flynn envisioned Patty Naylor Cummings as a slightly harried housewife.

"I don't see my brother very often," she told Flynn as soon as he said why he was calling.

"It's not that far to Nashua," Flynn said. "Any reason why not?"

"I could say we were never a close family, and that would be true," Cummings said. "It would also be true that my brother has always been a little creepy, and that he's gotten a whole lot creepier since he started writing those game books."

Flynn waited for an elaboration.

"The last time I was in Hardington, he had this giant map of a castle laid out in his bedroom. I mean, really detailed. And he talked about the ways into the castle and what weapons would kill what gorgons or whatever they were."

"I thought that was true of a lot of people who got into these games," Flynn said.

"I know some of those people," Cummings said. "They play for four or five hours at a stretch. George could go eighteen hours."

"But he was writing a strategy guide for the game," Flynn said. "He was presumably on a deadline."

"You don't get it, Detective," Cummings said. "This was six months *after* the guide was published."

Flynn felt it was time to update the chief.

"I thought I'd have it wrapped up," Flynn said as he stood in Chief Harding's office. "I've got the Framingham police looking for my two Brazilians, and the fact that I haven't heard from them yet gives me a feeling that they're hiding. My next step may have to be to bring the Oliveiras down here for a formal statement."

"I can't rule out Mary Ann Mandeville," he continued. "If the Stamford detective is right, she killed her first husband. While I don't have a motive other than 'jilted lover', as evidenced by a knee to the gonads on camera, something about Mrs. Mandeville just doesn't seem right. My problem is that she isn't being helpful."

"My principal suspect right now is George Naylor. He lives in Hardington Meadows."

Chief Harding held up a finger. "Tom and Christine Naylor's boy?"

Flynn flipped through his notes. The names of the deceased parents matched. "Yes," he said.

"Strange kid," Chief Harding said. "Weird kid. Parents were salt of the earth. Had a house in town. Came here about 1960. Newlyweds. Had two children, George and a sister - Patty. Sold the house after Tom had his first heart attack. Doctor said 'no more house maintenance'. Moved into the Meadows. Tom was president of the Rotary for about five years."

"George Naylor," Chief Harding continued. "Kind of a misfit. He'd take off from school in the middle of the day and we'd find him wandering around the sanitarium back when there were still about a thousand people up there. He'd be talking to those people, asking them questions, writing down the answers in a notebook. You have to understand that locals stayed away from that place unless they worked there."

Flynn listened to learn if there was more. Chief Harding seemed to have run out of recollections. "George Naylor went to

Fred Terhune's law firm two years ago, looking to sue a ski resort for negligence," Flynn said. "When Terhune suggested that he should settle for getting his hospital bills paid and a couple of thousand bucks, Naylor turned around and sued Terhune. Kept him wrapped up in legal knots. Really distracted Terhune from his law practice."

"News to me," Chief Harding said.

"Joe Hunt – his partner – said Naylor had gone through three attorneys and, from my conversation with him this morning, he hasn't lined up a fourth one yet," Flynn said. "That implies desperation. And, if Naylor is as out of touch with reality as his sister says, he just might have decided that killing Terhune was just the next step in winning the game."

Chief Harding pressed his fingers together and looked pensive. "That's an insanity defense if ever I heard one."

"That assumes a plea," Flynn said. "I've also got bupkus for physical evidence. So far, I have George Naylor in a lie – he said he wasn't at the party Sunday night but the video shows him there just before ten – but nothing to tie him to the crime. I've got a blood trail now but, without a murder weapon or fingerprints, we're looking at circumstantial evidence only."

"You may want to talk with Charlie Harris," Chief Harding said.

Flynn looked at the chief blankly. "And he is…"

"Was. Guidance counselor up at the high school. Retired two years ago. He was there back when Naylor was in school. Tell him I said you need his help." Chief Harding wrote down a number on a slip of paper. It had only four digits; the 'townie' convention of assuming everyone knew the area code and prefix.

"Do you need outside help?" Chief Harding asked as he handed Flynn the paper. "Your buddies at the state police keep calling to remind me that you're not calling them with updates."

"You may want to remind them that they had their crack physical evidence team out here all Monday morning yet it took

Eddie Frankel about an hour to find the attack site. Maybe they ought to figure out that sometimes you have to work past five o'clock. They have the video of the blood, which ought to keep them busy. Oh, and after 48 hours, they haven't showed me squat," Flynn said. "As to assistance, give me another day. My sense is that there's a lot more evidence and motive out there. I just haven't seen it yet."

Flynn continued. "I had hopes for the crime scene. Something left behind, perhaps. But Eddie went over it carefully this morning and, apart from the blood and the possibility of distinctive fingerprints on something like the tarps, it's clean. All I really know is that whoever clocked Terhune over the head intended to kill him."

* * * * *

The Wednesday five o'clock update meeting produced only good news. Construction was on schedule, materials were in place for Thursday's work sessions, and the flow of qualified volunteers was exactly as needed. The conversations began to shift from Hardington to the group's next project, an extended family of ten near Princeton, New Jersey, who were currently living in an antiquated three-bedroom apartment. Several of the family's children were adoptees and two were wheelchair-bound. *Ultimate House Makeover* planned to convert a vacant farmhouse into a five-bedroom home with full handicapped access.

"Are there any holes left in the volunteer schedule for Hardington?" Don Elwell asked Barry Zimmerman.

Zimmerman shook his head. "We look good."

"Then, if Liz can hold down the fort," Elwell said, "I want you to go down to Princeton tonight and make certain everything is going smoothly for next week. The way I see it, we need a minimum of five hundred qualified volunteers for that project and the coordinator down there has less than half that number processed." Elwell turned to Liz. "Liz, everything I hear tells me you've got things running like clockwork. If you need backup, come see me and I'll get it for you."

And, with that, the meeting was over.

Janey Matthews was waiting in the Volunteer trailer when Liz returned. And, once again, Liz felt the pang of loss at her own daughter's distance and adulthood. Perhaps it was the way the arms and legs dangled as she sat in a chair, the continuous kinetic energy of youth that required constant motion. It was a pose Liz had seen in her own daughter every day for years, and she had never appreciated its expressiveness.

Janey saw Liz staring. "I was going to go to the Cardozo's and see if I can help out before I went home," she said.

"You never told me about your friend," Liz said. "Did you ever go see her yesterday?"

Janey nodded. "Yeah, sort of. She's like, still grounded, but I think her mom is getting over that. But Michelle didn't want to see me. Her mom says she just stays in her room and listens to music."

"Janey, I grounded my daughter a few times," Liz said. "And she reacted the same way sometimes, staying in her room. But what she really wanted was for her friends to come around and see her. Friends were really important to my daughter, and I'll bet they're important to Michelle, too. So, if you really want to help someone out, go back over and see your friend. Spend some time with her. There are plenty of volunteers over at the Cardozo's."

Janey seemed to absorb the advice. Then, her head bobbing, she said, "OK," and bounced out of the chair.

Liz sat down at her desk. There were no more messages, no reason for her to stay. She should go home and relax, or work in the garden. But she felt like doing neither. For three days, she had been a vital part of an enterprise, an anchor upon which other people depended. It felt good, it felt natural.

David had asked her on many occasions, why she didn't go back to work.

'You need the challenge,' David had said. *'Liz, that garden club takes two or three days a month.'*

'But we don't need the money…' she had countered.

'It isn't about money. It's about challenging yourself,' had been David's response.

And he was, as usual, right. Three days of rounding up volunteers had given her renewed purpose. Seeing Janey had reminded her that her one-time role as full-time mother was now long past. But now Liz imagined a new element to that conversation.

'If you weren't away all of the time, we could travel and do things together,' she would say.

'Travel gets old, very quickly. What you need is a new interest,' David would likely have responded.

'What kind of 'interest' do you have in mind?' she would have fired back.

Liz was awaiting her husband's imagined response when her cell phone rang.

"Liz, it's John Flynn."

She nearly dropped the phone. "What did I do right to deserve this?"

"I owe you for that awful dinner Monday night," Flynn said. "I've got another hour or so of work here, but I'd like to bring you up to speed on what I've found and get your ideas. Is there a place…"

"Come by my house," Liz said. "Seven-thirty."

"I was inviting you out to dinner," Flynn said.

"And I'm accepting. We're dining at Chez Phillips."

Liz turned off her phone. *Oh, my God. What have I done now.*

* * * * *

Flynn hung up the phone. He had sweat stain under his arms. *Jesus Christ,* he thought. *Call her back. Tell her you can't do it.*

Can't do what? Have dinner?

His invitation was at least in part a reaction to the frustration of a case in which progress had slowed to a crawl. Two calls to the Framingham police produced only a promise that, 'we've shown the picture to a lot of people.' A lengthy conversation with Detective Jared Millman of the Stamford Police, in which Flynn read back Mary Ann Mandeville's statement that detectives had refused to look at her husband's labor union clients as suspects, was met with derision.

"The law firm was clean, the clients were clean," Millman said. "Believe me, we checked it out. Yes, he had the locals of a couple of labor unions as clients, but it was a dead end. No RICO indictments, no pending investigations beyond the usual stuff."

Two calls to the state police crime scenes lab produced two opportunities to leave voice mail. His first message was reasonable and asked for a prompt call back. His second was considerably more caustic.

He buried himself in work for the next hour. Slowly, he constructed a profile of George Naylor. Chief Harding's recollections, while rambling, helped pull the picture together. Naylor was the kid who didn't fit in, the last one chosen for the team.

His conversation with retired guidance counselor Charlie Harris had been marginally productive. School records were nominally sealed from inquiries from law enforcement agencies, and so Harris had provided only some broad-brush perspective of Naylor as a loner and someone who made few friends. "Call him intelligent, but misdirected," Harris had said. "He would obsess over things. Scared the hell out of a couple of his teachers."

Naylor's father had died soon after he graduated from college, his mother a few years later. Such a turn of events twenty or thirty years earlier would have left less of a mark, but kids who came of age in the 1990s and later had a far different relationship with their parents. They were dependent far longer, both financially and emotionally. The loss of both parents to illness must have been devastating.

And, Naylor was still in the family nest. Calls to his employers had failed to produce a reason for dismissal, or even an acknowledgement that there was a dismissal. Instead, it was the ubiquitous, 'lack of work' and 'company reorganization'. When pressed and told that the information was part of a police investigation, one human resources manager said only that 'Naylor left no footprints'. He was unremembered.

His work as a writer of video game guides was especially telling. Flynn read more than fifty pages of *Grand Larceny - Las Vegas*.

'Get injured in a casino. Fall down or twist an ankle. Demand that the casino give you a suite and chips. Don't take their first offer. Never take anyone's opening offer. Use the suite as a base to case the stores you'll rob later…'

'Don't be afraid of setting off the alarm in the Aztec jewelry store. It doesn't ring through to the police station. Hit the night guard over the head with anything metallic, but be sure not to leave your weapon behind…'

Was the original lawsuit against the ski resort an outgrowth of learning ways to win at a video game? Was the advice to 'hit the guard over the head' just coincidence, or the deadly playing out in real life of lessons learned on a computer?

At 7:15, Flynn assembled his notes and turned off his desk lamp. He studied himself in the men's room mirror. *There's more gray than there was last year. You need to exercise more. You've been wearing that same damned sports jacket all summer. You're 57 years old and you're one sad excuse for human being.*

At Hardington Wines and Spirits, Flynn decided that decisiveness was better than endless comparisons. "Give me the best chilled sauvignon blanc you sell for twenty-five dollars a bottle," he told the man at the counter. Two months earlier, he had spent an hour in this same store and come away empty-

handed. Surprised by the directness, the man promptly came back
with a bottle. Flynn didn't even look at the label.

* * * * *

Liz stood in the middle of the voluminous master bedroom
closet, her cat rubbing her legs. Her clothes swept in two long
rows down one side of the closet, turned a corner, and came half
way up the other side, where they ran into David's modest
assortment of suits and shirts. Thirty linear feet of clothing, she
calculated, and she did not know what to wear. A dress was too
formal. Slacks were too informal. Skirts were too long or too
short. Blouses were either Mary Jane-prim or come-hither
diaphanous.

She wanted to scream.

Twenty minutes after walking into her closet and after having
tried on and rejected six outfits, she emerged with a white skirt and
pink blouse that seemed to say, 'adult'. She placed the clothes, still
on hangers, on the back of the closet door and walked into the
master bathroom, where an eight-foot-long mirror called attention
to every hint of gray in her roots and every line in her face.

Why does it have to be this hard? Liz thought. She traced a line
around her mouth with a cream and rubbed gently.

*This is not a date. You are not going to the prom. You are not going
necking. You have invited a man with whom you share professional interests
over for dinner.*

She applied a minimum of makeup and changed clothes. She
again passed the perfume on her dresser. She again sprayed a mist
and stepped through it.

Liz went downstairs and gasped at the time: 7:15. *How long was
I up there?*

A plan formed. It was one of necessity but, when the doorbell
rang promptly at 7:30, she was ready.

John Flynn stood at the door.

"I thought a wine was better than a cactus," he said, holding
out the bottle. "I hope it doesn't reveal as much personality."

"I'm going to pour us a couple of glasses, and then take you on a tour of the garden," Liz said. She noted that the wine was chilled and was from a vineyard whose wine she admired.

"Cakebread," she said. "You have excellent taste."

"The guy at the wine store has excellent taste," Flynn said. "I get no credit for this one."

Liz opened the bottle and returned with two glasses. For the next twenty minutes, she walked Flynn along paths through two acres of late-summer perennials, made more colorful by the rays of the setting sun. White and pink Japanese anemones played off of Campanula, and a light breeze made flower heads sway gently.

"I have a confession," Flynn said as they walked. "The first time I ever came here – the day of Sally Kahn's murder -- I took one look at all of these flower beds and made an immediate assumption that you had about a dozen migrant laborers working for you to make it all look like this. I know now that you do it yourself, I'm just not certain how you do it. It's amazing."

"I'll take it as a compliment," Liz said. "This is what I've made. There was nothing here. Or, to be more precise, whatever had been here before had been ripped into oblivion by bulldozers. I had no plan, I only knew that I wanted to create something attractive and lasting, and that I didn't want some lawn service coming in every week and cutting a perfect lawn to a perfect height."

"I'd say you accomplished what you set out to do," Flynn said.

They were rounding the corner of the house when the truck pulled down the driveway.

"Dinner," Liz said and smiled.

A teenager carried a large pizza box.

Dinner was on the large back deck, a gingham table cloth over the outdoor table.

"Tell me about the case," Liz said.

Flynn chewed a slice of pizza. "If I said 'Naylor', would that mean anything to you?"

Liz thought for several moments. "Nothing."

"Tom and Christine Naylor were the parents," Flynn said. "They both died about ten years ago. Two kids, Patty or Patricia, about thirty-two now, and George, aged thirty-five. The parents lived in Hardington Meadows before they died."

"No connection," Liz said, shaking her head.

"George has come out of nowhere to become my chief suspect. He fits the profile – if you believe in profiles of people who murder outside of their immediate family. Loner and misfit. He makes his living writing how-to-win guides for those action-adventure video games. And some of the stuff he writes comes awfully close to what happened to Fred Terhune."

"What's his connection?" Liz asked.

"Naylor got banged up at a ski resort in the Berkshires two years ago," Flynn said. "It may or may not have been the resort's fault, but Naylor went to Terhune's firm and wanted to sue for half a million. Terhune took the case, made a few calls, and told Naylor that he should be happy to get his doctor's bills paid and a small check for his trouble. Naylor turned around and sued Terhune for shoddy representation."

"Can you do that?" Liz asked.

"You can in Massachusetts," Flynn said. "The suit tied up Terhune's law practice very badly. But once Naylor's lawyers figured out their client was a nut case, they dropped him. Apparently, the third firm hired quit fairly recently and Naylor can't find anyone to pursue the claim. He may have cracked and decided to come after Terhune directly."

"Was he at the party?"

Flynn nodded and chewed a slice of pizza. "Naylor says no, but the camera doesn't lie. He was there. Unfortunately, everything is circumstantial. There's no physical evidence. Idiot that I am, I let the staties do the crime scene investigation. That was two and a half days ago and, for all I know, they've outsourced it to someone in Alabama. I can't even get anyone to return a call."

"What about the murder weapon?" Liz asked.

"No sign of it. I found where Terhune got whacked – it was right in back of the Winnebago you're in. Naylor – or whoever did it – probably made some kind of noise outside of the RV, knowing Terhune was inside. Terhune came out to investigate and got something round and metallic on the side of the head. Terhune was dragged about fifty feet to where he died, then was dragged to where you found him."

Liz considered the gruesome nature of the crime as she ate a wedge of pizza. "If Naylor killed Terhune, Naylor had to risk being seen. Why not just attack him inside the trailer? I mean, walk in, close the door, and hit him. Why lure him outside?"

"I don't know," Flynn said. *And I hadn't thought of it, either.*

"What happened to the two guys in jeans?" Liz asked.

"Apart from knowing that they work – or worked – for MetroWest Construction, they're off the map."

"What does that mean, 'off the map'?"

"It means that no one among the Framingham detectives' squad recognizes them and that's a bad sign," Flynn said. "Bad guys don't usually graduate directly from digging ditches to murder. They get a reputation along the way and become known to the local police. You know, they get brought in for questioning for something but released for lack of evidence. In this case, you have two guys who go straight to the head of the class, and that takes a stretch of the imagination."

"How did they know where to find Fred on Sunday night?" Liz asked.

Flynn paused. *Another damned good question.* "If MetroWest sent them, then the Oliveiras passed along the information, or the guys were watching Terhune's house."

"Which means someone in the neighborhood would have seen them," Liz said. "That's a very close-knit part of town. Families there have lived in the same houses for generations. You hang around on a street corner, watching a house, and people notice."

Flynn kicked himself mentally. *If I had more people…*

"But it still begs the question: why confront him in a crowd?" Liz asked. "Why did they need to do that? That's asking for there to be witnesses. The only reason I'd go looking for someone under those circumstances would be to shame them into something."

"You're right," Flynn said, quietly.

"I'm right about what?" Liz asked.

"I've been dazzled by the technology," Flynn said, shaking his head. "I have two cameras pointing at a man during the last few hours of his life, and I think it represents his entire world. I'm seeing one facet of that world without connection to any other part. I see some people do something – interact with Terhune in a certain way – and I start ascribing motives for murder."

"Of course those two guys aren't the murderers, Liz. They'd be stupid to set up a public confrontation. Even if there weren't cameras, there would be a dozen witnesses and I'd have a composite sketch that was every bit as good as the video. Jesus Christ, I'm stupid."

"Stupid is getting a little carried away," Liz said.

"Maybe," Flynn said, "but that's why people have a partner. Abbott had Costello, Lennon had McCartney. One partner curbs the excesses of the other. And, working out here, I've been doing it all alone. I've gone off on a damn tangent and lost three days."

"Naylor doesn't sound like a tangent," Liz said.

"But it took me two days to get his name," Flynn said. "The damned technology gave me two attractive suspects right off the bat and so I didn't even bother to canvass the neighbors. That's a rookie mistake."

"What about Mary Ann?" Liz asked.

"Again, a little personal drama, caught on camera, and so, magnified. Could she have done it? Yes, but I see no motive. And, why kill him at the party?" Flynn poked at the pizza. "I think I'm personally responsible for your pizza getting cold."

"I've had plenty, but I'll take some more of that wine," Liz said, holding out her glass. "You said there wasn't a lot of physical evidence. What does that mean?"

"It means that for as much blood as Terhune lost, we didn't get lucky on footprints or a murder weapon," Flynn said, pouring out the last of the bottle. "Either one of those could have cracked the case wide open. There's nothing like a size eleven Adidas with a distinctive tread-wear pattern to nail down the identity of an assailant. But whoever did this got a lot of blood on them, no question. And, they either hid the murder weapon really well, or else they took it with them. If they hid it, and possibly some blood-stained clothes, then they'd need to come back to collect and dispose of it."

"Oh, my God," Liz said, putting her hand over her mouth.

"What?"

"When we were at the construction site yesterday, I told you Mary Ann had been up to the sanitarium to see me," Liz said.

"I remember," Flynn said. "She told you her side of the Kevin Rundle murder."

"A few minutes after she left the trailer, I saw something out the back window of the trailer. It didn't register at the time."

"What was it?"

"Mary Ann Mandeville," Liz said. "Carrying a black, plastic – and apparently heavy – trash bag."

"Could she have been carrying trash?" Flynn asked.

Liz considered the possibility. "She did say she was there to volunteer and was looking for some way to help."

"Then, unless something else comes up, we're going to assume that sometimes a trash bag is only a trash bag."

Flynn's cell phone rang. He opened it and said, "Flynn." There were several "uh-huh's", and then he hung up.

"Who was that?" Liz asked.

"Vince Galanti, chief of detectives of the Framingham Police Department," Flynn said. "He found my Brazilians, and he's holding them. He wants to know if I can have a chat with them this evening."

"I guess this is where we say 'goodnight'," Liz said, rising from her chair.

"The perils of inviting a cop to dinner. I'm sorry." Flynn, too, pushed back his chair and stood. There was an awkward moment of parting and Liz busied herself with picking up the detritus from the table.

Flynn came into the kitchen, gave Liz's hands a squeeze, and he smiled.

When David called at 10 p.m., Liz made no mention of the dinner.

* * * * *

Flynn gathered up the crime scene and coroner's photos, and made the drive to Framingham. Galanti, along with a second man, met him at the reception desk.

"This is Paul Torres," Galanti said, indicating the other detective. "He's the one who spotted your perps. It's also likely that they're going to plead a lack of linguistic skills to carry on a conversation, even though Paul says their English is quite passable. Paul can translate as needed."

"What kind of priors do they have?" Flynn asked.

"None," Galanti said. "I asked Paul to keep an eye on MetroWest Construction in case they turned up there. They were on their way into the building at six o'clock."

"Detective, you need to know these guys are illegals," Torres said. "They paid a lot to get here. They're scared of being put on a plane in addition to everything else."

"Do you think they'll cooperate?" Flynn asked.

"They don't really understand due process. They're thinking 'immigration police'. That works to our advantage."

"Let's go see them," Galanti said.

Flynn, Torres, and Galanti walked to an interview room. "Detective Flynn, meet Marco Menezes and Jorge Medeiros," Torres said.

The two men stared at Flynn.

"I have some questions for you about your whereabouts Sunday night," Flynn said.

One of the men said something in Portuguese. Torres fired back something else and a brief exchange took place.

"They claim limited English proficiency, Detective Flynn," Torres said. "I have told them that I will provide translation for each side, if necessary. They ask that you speak slowly."

Flynn nodded. "Were the two of you at a party in Hardington Sunday evening?"

One of the men said, in English, "We don't remember."

Flynn pulled the printed-out video frame from the party and placed it in from of them. "Does this refresh your memory?"

The two men looked at the photos and one another. One whispered in the other's ear.

"We were at the party. It was open to all."

Flynn took out a photo of Terhune. "And you spoke with this man?"

"Maybe," one of the man said.

Flynn sighed and took out a photo of the frame with the larger of the two men jabbing his finger into Terhune's chest, a frightened look on Terhune's face.

"Does this refresh your memory?"

More exchanged looks and whispering. "Who took pictures?" one of them asked.

Torres jumped in with a stream of Portuguese that Flynn assumed amounted to, "cut the crap and answer his question."

"Who told you to talk to this man, and how did you know who he was?" Flynn asked.

Menezes and Medeiros looked at one another and then at Torres. "We not hurt him. He fine when we leave."

"Who told you to talk to this man, and how did you know who he was?" Flynn repeated.

"We paint his house," one of the men said.

"What do you mean, you 'paint his house'?" Flynn asked, incredulously.

"He hire us to paint his house," the man said and shrugged. "He pay with bad check. We tell him we want cash."

Fifteen tortured minutes later, Flynn had extracted the full story. Menezes and Medeiros had worked for MetroWest until they were laid off in May when MetroWest lost the sewer contract. Fred Terhune had periodically spot-checked their work and had come to know the pair, who let it be known that they painted houses on the side. Three weeks earlier, Terhune had called them and asked for a quote on painting his Hardington home. They had worked two weeks on the project – the two fingers Menezes had held up in front of Terhune. On Thursday, Terhune had given them a check – for $4,000 and made out to cash – which they took to a check-cashing store. On Saturday, they had been told that the check had bounced, and that they owed a $150 service fee.

Menezes and Medeiros had gone to Terhune's house and waited for him on Saturday and Sunday – Terhune was shuttling between the sanitarium and the construction site both days. Sunday evening, a neighbor suggested that Terhune was likely to be at the party at the sanitarium. Menezes and Medeiros had gone with the intention of both pressing their demand for cash and to throw in a measure of public humiliation at cheating honest working men out of their wages.

Now the conversation snippets overheard by Karen McCarthy and related in her living room Tuesday morning made sense. "*...Fred hadn't done something, and he – Fred – was 'going to pay'. At the end, one said, 'two weeks'. That's when Fred said something like, 'you have to give me time'...*"

"I apologize to both of you," Flynn said to Galanti and Torres as they left the interrogation room. "This is one colossal screw-up on my part. In fact, this entire investigation is turning into one colossal screw up."

Galanti stopped and looked at Flynn. "I checked you out after that first conversation," he said. "You know what? Everything you said about yourself was true, except that you were being modest. You are considered by your peers as have been one of Boston PD's best. I remember some of those cases you cracked. That company president that whacked his girl friend? That was brilliant detective work. We talked about that one for a week out here, no kidding."

"You want to know what I think, Detective Flynn?" Galanti added. "I think it happens to everyone once in a while. You chase the wrong mope for a couple of days. Forget about it. Now go catch the real murderer, and let me know if I can help."

9. Thursday

Diane Terwilliger was punctual and appreciative of the muffins Liz had baked. They sat at a kitchen table that afforded a view of the heart of Liz's garden. A pot of tea steeped, jars of jams were laid out.

"I keep forgetting how nice a place you and David have out here," Terwilliger said. "But, if you're going to jail, I guess it's going to grow up in weeds. Too bad. So, tell me what you've done." She broke apart a muffin and spooned on some jam.

Liz placed the DVD in its jewel case on the table. Terwilliger looked at it but made no move to pick it up.

"I'm volunteering on the *Ultimate House Makeover* program," Liz said.

"From what I hear, you're practically running it," replied Terwilliger, pouring some tea.

"I'm the 'volunteer coordinator'. I'm picking up where Fred left off. I call people and tell them where to be and when to be there."

"Very noble."

"On Tuesday," Liz said, "I was asked by someone on the production staff to take pictures of eighteen volunteers. They gave me their information sheets. All women, all essentially college-age. I sent one of my runners to get the photos, I turned the photos over to the guy who edits the video."

"No laws broken so far," Terwilliger said. She took a bite of a muffin and nodded appreciatively.

"Yesterday morning, I went back to the production trailer and caught a glimpse on a big video screen of one of the women whose photo I had caused to be taken. Except that it was – let me call it a seduction scene – being played out with..."

"Don't tell me who," Terwilliger said.

"Anyway, it had been captured on video, and the video editor and… this other person… were watching it. And, on the console of the video editing machine or whatever it's called, there was a disk like this one, and it said, well, 'Greatest Hits – Hardington' on it."

"And you saw this for just an instant?" Terwilliger asked.

"As soon as they saw it was me, the video guy did something that made the screen go blank. It wasn't even a second. Just long enough to register."

Terwilliger took a thoughtful bite of her muffin. She topped off her cup of tea and sipped it. "Do you have reason to believe that the woman was being coerced?"

"It looked voluntary to me," Liz said.

"Do you think she knew she was being filmed?"

"I couldn't tell."

"Well," Terwilliger said, "It all comes down to intent and informed consent. If the woman is over eighteen, she is above the age of consent. If she was aware that she was being filmed, then she gave informed consent. If she did *not* know there was a camera in the room, the person who did the filming invaded her privacy. The legal basis is that sex between two persons is always a private act and that each person is entitled to an expectation of privacy both during and after that act."

"Which brings me to the two men," Terwilliger said. "Person A records the scene and gives it to Person B to edit and put on a disc. That gets us into the realm of a conspiracy, and possibly possession of pornography with intent to distribute. Persons A and B would say that the disc was for their private enjoyment and, if it were just one person filming and editing, it would probably fly at trial. But two people with a professional editing suite make it plausible that they intended to make multiple copies. They are, in fact, employees of a company that is in business to produce television programs."

"Now, let's talk about you," Terwilliger said, and took a sip of her tea.

"The more I thought about what I saw, the angrier I got," Liz said. "So, yesterday afternoon, when no one was in the production trailer…"

"Stop," Terwilliger said.

"I thought I was telling you what happened," Liz said.

"Let's talk hypothetically," Terwilliger said. "Let's say – hypothetically – that you found yourself alone in that trailer and you saw that disc…"

"Which had hypothetically now become 'Greatest Hits Parts 1 and 2'," Liz said.

Terwilliger nodded. "And that you found you had one of those discs in your possession when you left the trailer…"

"Or a copy of one of the discs," Liz said.

"If such a thing had happened," Terwilliger said, "then you could be charged with illegal entry if the door were unlocked, or breaking and entering if it were locked."

"Hypothetically, the door was unlocked," Liz said. "And I had been told previously by the video editor that I shouldn't waste his time by knocking."

"Depending on the monetary value ascribed to what's on the copy of the disc, you could be charged with either petty theft or grand theft," Terwilliger said. "That you hypothetically took only a copy of something rather than the original is not at issue. It is the content of what's on the disc, not its physical value. Although somehow, I doubt that this is copyrighted material."

"More important, however, is that the disc was illegally obtained," Terwilliger said. "If you took that disc to the police, it would undermine any potential to prosecute those who made it. If you *described* what was on that disc, it would have the same effect. You have only two legally obtained facts: that you saw a glimpse of a sex video incorporating the image of a woman who may not have known she was being filmed, and you saw one disc – not two discs

– that said 'Hardington's Greatest Hits' that appeared to be the source of the video you saw."

"I shouldn't look at the hypothetical disc," Liz said.

"If you did, and you were subsequently asked about the content of that disc – including being questioned under oath -- you would find yourself on very precarious legal ground," Terwilliger said. "I would think long and hard about how it would affect a prosecution's case."

"I should lose the disc," Liz said. "Hypothetically."

Terwilliger looked at Liz directly, with an unwavering gaze. "There is on this table an unlabeled disc which may be blank, or it may contain a group of songs you legally downloaded from iTunes, or it may be your favorite episode of *Dancing with the Stars*. I don't want to know anything more about this disc. And, neither does anyone else."

"What do I do with my information?" Liz asked.

"You need to find a way to determine whether the young woman in question knew she was on camera," Terwilliger said. "That won't be easy because, if the answer is 'no', that young woman is going to be extremely upset, and she will likely take out that anger on you, and then she will take it out on whomever she was in bed with."

"But, if the answer is 'no'," Terwilliger continued, "then you will have every reason to bring it to the attention of the police, who would then have probable cause to obtain and execute a search warrant. And in the course of that search, they would likely find both volumes of the 'greatest hits', unless there is a third one by that time."

Liz nodded. *How do I get myself into these things?* she thought.

"I think I know what I need to do," Liz said.

"The muffins were wonderful," Terwilliger said. "Every time I talk to you I kick myself that I never pursued criminal law. Good luck."

* * * * *

Flynn was at his desk at 7:00, a thermos of Dunkin' Donuts coffee and a bag of muffins arranged in front of him. Wide awake two hours earlier, he had written:

- *Coroner's report*
- *Crime scenes team report*
- *Re-sweep trailers*
- *Mary Ann Mandeville 'black garbage bag'*
- *Canvass Terhune neighbors – confirm painters' story and check for other visitors*
- *Weekend police logs*
- *Canvass Naylor neighbors*
- *Other 'coincidences' in book?*
- *Prior Naylor attorneys – anything not privileged*
- *Naylor formal statement*

The duty roster showed that Eddie Frankel was working the day shift, and Flynn made certain that the desk sergeant knew that street patrols were going to be down a man for the day.

When Frankel made his appearance, Flynn filled him in on the Brazilian painters fiasco and handed him the assignments of talking to Terhune's and Naylor's neighbors. "We're practically back to square one," Flynn said. "Anything you hear that sounds helpful, call me."

By 8:00, Flynn had called and emailed the coroner's office, placed yet another blistering call to the state police crime scenes unit, and read 150 pages of the *Grand Larceny* guide. The recurring theme of the game – and of Naylor's advice – was to 'shadow' opponents.

'Stay close enough to see who they talk to and where they spend their 'unstructured' time. Being part of a crowd is an especially good way not to be noticed. But, if you are spotted, don't flee the scene. Instead, find another place to hide. Your opponent has too many things on his mind to pursue you.'

Flynn thought back to the video and Terhune's look of concern upon seeing something or someone across the tent. There was no question but that Naylor had been at the party, standing in the shadows, blending into the crowd.   Was it the innocent behavior of a social misfit or a bizarre case of someone believing that his life was a re-enactment of the games about which he wrote?

And, why had he lied about not being at the party?

As a suspect, George Naylor just kept looking better and better.

Flynn read through the full patrol reports for Sunday evening. There had been three minor accidents in the hospital parking lot Sunday evening.   Two of them had occurred before 10 p.m., but one of them was shortly after 11 p.m.

Timothy and Jill Keating, 118 Church Street, Hardington, 2003 PT Cruiser incurred passenger side damage as a result of being backed into by Gerald LeProvost, 32 North Walnut Street, Hardington. LeProvost cited for failure to yield way. Officer Winn investigated.

It was worth talking to them, Flynn decided.   There were apparently few people not associated with the production who remained after 10:30.

There had been a pair of DUI arrests on Hospital Road. Both were between 10 and 10:30.   That was too early to have been useful.

The last report was of a fifteen-year-old girl who had told her parents she was going to the party.

The first call logged by the dispatcher was at 11:12.   *Evelyn Spencer, 244 Dover Road, reports daughter Michelle Spencer, WF age 15, has not returned from UHM reception. Asks for patrol to check site. Officer Winn dispatched.*

11:18 p.m.   Officer Winn reports no person matching description at reception.

11:20 p.m. Called Spencer residence to advise daughter not present.

12:55 a.m. Evelyn Spencer, see above, reports daughter home.

Thirty-five years of police experience told Flynn there were many explanations for the daughter's whereabouts. She could have indeed been at the party earlier but may have gone elsewhere afterward. The parents had waited until after eleven to contact the police, indicating they had likely first called friends and neighbors. Dover Road was one of Hardington's 'nice' streets and, on such a street in a town like Hardington, notifying the police would have been a last step, one taken only after the logical avenues were exhausted. The daughter could have been at an unknown boyfriend's home, or she could have been in the nearby woods, drinking or smoking. Fifteen was a difficult age.

He made a note to contact the mother.

Flynn's desk phone rang. It was the state police Central Laboratory. Flynn resisted the urge to scream and, instead, asked how quickly he could obtain the report and review the evidence the team had collected.

"If you're willing to come to North Sudbury, you can have it right now," the officer at the other end of the phone said. "We would have had it finished yesterday, but part of the material got sidetracked and went to the other Sudbury lab."

Two state crime labs in one town. Flynn swore silently but said he would be there in thirty minutes.

Anywhere else in the country, a state highway funneling traffic from half a dozen reasonably populous suburban towns onto the loop highway around a major city and into the metropolis beyond would have long since been widened to four or even six lanes. But in New England, and especially in Massachusetts, such roads remained two lanes, regardless of traffic congestion. Flynn traversed this road twice a day, but always well before or after the morning and evening rush hours. Now, he joined the slow, snaking caravan of inbound commuters.

At the turnoff for Post Road, he noted the wayside garden that had once been tended by Sally Kahn. She had been murdered two months earlier, the first such homicide in Hardington in more than a dozen years. The wayside garden now flourished in late summer; someone else was caring for it with the same dedication that Sally

Kahn had shown. The investigation of that death had first brought him into contact with Liz Phillips.

What would have happened if you hadn't gotten that call from the Framingham police last night?

Nothing, of course.

Nothing, hell. She invited you to her home for dinner. She smelled wonderful. She looked wonderful.

Admit it: you wanted to put your arms around her and kiss her.

And she would have slapped me silly.

The hell she would have. She is a lonely woman with a husband who sometimes comes home on weekends, and she is looking for that missing love...

A horn sounded behind him, shaking him out of his contemplation. He made the turn onto the Post Road, bypassing six miles of congestion.

No. Don't go there. You have been married for thirty-five years and you don't need this.

It's not a marriage, it's an arrangement.

Another horn implored him to move through the stop sign at Boggestow Street. From there on, he focused on driving.

At the state police Central Laboratory in Sudbury, Flynn found the Crime Scenes Services Section. Any resemblance between this operation and the identically named ones that multiplied like rabbits on television networks was coincidental.

Officer Robert Alsop greeted him perfunctorily and showed him the evidence box.

Flynn looked at the cubic-foot-size box, which was half-filled with items in plastic bags.

"Where's the rest of it?" Flynn asked.

"I'm not sure what you mean," Alsop said. "This is it."

"Jesus Christ," Flynn said. "Tell me there's a report."

"Right here," Alsop said, extracting a document from the side of the box.

"Two pages," muttered Flynn. "Give me ten minutes," he said to Alsop.

The two-page summary was, at best, superficial. The chest into which Terhune's body had been placed bore hundreds of fingerprints, therefore no effort had been made to identify any of them. There was no DNA under Terhune's fingernails, no foreign blood or hairs on his shirt. A dozen cigarette butts had been meticulously collected, bagged, numbered and tied to a crime scene diagram; but there was no analysis. Everything in a twenty-foot circle around the chest had been vacuumed and bagged, but no one had performed anything beyond a cursory examination, such as 'three hairs – probably human.'

If I am to make this case, it will be without the physical evidence, Flynn thought.

Alsop returned.

"This doesn't seem to cover the blood trail your guys went out to investigate early Wednesday morning," Flynn said.

Alsop went to a computer workstation and entered a query.

"That's still in the lab," he said.

"Tell them not to waste their time," Flynn said. He started to collect the box of evidence.

"You can't take that," Alsop said. "It's property of the Massachusetts State Police and is part of an ongoing criminal investigation."

Flynn suppressed the urge to ignore the command. He put down the box. He walked back to his car and drove to Dedham and the Norfolk County coroner's office.

Minal Sajahada, the medical examiner who had conducted the autopsy of Fred Terhune, was in a cubicle the size of a phone booth, typing at a computer.

"Do you do autopsies in here, too?" Flynn asked, hoping it would be taken as a joke.

Sajahada looked up over her glasses. "I store the interesting body parts in a small refrigerator under my desk. Welcome to my very little world, Detective Flynn."

"I've had a rotten morning, Doctor Sajahada," Flynn said. "Please make it a better one."

"You're not in Boston any more, Detective Flynn. We are understaffed and under-funded. I have had eight autopsies so far this week, three of them requiring detailed analysis. But yours is done. I finished the report last night." Sajahada reached into a briefcase and pulled out a dossier of at least thirty pages.

"Do you want the oral summary, or are you more of a reading man?" she asked.

"Both," Flynn said, thumbing through the report. "You should have a talk with your buddies at the state police CSI unit about attention to detail."

"I don't get to choose which investigations I go out on, Detective Flynn. Now, let us talk about Mr. Terhune. He died between 12:30 a.m. and 1:00 a.m. I would lean closer to the later time based on body temperature. He died of one massive blow to the skull, almost certainly administered by a right handed person. The object that hit him was almost certainly metallic, because it left no glass, plastic, wood, or other identifying residue. The part that hit him was round and about six inches in diameter, less than an inch in height and beveled slightly inward. There is nothing in my database to indicate that something of this shape has been used in another killing, therefore I conclude it was likely a handy object rather than something the perpetrator brought with him or her for the purpose."

"I described the shape to someone and they likened it to lamp base," Flynn said.

Sajahada considered it for a moment. "That would be one possible match."

"Death was due to loss of blood," she continued. "The blow crushed the skull and severed the middle cerebral artery. The victim bled both internally and externally. Death took about ten minutes."

"If the perp had shown remorse and called for assistance, could Terhune have lived?" Flynn asked.

Sajahada shook her head. "It is very unlikely. In addition to the blood loss, the skull fracture introduced bone fragments into several areas of the brain. This was blunt-force trauma. Even if the bleeding could have been contained – and repairing cerebral arteries are highly specialized procedures – the victim would likely have died."

"Do you see evidence of premeditation?" Flynn asked.

"The choice of weapon argues against it, but the decision to let the victim bleed to death was a fairly callous one. Someone watched him die. Even if you don't have premeditation, you have depraved indifference."

"You sound like a prosecutor," Flynn said and smiled. "Tell me, counselor, was it a man or woman?"

"Terhune was sixty-seven inches high and weighed one-fifty-eight," Sajahada said. "I'm five-four and I could have inflicted that blow. Anyone in reasonable shape, man or woman, could have dragged him to the tent and put him in the box."

"What did you find that can help identify the killer?" Flynn asked.

"You're looking for someone with longer than average fingernails," she said, turning pages of the report to one with a photograph. "This is the area under Terhune's arms. The person who dragged him got a good grip and left fingernail impressions in the skin through his shirt. There's nothing distinctive, though the total width of the four fingers indicates someone with small hands. But they had fingernails long enough to be noticeable."

"How about nail polish on the shirt?" Flynn asked.

"I checked. There was none, which is inconclusive."

Flynn tried to visualize George Naylor's hands and fingernails. He had not focused on the hands. Naylor did stand a few inches short of six feet, but that proved nothing.

"This is very helpful," Flynn said.

"I wish it were more so," Sajahada said. "I've told you how he died, but I fear I haven't told you who did it."

"You've answered your part of the question," Flynn said. "Now, I have to go answer mine."

* * * * *

Liz arrived at the sanitarium by eight o'clock and found more than two dozen urgent requests for painters, persons to lay and sand floors, masons, and trim work specialists. It was apparent that, with less than two days remaining to complete the home, the construction foremen had worked through the night, creating a 'punch list' of open projects to get every part of the house exactly right.

She also found 220 color photos of Whit Dakota with various Hardington residents, ready for a personalized autograph. A Sharpie pen was atop the photos. These, she set aside to deal with later.

She worked steadily through the morning, matching volunteers to assignments. At the same time, she drew up her own list of completion items:

- *Find and talk to Linda Harper*
- *Find out if there is a camera in Whit Dakota's trailer*
- *See if anyone else has a copy of the 'greatest hits' video*
- *Tell John about videos*

In drawing up the list, she realized she had placed the selection and purchase of New-England-hardy plants entirely in Eva Morin's hands. The catalyst that had first brought her to this trailer on Monday morning was now someone else's worry, and she was entirely focused on things that she could not have envisioned three days earlier.

Fate.

Liz ran her finger down the list, pausing at the last item. *Tell John about the videos.* It had taken a so-far senseless murder to bring her back into contact with John Flynn. But in contact she was, and last night had proven something to her.

She was attracted to John Flynn.

It wasn't about looks, though he was ruggedly handsome. With few exceptions, the men she knew in their mid-fifties seemed to fall into two groups. The first were those who had given up the battle to keep any semblance of a waistline or of other physical conditioning. The second – and her husband, David fell into this group – were intent upon postponing middle age indefinitely. They used gyms, tanning salons, and even liposuction to hold the aging process at bay. David had treated his receding hairline as an affront to his masculinity and had undergone months of 'hair restoration surgery' to achieve a desired look.

But John Flynn appeared to have simply stopped aging ten years earlier. Some graying at the temples and a network of lines at the corner of his eyes were the lone signs that this was a man within a few years of sixty. There was no protruding belly, no incipient jowls. And, neither was there a vanity about his appearance. John Flynn showed no sense of self-consciousness about clothing, cars, or personal adornment. As far as she could tell, he had worn the same sports jacket every day of the week.

What was the attraction?

It had something to do with the way he listened. When Liz spoke, he paid full attention. As they had walked the garden, there had never been a moment when she thought his mind was anywhere but on understanding her design for the garden and choice of plants. He had posed intelligent questions that showed he had been listening and he drew connections to things she had said earlier.

But this was his job. He was a detective. He was good at his job precisely because he knew how to listen and to draw connections. On the other hand, Liz knew many people – men and women – whose livelihoods depended upon their ability to listen and interpret, and who turned off those skills the moment they left their place of business. John Flynn was still listening long after the work day was over.

It also had something to do with his sadness. There was something in his past – or his present – that had left him with an ineffable sense of loss. It was not melancholy or despondency, and it was not overt. But it was there, in his eyes.

Two months earlier, she had asked him about his marriage, and he had replied that it was 'complicated.' He would say nothing more. He apologized, he was even embarrassed by his unwillingness to respond. Yes, some of the sadness was his marriage, but she sensed there was something more. She wanted so much to ask. She wanted so much to know.

Which brought her back to her phone calls with David of last night and this morning. Last night, he had been ebullient. He was in his element now, wheeling and dealing. Prospective buyers were being played off against one another. Hints were being dropped among competitors that other interested parties were circling, perhaps thinking of outsized offers. It was all being done by the books, but it was all part of a hunt as old as Cro-Magnon man and the mastodon.

"Oh, and the process might take an extra thirty days," he had said.

He had left out this detail until the end of last night's call. Nothing definite, of course. Just some court-mandated folderol. But the end of September might be the end of October.

It was to have been over in June. He had promised before he boarded that first flight to Pittsburgh in mid-January.

And the worst part was that he had not been the least bit apologetic last night. To the contrary, there was a note of detachment in his voice. It infuriated her.

And so, when he called this morning, she had exploded. No, not exploded. She had followed a carefully thought-through script intended to provoke an honest discussion. She listened to his litany of things he had to do today, waiting for the words of contrition; words like, "I wish it were otherwise." Words like, "I miss you so much." Instead, she heard a calendar of upcoming events in the life of David Phillips, corporate savior.

She interrupted him. "David, why don't you ever choose assignments that would let you work from home?" she had asked.

"Because I haven't been offered any interesting ones in or around Boston," he had replied.

"Have you been offered any un-interesting ones locally?" she had parried.

"Anyone can manage a plain-vanilla turnaround," David had countered, still unaware of where the conversation was headed. Liz thought he sounded smug.

"So being away at least five days a week for eight or nine months doesn't bother you because it's all about the challenge." There. She had said it.

"Liz, what's this about?" David had finally figured out that this was not going to be his usual good-morning-and-have-a-nice-day call.

"It's about me waking up every morning to an empty house and you dropping a bombshell on me last night that this could drag out until November."

"I never said 'November'. And nothing holds you captive in that house. You could be in Paris this morning or at that spa in California you loved. Liz, if you told me this morning that you're catching a flight for Buenos Aires because you always wanted to go there, I'd cheer for you. We can afford it. How many people can say that?"

"This isn't about traipsing around the world," Liz had shot back. "This is about it being August and you and I have spent about thirty days together this year. Doesn't that bother you?"

"Liz…" he had started.

"And your next assignment?" Liz had asked. "Have you already got it picked out? Is it off to St. Louis this time? Or maybe North Carolina?"

He didn't answer. Instead, he snapped back, "Liz, I don't know where this is coming from, but I haven't got time for this. I've got back-to-back meetings starting in fifteen minutes. I just wanted to check to make certain you're OK."

"Well, I'm OK. The house is OK. The garden is OK. It's our marriage that isn't OK because you're never here."

"Liz, I'll call you tonight when you calm down."

That is where the call had ended. She could have sought some common ground. She could have agreed that they could pick up the conversation that evening. She could have defused the tension with a joke. Instead, she said... nothing.

And in saying nothing, she made no mention of the evening's dinner with John or of Diane Terwilliger's pending visit or its subject matter, or why she was baking muffins at six o'clock in the morning. Mary Ann Mandeville and the Brazilian men disappeared from the radar screen.

Nor had he offered to stay on the phone, or to cut short his work-week. Her translation: he wasn't especially interested. When the cavemen hunters plotted strategy to bring down the wooly mammoth, the schedule of the women of the clan was of no consequence.

Playing back the call in her mind, the most galling part of the exchange was his saying he was just checking to 'make certain you're OK'. It was the same kind of call they placed to the pet sitter who minded Abigail when they were on vacation. *We just wanted to check to make certain she's OK...'*

Liz was startled out of her funk by a knock on the door. Janey. "I'm sorry I'm late..."

"I've been busy myself this morning, Janey. I'm not sure I would have had very much for you to do until now." Liz smiled. "But I'm glad you're here."

There was something on Janey's face. A slightly different look. Liz could not read it; she did not know this girl well enough. But there was something. When Sarabeth had shown such a 'different look', Liz had always been able to instinctively divine the cause and quickly help or allow her daughter to sort out the problem. With Janey, she could only wait.

But she also needed Janey. "Have you been to the site this morning?" Liz asked.

Janey shook her head.

"Would you go down and look for someone for me?"

Janey quickly nodded. "I've got my bike. I'll go." *She is looking for something to take her mind off of whatever is bothering her*, Liz thought.

"I need to find Linda Harper, one of the girls whose photo you took on Tuesday. Do you remember her?"

Janey nodded again. "I still have her photo in my camera," she said.

"I need to see her here," Liz said. "It isn't urgent, but it has to be today."

Liz handed her the message slips from the construction foremen with her comments on who would be reporting for duty and asked her to give them to the production assistants. A few minutes later, Janey was gone.

And now for Whit Dakota's trailer, Liz thought.

The massive motor home was locked, as she expected. But the door to Don Elwell's trailer was open. Liz knocked. Sam Hirsch, Elwell's production assistant, appeared in the doorway.

"I need to see Don for just a moment," Liz said.

"He's talking to the network," Hirsch said.

"I need to get into Whit's trailer. I've been volunteered to forge his autograph on the 'thank you' photos. I need some writing samples."

Hirsch closed his eyes and mumbled something under his breath. His attention was clearly focused on the conference call going on just inside the door. "Can't it wait?"

"Not if you want those photos tomorrow," Liz said.

Hirsch clenched his jaw, disappeared for a moment and came back with a key. "Please bring it right back."

"I promise," Liz said.

Liz quickly went to Whit's motor home and let herself inside. She quickly found enough innocuous handwritten notes to back up her reason for being in the trailer. She then went back in the trailer to the bedroom and opened the door.

This is what 'money is no object' means, Liz thought as she went into the bedroom. It was a true king-sized bed and not some fold-away substitute. The mattress was firm, the sheets expensive. The room built-ins were solid wood, not veneers, and the workmanship was excellent. The bathroom, while small, was superbly appointed.

It took only a minute to find the cameras. There were three. All were discreetly hidden; two were blended into the woodwork of the built-in armoires that flanked the bed, and one had been placed overhead. Each provided a different angle, but there was no question but that all had the single purpose of capturing what was going on in the bed.

What kind of man is so vain that he needs to record his sexual conquests? Liz thought.

Opening one of the armoires to inspect a camera, she saw that there was no recording device attached. The camera apparently provided a wireless feed somewhere else. Perhaps, she thought, to the production trailer, which was less than fifty feet away.

Liz had found what she came to see. She closed the bedroom door and retreated back though the galley and into the lounge area where she had met with Whit and Chip Gilman when they wanted her to contact Tom Snipes on their behalf.

There, on the shelf, were the awards Whit Dakota had so proudly pointed out on their first meeting. *"Two Emmys and three People's Choice,"* he had said. Now, Liz saw the awards for what they were: slick tools of seduction in pursuit of something much darker. *"Come on over this evening and I'll show you my Emmy. And when we have sex, I'll have three cameras rolling."*

The thought made her ill.

She left the trailer, re-locked the door, and returned the key to Sam Hirsch. Total time elapsed, six minutes.

* * * * *

Jill Keating squeezed icing onto cookies as she spoke to Flynn.

Flynn, in turn, could not help but notice that this was no ordinary mom-baking-cookies kind of event, and said so.

"I had no idea there would be this kind of demand," Keating said. "I always loved to bake, and I found a recipe for a cookie that both tasted good and didn't break easily. I started making different colored icing borders and brought them to a birthday party one of my sons was attending. The mother went 'wow, where did you buy that?' and a business was born."

"I could do a hundred dozen a week if I had time," she said. "Birthdays, Halloween, football parties, you name it. Each one with a custom design, all with the pretty borders."

"Do I want to know how much?" Flynn asked.

"Twenty dollars a dozen," Keating said and shrugged. "A little less if it's for ten dozen or more."

Flynn whistled. *Colorful cookies. Nearly two bucks each.*

"I need to ask you about Sunday night," Flynn said.

"Jerry backed into us, pure and simple," Keating said. "I thought it was dumb to call the police, but Tim said we'd need a report for the insurance claim. Jerry and Tim are both over at the Cardozo house painting this morning, if you'd rather talk to them."

Flynn shook his head. "I'd rather hear your take on it. The accident took place after eleven. Were you in the tent up until the time you left?"

"Pretty much," Keating said. And then stopped as she recognized the underlying question. "Oh, God, is this about that selectman's murder?"

"Yes, it is," Flynn said. "You were apparently one of the last people to leave the party,"

"Well, it had pretty well broken up," Keating said. "They had closed the bar, but Tim – my husband – found a bottle of wine, and we drank it with a group of friends while we talked."

"Tell me how the party wound down," Flynn said. "I saw a video of Whit Dakota giving his speech at nine o'clock. That took about fifteen minutes. It looked like the crowd just slowly drifted away after that. There was no video after ten o'clock."

Keating checked a batch of cookies coming out of the oven. "I guess there were a small group that thought as long as they didn't turn out the lights, it was a great summer night to enjoy being out of doors. I guess ten of us altogether. Well, I mean ten in our group."

"There was another group?" Flynn asked.

"Whit Dakota stayed a little while. He had half a dozen girls hanging onto him." Keating readied the next batch of cookies to go into the oven. "I guess he was gone by about ten-thirty. Then all these guys in identical tee shirts started banging things around, you know, cleaning up, moving things. Around eleven, the wine ran out and we figure our welcome had run out, too."

Flynn took three photos out of his jacket pocket. The first was of Fred Terhune.

"Do you remember seeing this man leave the party?"

"That's Fred Terhune, isn't it?" Keating said. "The man who was killed. His picture was in yesterday's *Chronicle*."

Flynn nodded.

She took the photo and studied it. "He was in the tent for a while. He probably left about the same time as Whit Dakota, though they didn't leave together. No, he left just before. I remember Whit still had two or three girls there."

"Did you know any of the girls?"

Keating shook her head. "No, they were all older – late teens, twenty. College girls. My oldest is nine."

Flynn pulled out the photo of Mary Ann Mandeville. "Do you remember this woman leaving the party?"

"Mary Ann?" Keating said. "She was part of our group. She sold us this house. When we left, she was still flirting heavily with Dan Keegan." She paused. "Well, maybe not 'flirting'. Mary Ann's married. But she and Dan were certainly enjoying themselves. Dan's our stock broker."

He pulled out the final photo. George Naylor. "Does he look familiar?"

Keating again took the photo and studied it. "I *remember* him. He just stayed right outside of the tent and watched. When it got down to the last few dozen of us, he went over to one of the trailers and stared. Creepy."

"When did you last see him?"

"Around ten-thirty," Keating said. "I think I stopped paying attention to him after that."

"So, when you left the tent a little after eleven, who was still there?" Flynn asked.

"Mary Ann, Dan, and Pete and Loretta Mott, and Jerry LeProvost," she said. "And Jerry apparently left right after we did because he backed into my door while we were still buckling up."

Flynn got addresses and phone numbers for Dan Keegan and the Motts. Jill Keating gave him two cookies to tide him through lunch.

There was no answer at the Motts, but Dan Keegan, who ran the Hardington office of Edward D. Jones, a brokerage firm, was at his desk.

"I don't run the office," Keegan laughed when Flynn asked if he ran the office. "I *am* the office. All our offices are one-man shows. No one to blame for failure, no question about success. Retirement planning, portfolio management, insurance. One man to see, one place to visit."

Flynn explained that he was attempting to determine who was still at the reception at its conclusion.

"I guess it was the Motts, Mary Ann Mandeville and myself," Keegan said.

"They were still there when you left?"

"Yes," Keegan said.

Flynn heard a quaver in Keegan's voice in that single word. What he has said was technically true, but not entirely true. Flynn let it pass.

Flynn showed him the photo of George Naylor. "Did you see him?"

Keegan squinted at the photo. "I didn't pay that good of attention. I don't remember seeing the guy."

"Whit Dakota apparently still had a group of women around him as late as half past ten. Did you know any of them?"

Keegan nodded and grinned. "Them, I paid attention to. I knew two of the finalists, there were two or maybe three others I didn't recognize. That's what Pete Mott and I were calling them, 'the finalists'. Ole' Whit was culling the herd, so to speak. Lisa Pittman was one. That's John and Marge Pittman's daughter. She's going to be a sophomore at Colby College next month. The other was Marie Casuscelli. She just finished her freshman year down at Fordham. Dom and Elena Casuscelli are clients of mine. I put together their college loan package, in case you have children of your own, Detective."

Flynn smiled. "You're too late, Mr. Keegan. But I thank you for your interest."

Flynn got addresses and telephone numbers for the Pittmans and Casuscellis.

Back in his car, Flynn wrote in his notebook, *Mary Ann Mandeville lied about leaving the party at 10. She did not leave until after 11. George Naylor was still at the party long after he had any good reason to be there. He, too, is lying.*

As he wrote, he thought to himself. *Why am I pursuing Whit Dakota's adoring fans? Because one of them may have gone back to Whit's trailer with him. And they just may have seen or heard something.*

10.

Liz and Roland Evans-Jones sat in the trailer, forging Whit Dakota's signature and adding cheery notes like, 'Thanks Earl and Nancy for all your help!' and 'Fun working with you, Jeff!'

"I don't think I've written so many exclamation points since junior high school," Roland said as he finished another photograph. "I just hope no one compares the autographs between your pile and mine."

"Just think of it as your modest contribution to making a better life for a Hardington family," Liz said, checking names against the contact sheets.

"I've been waiting for you to bring me up to speed on the investigation," Roland said. "In fact, it's the only reason I'm here. It's the only reason anyone would be in this miserable, hot, stuffy trailer."

Liz kept signing photos. "Roland, all I can tell you is that there are suspects."

"Do I know any of them?" Roland asked.

"Roland, the police aren't going to confide in me. That's not the way it works."

"You are the world's worst liar, Liz Phillips."

Liz sighed and put down her pen. "All right, there's a guy. He's here in town and he had a legal kind of run-in with Fred. He's a nut case who thought Fred should have pursued a big lawsuit against a ski resort. When Fred came back and said, 'you should settle for a few thousand dollars,' the guy went ballistic. That was two years ago. Since then, the guy has been hounding Fred with negligence lawsuits, except that the guy's lawyers keep quitting."

"Who is he?" Roland asked.

"If I tell you that, John would never talk to me again," Liz said. "I don't know the guy and I doubt that you do, either. He writes 'how-to' guides for these gory video games. John theorizes that he may be in this fantasy world and is just acting out one of the games. Fred had the wrong guy for a client. End of story."

"When is he going to arrest him?" Roland asked.

"When John finds the evidence…"

Liz's answer was interrupted by a knock on the trailer door. Linda Harper, an attractive woman of about twenty, dressed in paint-spattered jeans and a DUKE tee shirt, stood in the doorway.

"Roland, could I have a couple of minutes?" Liz asked. "There are some soft drinks over at the refreshment tent."

Roland excused himself and left the trailer.

"Janey, your runner, said you were looking for me," Linda said.

"Well, I hope it's you that I'm looking for," Liz said. "If you're not the right person, this could be embarrassing."

Linda's interest was piqued. She sat down in the chair Roland had occupied.

From her purse, Liz extracted a multi-colored-stone bracelet. She had found it that morning in Sarabeth's room, an inexpensive piece of jewelry dating to her daughter's college years, left behind when she moved to Seattle.

"Whit thought this might be yours," Liz said, holding out the bracelet in her hand. "He found it in his… well, he found it this morning and asked me to return it."

Linda looked at the bracelet but did not take it from Liz. Her face reddened slightly. "I'm afraid it isn't mine."

"Oh," Liz said, and paused for several moments. "I must have misunderstood the name. I'm terribly sorry…"

"I'm sure you heard the name right," Linda said, her voice betraying some embarrassment of talking to a woman her mother's age. "I mean, if you were saying that Whit found it in his motor home and thought it may have belonged to Linda Harper, then I'm the right Linda Harper. But I don't own a bracelet like that. I guess it belongs to someone else."

Liz sensed a hint of disappointment in Linda's voice in the last sentence she spoke. A recognition that she had been neither the first nor the last woman to share Whit Dakota's bed for a few hours. It gave Liz the courage to ask the next question.

"Linda, have you ever seen one of these, *Girls Gone Wild* videos? You know, the ones where the girls are asked to…"

"I know what they are," Linda said, quickly. "They're kind of frat boy humor. Spring break stuff."

Liz plunged in. "If someone asked you to be in one, would you?"

"No," Linda said immediately, a look of scorn on her face. "I mean, I'm no prude, but that's kind of over the edge…"

"I understand," Liz said. "I was just wondering… how much things had changed since my daughter's college days. She's twenty-six. Married…"

Linda Harper was not going to be sidetracked. "Why did you ask that question?" Her voice had an intensity to it. Her teeth were gritted.

"Whit didn't have a specific reason… I'm sure he didn't have anything specific in mind. He just…"

"Because I would *never*…"

"Linda, I'm sorry I even mentioned anything…"

"And you can tell Whit Dakota to go screw himself." Linda got up from the chair and left the trailer without looking back.

Liz absorbed the exchange. It hung in the air with the heat. She had her answer, now she had to decide what to do with the information.

* * * * *

Flynn and Eddie Frankel sat at Flynn's desk in the Hardington police station. Frankel paged through his notes, reeling off highlights.

"Naylor's neighbors tell you they aren't the nosy kind, but you give them any kind of opportunity, and they're off and running," Frankel said. "They're all retired, and watching out the window seems to be their principal form of entertainment. Naylor hasn't had a visitor in his apartment in probably a year. He has no girlfriend. What he does is work at his computer, including a lot of playing 'shoot-em-up' video games with loads of sounds effects."

Frankel flipped a page. "Naylor goes out every day for at least a couple of hours. Sometimes he walks, most times he takes this old Toyota. Eats a lot of carry-out from the Chinese restaurant. Very seldom talks to his neighbors but, when he does, he says he's a big-shot author and tour guide writer. They don't believe a word of it. He never mentioned Fred Terhune to any of them. But when he busted up his leg two years ago, he made a really big deal out of it and said he was going to get some huge settlement out of the ski resort and he was going to be fixed for life."

"This one's important," Frankel said, turning a page in his notebook. "One neighbor who lives up against the parking lot remembers Naylor going out Sunday night a little after nine. The neighbor went to bed about eleven thirty and Naylor still wasn't back."

"I've got people from the party who place him at the sanitarium after eleven," Flynn said. "That ties, but it's circumstantial."

"Monday morning, people remember Naylor taking his trash out early, and he stayed indoors for the rest of the day," Frankel said.

"Don't tell me," Flynn said. "The dumpsters get picked up Monday."

"Ten o'clock," Frankel said. "Just like clockwork."

"So anything he threw away – like evidence – went to the incinerator in Millbury the same day," Flynn said.

"I am the bearer of that bad news," Frankel acknowledged. "On the other hand, we have Fred Terhune's neighbors, who have been watching over him since he was a kid in that house."

"While it's no surprise, the painters' story holds up," Frankel said, turning to a new page. "They were there for two weeks and did a real nice job. They finished up, went away for a few days, then were back last weekend, waiting around on the steps. They finally went door to door until one old lady told them Fred was up at the sanitarium and would be there Sunday evening. Drew them a map and everything."

"But here's the surprise," Frankel said. "Naylor's also been hanging around. I've got two people who described his car right down to the rusted door panels. Naylor would drive his car into the neighborhood about the time Terhune was expected home. If Terhune went back out, Naylor would follow him. That started a couple of days before Sunday."

"And no one felt the need to call the police and report this?" Flynn asked.

"The guy didn't do anything," Frankel said. "Never got out of his car, never tried the door to the house when Terhune wasn't there."

"Just shadowing him," Flynn said.

"Stalking him," Frankel said.

"No," Flynn said. "Shadowing him. Just like it said to do in his video game books."

There was no answer at either the Pittman or Casuscelli residence, the two names supplied by Dan Keegan, the broker who had watched as Whit Dakota chose his 'finalists'. Flynn drove out to the construction site, where over a hundred people appeared to be working on every aspect of the house.

From the outside, the Cardozo house now looked complete, though there was neither lawn nor shrubbery in place. Workmen were in the driveway, a dozen men with tamps and rakes forming the asphalt into place, a roller idled nearby.

Flynn spotted one of the production assistants in the distinctive *Ultimate House Makeover* tee shirts. "I'm looking for Lisa Pittman or Marie Casuscelli,"

The young man shrugged. "I have no idea who these people are. Just ask until you find someone who knows them," he suggested.

Ten minutes later, he tapped on the shoulder of Marie Casuscelli. Cascades of black wavy hair flowed from under her painter's cap. Flynn introduced himself and asked that they find a quiet place to talk.

"Sunday night, you were at the party up at the sanitarium, and you were part of a group talking with Whit Dakota around ten-thirty," Flynn said.

Casuscelli squinted for a moment. "Sounds right. I left about that time."

"Do you remember who was still there when you left?"

"Lisa Pittman," Casuscelli said. "Her I know. We were in the same class in school. There were two – no, three -- other girls there. Heather something. She just graduated in June. And two girls I didn't know. They looked like they were still in high school."

"At the risk of being blunt, Ms. Casuscelli, was Whit looking for a bedmate for the evening?"

"He certainly wasn't turning away any offers," she said. "The guy's cute, but he's thirty-something. That's a little old to be hanging around with the sweet young things in thongs."

"Do you think he invited someone back to his – what – trailer? Winnebago?"

"His 'Vectra' is what he kept calling it," Casuscelli said. "'It's like a house on wheels,' he said. 'Best sound system you ever heard.' He wanted to show us his Emmys. The more I listened to him, the less interested I was."

"So, do you think he took anyone back to his Vectra?" Flynn repeated.

"If he did, it wasn't me and it wasn't Lisa," Casuscelli said.

"You asked?"

"I asked."

"Is Heather here?"

"I haven't seen her today," Casuscelli said. "I know she was here yesterday."

"How about the other two girls?"

Casuscelli shook her head. "I haven't seen either of them all week."

There was one more witness who could answer these questions, and up until a few hours earlier, she had been a suspect. Or at least she wasn't a suspect assuming the only thing in that plastic garbage bag Liz had seen her with was trash. It was time to go back and see Mary Ann Mandeville.

* * * * *

Janey was at the trailer door again. Liz smiled and beckoned her in and invited her to sit down.

"Janey, I worry that you're letting the last of summer slip away, and all you'll remember is that you shuttled messages back and forth between this trailer and the Cardozo house," Liz said.

Janey flopped in the chair. "This is fun," she said. "And, I'm being useful. My mom says I need to be useful and think about other people instead of just myself."

"Well, you've certainly been useful to me," Liz said and smiled. "But you need to make time to see your friends."

Janey was quiet for a moment. "I saw my friends already."

"Is Michelle still grounded? Was she happy to see you?"

Janey said nothing but looked pensive and worried.

"Janey?"

"Can I tell you something, Mrs. Phillips?"

"Yes, you can." And Liz smiled again. *This is what was bothering her this morning.*

"Michelle told me a secret. She made me promise not to tell. But I'm worried about her. She still won't come out of her room even though her mom says it's OK. And she said some things that were really scary."

"What did she tell you, Janey?" Liz asked softly. "You know, it's OK to tell if you're worried about her."

Janey bit her bottom lip as she gathered her thoughts. Liz waited. "Michelle went to the party Sunday night," Janey said after more than minute. "She only lives half a mile from here so her parents let her go."

"I understand," Liz said. *Encourage her.*

"Michelle said she'd be home by ten. But then Whit Dakota asked her to join a group of people to tell him about the town and stuff. You know, for the show."

"And she stayed late," Liz said.

"Michelle was like, 'Whit Dakota. Cool!' And he seemed really interested in what Michelle had to say. And pretty soon it was just Michelle and one other girl, Heather Lauricella. She's a senior this year. And Whit Dakota said, 'Hey, they're getting ready to kick us out of the tent, let's go back to my Vectra and I'll show you my Emmys.' And they get to the trailer and Heather says, like, 'I gotta get home' and she practically runs off. And Whit Dakota says to Michelle, 'That's good, because you were the one I wanted to talk to anyway.'"

"Take your time, Janey," Liz said.

Janey looked at Liz with tears in her eyes. "I promised her I wouldn't tell, but isn't right."

"Sometimes, doing the best thing for your friends means telling someone else, if that person can help," Liz said, putting her hand on Janey's.

"So Michelle went into the trailer with Whit Dakota," Janey said. "And he's showing her all of these important television awards he's won. And he goes over to the refrigerator and says, 'I'm having some wine. Can I pour you a glass?' And Michelle is totally, like, not believing that this huge star is talking to her, and she's all alone with him, and he's just this totally cool guy. And they talk some more and then he says, 'Michelle, you are just the most beautiful girl I've ever seen, and I've just got to kiss you.'

And he kisses her. And Michelle is thinking, 'Oh, wow, I just got kissed by Whit Dakota.' And he says, 'That was fantastic. I've just got to do it again.' And this time, he really kisses her and keeps telling her that she's so beautiful. And he's telling her that he knows lots of people in Hollywood and they're always looking for 'fresh faces' and she ought to be an actress and he could help her get parts on television."

"I think I know what happened, Janey," Liz said softly.

"He took off her clothes." Janey was crying.

"It's all right, Janey."

"And Michelle kept saying to herself, 'I can't believe that he chose me. That he loves me.'"

"You don't need to finish, Janey. I know the rest."

Janey looked at Liz, sobbing. "And when it was over, Whit Dakota gets on that walkie-talkie thing they all carry and says, 'Chip, I think my guest needs a ride home. Can you pick her up?' And that's it. Two minutes later, that guy Chip knocks on the door and kind of leers at Michelle, and says 'Your chariot awaits'. And Whit Dakota just waves from the door because he's talking to someone on the phone. And on the way home, Chip looks over at Michelle and says, 'You are eighteen, aren't you?' And Michelle says, 'Sure.'"

"But Michelle is fifteen, right?" Liz asked.

Janey nodded. "So Chip lets Michelle out at the end of her driveway, and she walks in the door and her mom and dad started yelling at her for being out so late. And they send her to her room and say she can't come out until she's ready to apologize for 'breaking their trust'. That's what they always say to her. 'Don't let us down by breaking our trust.' And Michelle wants to say, 'It wasn't my fault' but she can't."

"So she wanted to know if Whit Dakota had asked about her or said anything, and I told her that he's at the Cardozo house all the time. She told me she wants to go see him to find out if he really loves her, but then she said she knows that he just wanted to…."

"You've said enough, Janey," Liz said, hugging the girl. "And you did the right thing. You're Michelle's best friend, and you're the person she trusted to share her secret. But now you've got to keep it a secret, at least for a little while."

"What are you going to do?" Janey asked.

"I'm going to try to help Michelle and put it right," Liz said. "Whit Dakota shouldn't have taken advantage of Michelle. He needs to know that he did something wrong. But whatever we do we have to be very careful. We don't want to hurt Michelle any more than she's already been hurt. That's what I've got to figure out. You need to give me some time to make it right for Michelle. Can you do that? Can you keep your secret?"

"From my parents?"

Liz hesitated. *Don't put me on this spot.* "If they ask you directly, you have to tell them. That's the way it is with parents. But don't tell them if you can avoid it. And, if you go back to see Michelle, it's really important that you don't tell her that we talked."

Liz offered Janey a ride home but Janey shook her head and said she had her bike. She needed time to think.

As soon as Janey was out of sight Liz took out her phone. *John, you'll be involved soon enough, but right now, I need professional help, not the police.*

She dialed a number. It was picked up on the second ring.

"Felicity, do you still have those adolescent psychology degrees? Well, dust them off. I know someone who needs every bit of help you can give them."

* * * * *

Twenty minutes later, Liz was at Felicity Snipes' home on Blueberry Lane, recounting the story Janey had told her.

Felicity kept coming back to the timing. "This happened Sunday night? Michelle has essentially been in her room alone for three and a half days? She just confided to Janey this morning?"

"Leaving aside the issue of statutory rape – and a girl of fifteen cannot give consent – we're almost certainly dealing with post traumatic stress syndrome," Felicity said. "Michelle was used and then cast aside in just about the most callous way imaginable. She went home and was told it was all her fault. And now, she's had more than three days to internalize this stress."

"Did telling Janey help?"

"She confided to a friend and that's good," Felicity said. "Sometimes a child has no one they can trust and then it really gets brutal.   But this is a girl who has gone through something no fifteen-year-old should ever have to.   And every hour nothing is done for her, the deeper the long-term effect."

Felicity tapped the color photo of Michelle with Whit Dakota's arm around her waist. "You're right, Michelle doesn't look fifteen. And girls grow up a lot faster than we did, and they know more than we did. Blame it in television, blame it on music, blame it on anything you want, but it's real and there's no getting away from it. Things like oral sex happen down all the way into the upper grades of elementary school.   And, don't get me started about 'friends with benefits'."

Felicity shook her head. "But this was rape, pure and simple, dressed up with some preliminary kissing and 'gee you're beautiful' talk. Whit Dakota is a sexual predator who had to have known damn good and well that he was taking a minor to bed. And after four days of playing it over and over again in her mind, Michelle Spencer knows she was raped, and she's almost certainly thinking it was her fault."

"Do you think you know what's in Michelle's mind?" Liz asked.

"I suspect she's thinking that she led Whit on, and what happened Sunday night took place only because of things she did. She's too young to grasp that Whit maneuvered her into the trailer and into bed." Felicity said. "What's in her mind? The worst case is she's thinking suicide. Worst case, she's going to go see Whit

Dakota and, when Whit just waves and says, 'hey, babe' without remembering her name, she's going to go back into her sanctuary – her room – and open a vein. Very nearly worst case is that Michelle is an emotional basket case with a need for intervention for a very long time. And, unfortunately, that's also probably the best case. You don't get over this in a week. Most girls don't get over it in ten years."

"What we don't need – now or ever -- is for people to start whispering and for that whispering to get back to Michelle," Felicity said. "Because that will traumatize her further, and post traumatic stress is cumulative. If we can, we clean it up in such a way that Michelle's name never gets used."

"Then you need a good stiff drink in your hand, because there's more," Liz said.

"Oh, dear God, what?"

"Whit has his bedroom wired for video. Three cameras. It's all on tape, or in a computer, or however you store those things."

"You've seen it?" Felicity asked, incredulously.

"I saw a glimpse of his Tuesday night cutie, apparently when they were editing."

"'They'?" Felicity asked.

"Whit and his video guy. I suspect the cameras all feed back to this big Winnebago outfitted as a video production facility."

"We could just tie the entire production crew by their pricks to the back of my pickup truck and drag them through town for a few hours," Felicity said. "It wouldn't help Michelle, but it would make me feel one hell of a lot better."

"I just found out about the cameras this morning," Liz said.

"I suspect his on-screen days are at an end," Felicity said. "But first, we need – I need – to talk to Michelle. And, before I can do that, there's a protocol I have to follow. My clinical work is with adolescents and I've done my share of crisis intervention. Everything you've told me rings true, but it's all third hand: Michelle told Janey, who told you. The Mass Psychology

Association has a hotline for just this sort of thing and, ultimately, it's their call. What I've got to make them understand is that we need to do something now, not in a day or two days."

Felicity glanced at her notes. "Her parents obviously don't know, and there are privacy aspects we have to consider. And, as much as I want to see Whit Dakota roasted over an open spit, we can't bring in the police until Michelle is stable and can deal with it. Ideally, we'd meet in some neutral place – not her home – but someplace where she was comfortable, and we'd have our first talk there. But I don't think there's time. This girl may be building up to an explosion."

"Dear God," Felicity added. "And I let my husband go out and play football with that bastard."

11.

"If you want to talk to me, you'll have to meet me at a house I'm inspecting," Mary Ann told Flynn over the phone. Flynn quickly obliged.

They were standing outside of a Garrison Colonial in Metacomet Park, a modest 1960s-era subdivision prized by developers for its one- and two-acre lots that could support houses three and four times the size of the ones they replaced. Joe Haskell, the druggy friend of Tim Kahn, lived a block away from where they were now standing.

The house was still occupied, though Mary Ann made no effort to go in the house.

"Would you pay $375,000 for this house, Detective Flynn?" Mary Ann asked.

"I couldn't say," Flynn said, noncommittally.

"Well, within a week, Mrs. Maguire is going to have three offers in her hands, all with a promise to close on whatever schedule suits her. They will all be from developers, they will all be for $375,000 or more. Mrs. Maguire's husband died four months ago – of natural causes, I assure you – and it took me that long to convince her that the house was too large, that it was time to move on with her life, and then to find her somewhere else to live. I've found her a one-story condominium in an over-55 community in Cavendish. Five miles away so she can still see her friends. No more lawn to mow, no more house maintenance."

"Then, why do you need to be here today?" Flynn asked.

"Details, Detective Flynn. I deal in details. The developers need to know where the septic tank outflow is and how the utilities come into the house. I'll have that mapped out for them as they come to look at the house. The less it costs them in manpower and equipment to remove the existing structure, the more they'll be willing to pay."

"I guess selling the house 'as is' for a family of more modest means isn't in the cards," Flynn said.

Mary Ann studied the house's drooping gutters. "Not in Hardington, Detective Flynn. It would cost a minimum of $100,000 to update this house – and that's just the kitchen and bathrooms – and you'd still have a forty-year-old house with tiny rooms. That's a $475,000 investment and, for the same money, you can buy a brand new house just over the border in New Hampshire. No, Mrs. Maguire's house is coming down."

"We need to talk about details," Flynn said. "You told me you left the party at ten. I have people who place you there after eleven. You also told me you learned of Fred Terhune's insurance policy from his law partner. Neither of those statements was true, though I think I know why you lied."

"And why is that, Detective Flynn?" Mary Ann turned her full attention to Flynn.

"We can't just leave it at my being fairly certain that I know the reason?"

"There is a time for being coy and there is a time for bluntness, Detective Flynn. This is one of those times for candor."

"You spent the night – or at least some portion of it – with Dan Keegan," Flynn said. "And I would bet that Dan Keegan sold the Terhunes that insurance policy, and told you about it Monday morning after the news got around about Terhune's death."

Mary Ann smiled. "Bravo, Detective Flynn. You are a man of considerable talent. But I don't think you came to see me today to impress me with your powers of deductive reasoning. How can I help?"

"Well, first there's a matter of a trash bag," Flynn said. "You were spotted at the sanitarium yesterday afternoon carrying one around. Would you mind telling me what was in it?"

Mary Ann Mandeville laughed. "Empty plastic water bottles, Detective Flynn. I was trying to do my good deed for the day and, if I can't paint a house, at least I can police the grounds. I hope you have something more important to ask me."

"Whit Dakota had a group of women around him after ten o'clock," Flynn said. "By ten thirty, there were just four or five. Lisa Pittman and Marie Casuscelli were two of them. There was girl named 'Heather' and either one or two others. I need to find those women."

"Those 'women' were girls," Mary Ann said. "I didn't know Marie's name, though I did recognize her, and you're right about Lisa. 'Heather' is Heather Lauricella. She lives on West Street. Her parents are Hank and Marilyn Lauricella. She, at least, is eighteen. The other girl was Michelle Spencer. She's fifteen, though she looks older. She lives on…"

"Dover Road," Flynn said. "Jesus Christ. Her mother is Evelyn Spencer, right?"

Mary Ann nodded, but not comprehending why Flynn was suddenly so agitated.

"Thank you, but I need to go," Flynn said, and walked quickly back to his car.

"Is that it?" Mary Ann said, following him back to his car. "Is that all you want?"

"That is exactly it, Mrs. Mandeville," Flynn said, starting his car. "You may have just done your best good deed of the entire week."

As he navigated out of Metacomet Park, he scanned his notes, copied from the Sunday night police log. They were scribbled, but clear:

11:15 Evelyn Spencer, 244 Dover Rd, called HPD to report daughter Michelle Spencer, WF 15, not back from reception. Winn dispatched, checked site 11:18. E. Spencer called 12:55 a.m. to report daughter home.

Flynn drove the four miles from Metacomet Park to the luxurious homes on Dover Road in under six minutes. The houses were all on multiple acres, each set back at the end of a winding drive. He slowed only to check the oversized mailboxes that were at the end of each driveway for addresses. He was almost to 244 when he was nearly sideswiped by a green Jaguar.

Liz's Jaguar, Flynn realized. He blew his horn and the Jaguar's brake lights came on.

The driver's side door opened and Liz hurriedly got out. The passenger door opened and out stepped another familiar face: Felicity Snipes. Flynn came to a stop.

The two of them got into his car.

"If you're headed to see Michelle Spencer, don't," Liz said.

"How did you know…"

"Because you're a smart guy and you've figured out that Whit Dakota took Michelle back to his trailer Sunday night," Liz said.

"But you can't go up there," Felicity said. "Certainly not today and maybe not for a few days. Please. Michelle's life may depend on it."

"Tell me what you know," Flynn said. He turned off his engine.

"At the party Sunday night, Whit Dakota picked out Michelle," Felicity said. "He lured her back to his motor home, he may have gotten her drunk, and he definitely had sex with her. Except that she's fifteen and, being a policeman, you know better than I do that fifteen year olds can't give consent. Dakota may or may not have known she was underage, but that's not the issue. After two hours, he called up his toady and said, 'take her home.' Then he calmly starts making calls. The toady…"

"Chip Gilman," Liz added.

"The toady drops her off at the end of the driveway and that's it, "Felicity said. "Michelle goes into her house and gets reamed by her parents for staying out late. She goes into her room and starts thinking about what happened. In clinical psychology, that's called post traumatic stress syndrome and rape trauma."

"She's basically been in that room since Sunday night, with the trauma deepening and festering because she's almost certainly convinced herself that she brought it on through her own actions. She finally confided in a friend this morning, the friend told Liz. Liz came to me because I happen to have a PhD in clinical psychology with a specialization in working with adolescents."

Liz began talking. "That's just part of it. What I also know is that Whit films these one-night stands. There are three cameras, almost certainly all feeding into the production trailer. I caught a glimpse of Whit's Tuesday night date on the big monitor when I opened the door of the video trailer. Whit and Joel – the video guy – killed the screen, but I saw just enough to see it was one of the volunteers. I also saw a DVD on the console of the editing system that said, 'Whit's Greatest Hits – Hardington'. There may be more than one volume."

Flynn listened and absorbed. "You understand I'm trying to catch a murderer, and Michelle may have the key – she probably *does* have the key. She may even have seen it."

"She didn't tell her friend that, and she told her everything else," Liz said.

"These guys are leaving town tomorrow afternoon," Flynn said. "Once they're gone, there goes whatever evidence may exist." He thought for a moment and looked directly at Liz. "Liz, can you give me an affidavit on everything you've learned and observed? This afternoon? Right now?"

Liz nodded.

Flynn held his breath. "Will there be anything in that affidavit that could come back to bite us? I remember some of the things you did to get evidence in Sally Kahn's death that a defense lawyer could have had a field day with."

"We may have one or two things to talk about privately, but I'm reasonably certain that everything I've told you is legally supportable. I got some advice on the subject this morning."

"Give me the keys to your car, Liz," Felicity said. "If Michelle's parents let me in, I'm likely to be here quite a while. I'll drop your car back at the sanitarium or the police station when I'm done."

A moment later, Felicity parked the Jaguar, then began the long walk up the driveway.

* * * * *

Liz went over the details of what she had seen and heard as she drove with Flynn to the Hardington police station.

"You could have given me a 'heads up', Liz," Flynn said.

"To say what?" Liz said. "That Whit Dakota likes to hit on the sharpest looking volunteers? I didn't have anything solid until a few hours ago. And then I called Felicity because that was more urgent."

"You said you 'got some advice' this morning," Flynn said. "Do I want to know what that's all about?"

Liz pondered the question. "I was afraid that at some point it might be my word against Whit's. I wanted to be certain that, if it came to 'he said she said', everyone would know I was right even if it wasn't admissible. The advice that I got was that if I ever wanted to be able to testify truthfully in court, that I shouldn't look at... anything I might have come into possession of. And I haven't. For all I know, I don't have anything."

The first affidavit took an hour. Liz acknowledged that she was a volunteer working on the temporary premises of Hammer and Saw Productions. Her statement said that she had been asked to provide photographs of certain volunteers and that, on Wednesday morning, she had seen in the video production trailer a portion of a video that showed one of those volunteers, an adult female, in a compromised position. She had also seen in the video trailer a DVD bearing the title 'Whit's Greatest Hits – Hardington'. In talking to the volunteer on Thursday, Liz became aware that the video had almost certainly not been made with the permission of the volunteer. Also on Thursday, Liz had been given a key to a

Winnebago used by Whit Dakota by the assistant to the Executive Producer of Hammer and Saw Productions. She had gone into the trailer for the purpose of finding handwriting samples of Whit Dakota and had noticed partially hidden cameras in one part of the trailer.

The second affidavit, detailing what she knew about the rape of Michelle Spencer, took only a few minutes.

"It's hearsay, Liz," Flynn said. "Michelle told her friend, her friend told you. I can't act on that and, if I did, it could get everything I collect as evidence tossed out."

"But you've done your own investigation that took you to Michelle's house," Liz said.

"And, had I spoken to Michelle, I could act on it," Flynn said. "As it is, I have reason, based on independent investigation, to believe that Whit Dakota took a minor child to his trailer on Sunday evening. I can look for evidence that he did so and, if I find it, then we've got a ball game. Your first affidavit gives me the hunting license I need. The second affidavit goes into a folder, but I'm not showing it to a judge tonight."

Flynn had a squad car drive Liz back to the sanitarium. He spent the next several hours marshalling resources. His first step was to meet with Chief Harding. After closing the door and giving him Michelle Spencer's name, Flynn extracted a promise that in all conversations, public and private, she would be known only as 'the girl' or 'the kid'.

"I think you'll want your dress blues tomorrow, Chief, but you may want to put them on over a Kevlar vest," Flynn said. "We're likely to arrest a murderer, but we're going to piss off a lot of people in the process."

"You finally think you know what happened," Chief Harding said.

Flynn nodded. "Sunday night, Whit Dakota put the moves on a fifteen-year-old girl, took her back to his trailer, and seduced her. About twelve-thirty – the same time Fred Terhune was killed –

Whit had his aide, Chip Gilman, drive the kid home. I believe that when we execute a search warrant on Whit's trailer and the production trailer, we'll find evidence of that seduction in the form of a video. Apparently, Whit has been bringing women back to his trailer every evening for a little entertainment. One of the perks of being the star of a television show is that you can make a souvenir copy of the encounter. Without the other person's knowledge, of course. If we find any video, we arrest Whit, the video engineer, and the assistant on roughly a dozen charges having to do with possession of pornography with intent to distribute. If we find video of the fifteen-year-old, we tack on rape, at least for Whit, and accessory charges for the other two."

"I didn't hear you solve Fred's murder in there," Chief Harding said.

Flynn measured his words. "It is impossible that one of the three, or maybe all three, don't know what happened with Fred. One of them is going to roll as soon as we offer a deal."

"What about Naylor?" Chief Harding asked.

"I haven't ruled him out," Flynn said. "He was there after eleven, the question is whether he was there an hour and a half later. I'm bringing him in for a formal statement after I get the search warrants issued. The question is why, if Naylor killed Terhune and one of the three Hammer and Saw people saw it happen, they wouldn't have come forward long before now."

"Maybe because one of them had just had sex with a minor," Chief Harding said. I think under those circumstances, I'd not want to call too much attention to myself."

"Maybe," Flynn said. Chief Harding, for once, made a very good point.

"Can we keep the girl out of the story?" Chief Harding asked. "I think the world of that family, and I don't want them hurt."

"That's why I'm not going in until tomorrow morning," Flynn said. "I need resources we don't have, but I also want the girl and the family clear of the story when and if it hits."

As he drove into Dedham, he called Ray Missoni, his one-time partner at the Boston Police Department. Missoni had been injured several years earlier and now ran a 'resources' unit, doling out scarce or expensive people or equipment. While police departments beyond Boston had no call on the unit and few knew of its existence, Flynn's status as Missoni's former partner, coupled with a reputation for asking only for what was needed, meant that a reasonable request would be met.

"Ray, I need the best computer guy you can find," Flynn said, and then outlined the search warrant that would be executed the following morning. "I assume it's all on a hard drive, all under encryption, all protected by passwords. We have to assume that any password we're offered will either send us to a dummy site or, worse, erase everything. This is state of the art, high-definition video stuff, and it looks like a couple of million bucks worth of editing equipment."

"You don't ask for much," Missoni said.

"This one is for a worthy cause," Flynn replied.

"And you need this at eight o'clock in the morning? I'll see what I can do."

Judge J. Penrod Toles of the Norfolk County Superior Court looked over the application. "Two affidavits, one of them your own," he said. "And for this, I'm going to let you go crashing in on a television star's private trailer and disrupt the show's production?"

"The work is being done a mile away, Your Honor, and both trailers are considered offices rather than living quarters," Flynn said.

"Well, you were right about searching that Russian woman's home a couple of months ago," Judge Toles said. "On the strength of that, I'll go out on a limb for you. Heaven help both of us if you're wrong. I'll have a lot more time for golf." He signed the papers.

The Norfolk County District Attorney's office was Flynn's last stop.

District Attorney Jack Brady was incredulous. "You expect us to get on board with this on the strength of one visit, twelve hours before you execute a search warrant?"

Flynn shrugged. "I'm handing you a high profile target on a platter. You have the option of ignoring it when I bring you the evidence."

"And if it blows up?"

"You get to say that I came in with insufficient cause for a search warrant and you begged me to reconsider," Flynn said. "You can say you threatened to have me fired and revoke my pension if I insisted on carrying out such a stupid search warrant. If I'm wrong, you can say anything you want, and you probably will. But the truth is, you're salivating at this and you're just pissed that I didn't bring you in from the start. Because this time tomorrow, you're going to have both a murderer in custody and a TV personality who loves to secretly film his one-night stands. And there's some small chance that the murderer and the TV guy are one and the same. And, just to make you bullet-proof on this, I'm not going to call you until I find something admissible. And then you can tell the *Globe* and the *Herald* that this whole thing was your idea."

"But you won't give me the name of the underage girl?"

"I didn't mention her to the judge," Flynn said. "She's not in the warrant. If she's not on the videos, we pursue it a different way. And if she is on the videos, we carve out that part of the case. There's a fifteen-year-old who is in a very fragile condition. Neither you nor I are going to do anything that would hurt her further."

* * * * *

Don Elwell was waiting for Liz when she got back to the Volunteer trailer, and Liz noted that Elwell studied her every move as she put down her purse and settled into her chair. It was just after five o'clock. A police car had driven her from the station after she gave her statement, and Liz at first feared she had been seen getting out of the vehicle.

"We've been worried about you," Elwell said. "We're also a little worried about getting done on time."

"I had an emergency," Liz said tersely. She began thumbing through messages.

"Our problem is that we're depending on you," Elwell said, studying Liz's body language. "I sent Barry down to our next location because you said you could handle everything. Instead, I've got three construction foremen nervous as cats because they don't know if they're going to have a full complement of people tonight."

"I'm back and the emergency is solved," Liz said, trying to put courage into her voice. "And I've got a crew of fifty to landscape tomorrow morning."

Elwell kept his eyes on Liz's face without speaking.

He's trying to find out if I know anything, she thought.

"Really, no more emergencies," Liz said. "From now until the reveal, I'm twenty-four-seven." She thought she struck just the right note of enthusiasm.

"Your cell phone was off," Elwell said. "We tried to reach you a couple of times."

Yes, of course it was off. I was giving a statement and trying to save a life that a couple of your people have screwed up royally, Liz thought.

"I have a life, Don," Liz said, allowing irritation to creep into her voice. *Think on your feet. Go on the offensive.* "I was dealing with something that was going on before you came to town and that will still be going on after you leave. And it meant I had to be gone from here for a few hours, and yes, it meant I even turned off my cell phone. But it's taken care of for the moment and you can be sure that I'm here until the end. I won't let you down."

She watched Elwell's face as she spoke. *He liked what he heard but he didn't buy it completely.*

"Liz, these are good people doing very good things that help other people," Elwell said. "It doesn't mean that I always approve of some of their shenanigans. They can be kind of sophomoric at times. And these are guys who are on the road twenty-two weeks a year with very few breaks."

Linda Harper, she thought. *Linda Harper was still angry and she went to Whit Dakota and said something. And she mentioned me and the bracelet and maybe even videos. And Whit went to Don Elwell. And they're worried that I've figured it out. And if they're worried, they may have erased everything electronic and shredded everything else. Oh, my God. I may have loused everything up.*

"Don, I'm thrilled to help out," Liz said, choosing words carefully. "And I recognize that these guys are on the road a long time. My husband is on the road probably ten months out of the year. But I *don't* appreciate being asked to set these guys up with dates. That's above and beyond the call of duty."

Elwell visibly relaxed somewhat. He said nothing, but it was clear his mind was working, matching Liz's words with the second- or third-hand report he has received.

"Do you think I can't see?" Liz said. She pointed out the back window of the trailer. "Or do you think I'm not here in the evening? Tuesday morning, I'm asked to take photos of eighteen women. Tuesday night, I watch Whit lead one of them into that trailer of his. Two hours later, she still hasn't come out. How do you think that makes me feel?"

The relief on Elwell's face was palpable.

"My husband is a temporary CEO for hire," Liz continued. "He has been in Pittsburgh on an assignment for going on six months. I see him weekends, if I'm really lucky. Put yourself in my shoes…"

"You wouldn't want someone out there trolling for a date for your husband," Elwell said, finishing Liz's sentence. The relief was complete. *Middle-aged, menopausal broad is afraid her husband is banging some secretary while he's on the road. And so she fixates on Whit and whatever volunteer White screwed, and sees Whit as her husband and the volunteer as the cupcake, and she decides to confront the volunteer because she can't confront the secretary her husband is banging out there in Pittsburgh. And she's angry because she set up the date.*

Elwell smiled. "Liz, I think I understand. And I'm going to apologize to you right now, and Whit is going to apologize to you tomorrow morning. He had no right to ask you to take those photos for him, or to do anything else other than coordinate volunteers. And I'll tell you one more thing. It stops here. From here on out, no volunteer coordinator or anyone else from the community is going to be asked to do anything personal for anyone on my staff."

Liz smiled back. *You're lying through your teeth, Don, but you sure do sound convincing.* "Thank you for understanding, Don."

He was getting up when there was a knock on the trailer door.

"Felicity!" Liz said.

"I was just dropping…" Felicity started to say. She was holding Liz's car keys. She saw Elwell and stopped, giving Liz a quizzical look.

"Felicity, this is Don Elwell," Liz said. "Don is the executive producer of *Ultimate House Makeover*. Don, this is Felicity Snipes. Her husband is Tom Snipes, who is going to be joining us tomorrow."

Elwell jumped to his feet and extended his hand, his conversation with Liz forgotten. "I was hoping I'd get to meet you! What a pleasure!"

Felicity didn't miss a beat. "We're just as excited, Mr. Elwell." As she said it, she gave her blonde hair a toss. The athlete's brainless but beautiful wife. *Play to the stereotype.* "Tom's just rarin' to go." A hint of a southern accent had appeared in her voice.

"Do you have a moment?" Elwell said. "I'd like you to meet the rest of the staff." *That crocodile smile,* Liz thought.

"Oooh, sorry, Mr. Elwell," Felicity said, putting her finger on her chin. "But I met most of them the other day when Tom played football with them over at the high school. That Whit Dakota is even cuter in person."

All she needs is some gum to snap and the picture is complete, Liz thought.

"Well, I'll leave you two girls to chat," Elwell said. He left the trailer.

Felicity said inane things until Elwell was out of sight.

"Quickly," Liz said.

"The first intervention went about as well…" Felicity said.

"Wait," Liz said. *Could Elwell have had the trailer bugged? If Joel Silverman could wire Whit's trailer for three cameras, a hidden wireless microphone was simple.* "Let's go outside. It's too stuffy in here."

When they were outside, Felicity said, "The parents have a huge hurdle to get over. They're just starting to grasp that screaming at Michelle when she came home exacerbated the problem. Michelle is fragile but stable for now. All I can tell you is that there's a lot of work to be done. What do you hear from Detective Flynn?"

"He's fully on board," Liz said. "He was getting a search warrant this afternoon. They're going in tomorrow morning with full electronics experts. And Michelle's name is never used. There isn't even a mention of a 'minor child' in the warrant. He thinks he can get one of the people here to cooperate in return for reduced charges, assuming he finds what he's looking for."

"I brought your car," Felicity said. "My housekeeper is waiting to drive me home."

"I guess I'm going to be here for a while," Liz said. "Elwell was suspicious about my confronting the volunteer I saw on the monitor. I think I explained it away by sounding like some cuckolded shrew, though I managed to set back the cause of women's rights by a decade or so in the process."

"Honey, we both played to our audience," Felicity said. "I'm from Oregon, but I learned a long time ago that nothing puts a stupid man at ease like a little southern sweetness and a hair toss.

That guy heard what he wanted to hear because he saw what he wanted to see."

Liz went back into the trailer and worked steadily for several hours, arranging both the evening work schedule which included a crew to lay sod, as well as the Friday contingent, which would require a total of nearly two hundred people. If anyone was listening in, they were hearing a dedicated volunteer doing her job.

Just after nine o'clock, Liz closed down her computer and turned off the lights in the trailer. It was then that she looked out the back window of the motor home. Thirty feet away, she saw the door open to Whit Dakota's Vectra, the lights from inside the motor home illuminating the area around the door. Dakota stood outside, stretching and turning his neck to get the aches out. Right behind him was Chip Gilman, saying something to Dakota. Dakota clapped Gilman on the shoulder and waved. Gilman turned left toward his trailer, Dakota went back into the Vectra and closed the door. In walking to his trailer, Gilman passed within a few feet of the window out which Liz looked.

In that moment, Liz understood why Fred Terhune had been killed, and she had a very good idea of who had killed him. She carefully went outside of the trailer and placed a phone call.

12.

Flynn sat across from George Naylor in the conference room of the Hardington police station.

"I need to clear up some discrepancies from our conversation yesterday," Flynn said.

"I refuse to talk to you until I have a lawyer," Naylor said.

"You have not been charged with any crime," Flynn said. "To the best of my knowledge, you don't have a lawyer, and the town isn't going to supply you with one. In the meantime, you're impeding an investigation into a murder."

"I want a lawyer," Naylor said. "It's my right and it's perfectly legal. I'm not obligated to talk to you."

"And it is my right to call…" Flynn flipped to an inside page of the *Grand Larceny – Las Vegas* book, "…Primrose Publishing and let them know that you are refusing to cooperate and thereby lessening our chances of catching a murderer. I don't know if that's going to affect whether they want you to keep writing *Siege of Stalingrad* but, as you point out, you aren't obligated to help me beyond what any citizen is supposed to do. You and Primrose can work out any reservations they have."

"You can't do that!" Naylor said, startled that Flynn had a copy of the book he had written.

"Of course I can," Flynn said. "It's my right. It is perfectly legal."

"What do you want to know?" Naylor asked sullenly.

"Why did you lie about not being at the party Sunday night?" Flynn pushed the photograph of Naylor standing in the shadows across the table.

Naylor stared at it. "I didn't tell you because I heard Fred Terhune was killed that night."

"And you thought no one would notice you were there?"

"I didn't know anyone," Naylor said.

"Well, there you go," Flynn said. "What time did you leave the party?"

"You apparently already know," Naylor said.

"Call it the truth-meter test," Flynn said.

"About eleven thirty," Naylor said.

"Tell me what you did between ten thirty and eleven thirty," Flynn said.

Naylor was silent for a moment. "I studied the layout of the place."

"Let's be more specific," Flynn said, and pushed across a photo of Whit Dakota with his arm around a woman. "Do you recognize this man?"

"He's the carpenter jerk on that television show. I've never watched it."

"You followed him?"

"I know where he went."

"And you followed Fred Terhune?"

"Yes."

"Who left the tent first, Whit Dakota or Fred Terhune?" Flynn asked.

"Terhune."

"So, when Terhune left the tent, there were still four or five women with this guy?" Flynn indicated Whit Dakota.

"Yeah," Naylor said. "Four or five."

"So you followed Terhune," Flynn said. "Where he did he go?"

"He went to a motor home," Naylor said. "It was marked 'Volunteers'. He went inside and started working on his computer."

"And you staked out the trailer?"

"For a little while. I thought he was just going for a few minutes."

"While you were watching the trailer, did you see this guy go by?" Flynn again indicated Dakota.

"Yeah," Naylor said. "About fifteen minutes later."

"And did he have anyone with him?"

"Two girls," Naylor said. "One of them went back, though. Didn't want to go into that guy – what's his name again?"

"Whit Dakota," Flynn said.

"Yeah. She didn't want to go into his motor home," Naylor said. "He just bagged one babe."

"Could you see Terhune all this time?"

"Yeah. He was plugging away at that computer."

"Did he see Dakota go into the trailer with the girl?"

"I have no idea," Naylor said, shaking his head.

"Did he react? Come out of the trailer?"

"No, just kept typing in stuff," Naylor said. "I know what it's like. You get into the zone."

"So you just kept watching Terhune," Flynn said.

"For a while, anyway."

"Just like it says to do in your game strategy guide," Flynn held up the book. "Watch them, keep to the shadows, see where they go because it may be important."

Naylor feigned nonchalance. "I never thought of it that way. But the guy owes me half a million."

"Owed, Mr. Naylor. Fred Terhune is dead and you're never going to collect. You also started parking outside his house every afternoon."

"You can't prove that," Naylor said.

"I have three of Fred Terhune's neighbors who can describe, in detail, the rust patterns on a 1998 Toyota Tercel. Do you want to reconsider?"

Naylor was silent.

"Do you have any way to prove that you were home between midnight and one o'clock?" Flynn asked.

"I went home and went to sleep."

"Did you see anyone, or did anyone see you at your apartment building?"

"They all go to bed at ten," Naylor sneered.

"So all I have is your word that you didn't hang around until one o'clock and kill Fred Terhune?" Flynn asked.

"I didn't kill him," Naylor said.

"Too bad you don't have an alibi," Flynn said.

Flynn took a statement from Naylor, focusing on Naylor's observation of Terhune and Whit Dakota. By nine o'clock, he was weary, hungry, and ready for rest.

The phone rang.

"John, I'm up at the sanitarium," Liz said. "You need to see this. Come quickly, but come quietly."

Five minutes later, he had parked at the sanitarium grounds and had made his way to the Volunteer trailer. He had expected the trailer to have all the lights on inside. Instead, there was only a desk lamp for illumination.

Liz was standing outside. She put a finger to her lips, asking him to be quiet. She indicated the desk inside the trailer.

"We're out here because there's a slim chance that there's a microphone inside that trailer," Liz said softly. "I want you to go inside and sit at my desk. It's where Fred Terhune was sitting Sunday night. He had worked for several hours updating his spreadsheet of volunteers. He's tired, it's after midnight. He prints out a final volunteer schedule, then shuts down his computer. I want you to just sit there for a few minutes and observe. But don't move from that chair until I come back and get you."

She held the box of signed photos and left the trailer. Flynn did as asked and watched the open door, also looking around the trailer to see if what he was to observe was inside the trailer.

About three minutes later, he saw a light and turned around to look out the window on the back side of the trailer. Liz and Chip Gilman were standing in the doorway of Whit Dakota's Vectra. The door was open and Dakota was looking at one of the photos.

He appeared to be smiling and nodding agreeably. Then he went back inside. Chip Gilman and Liz walked by the window from which he now peered, and Liz threw him a knowing glance. She handed Gilman the box of photos, said something, and Gilman went into his trailer.

In that moment, Flynn, too, realized why Fred Terhune had been killed. Terhune had looked out this window Sunday night and had seen Whit Dakota's door open and fifteen-year-old Michelle Spencer come out, followed by Dakota. As a selectman, Terhune certainly knew a family with as much money as the Spencers, and he would have known that Michelle was their daughter. With two daughters of his own, Terhune would have been aware of Michelle's age, either exactly or approximately. Terhune had watched as Dakota casually started making phone calls and handed off Michelle to a leering Chip Gilman.

Flynn believed Terhune would not have raced out of the trailer. He would have waited at least until Chip had driven Michelle away. It was the decent thing to do. But at some point after that, Terhune would have confronted Dakota and perhaps Gilman and Silverstein, the video recording engineer, if he had stayed in the video trailer to watch the live feed of Dakota's latest conquest.

Chip Gilman would have taken less than ten minutes to drive Michelle home and return. And Whit Dakota would have been in his trailer the whole time. Those three, and perhaps others, had been witnesses to the death of Fred Terhune.

Now, all he had to find out was which one of them had killed Fred Terhune. And, preferably, find a murder weapon.

He rose from the desk and went outside into the warm, humid night air, knowing that, once again, it had been Liz Phillips who was really the person who cracked the case.

13. Friday

The phone rang at six o'clock. Liz had been awake and outside for an hour, pulling weeds from deep within her perennial borders, trying to keep at bay the worry that something she had said to Don Elwell might have caused him to order all evidence destroyed. She also worried that going to Chip Gilman's trailer with the photos and asking that Whit 'approve' the forged signatures might have been taken as a sign by the production staff that she was unstable.

But mostly she replayed in her mind one minute from the night before. She thought about the kiss.

It had been innocent enough, she kept telling herself. When she was certain Chip Gilman was back in his trailer with the door closed, she walked around to the Volunteer trailer. Flynn was outside, visibly excited.

"You've done it, Liz!" he had said. "That's it! Now it all makes sense!" And he had reached out and pulled her toward him, then kissed her. It was only for a moment and could hardly have been described as romantic. But it was a kiss, on the lips, and it had feeling behind it. What she still could not determine was whether it was premeditated.

While the entire incident took just a few seconds, she had noted certain things. His body was warm, his body quivered as he held her. When he pulled away, he seemed not to have noticed what he had done, though she could think of nothing else. He had said other things, but she had no recollection of them. She remembered only the kiss and the embrace.

And, she worried.

She worried that, if Flynn had kissed her again when he walked her to her car, she would have eagerly returned the kiss. Had he embraced her and kissed her neck, she would have wrapped her own arms tightly around him and prayed it would last.

And she worried that the feeling was not just the excitement of the moment but, rather, something different. She worried that her feelings had crossed an invisible line into some new and uncharted territory.

The phone continued to ring.

She answered in her sleepiest voice.

It was David. He had not called last night.

"I'm sorry as hell for what I said on the phone yesterday morning," David said. "And I'm even more sorry for not understanding what my schedule does to you. And I want you to know that it's going to change."

"Change how?" Liz asked.

"For one thing, I'll be home tonight," David said. "For another, I'm going to wrap this thing up in the next forty days and, if it isn't wrapped up, I'll manage it from home."

"David, aren't you tired of always being on the road?"

"It's my job," he said. "It's how I make a living. But I wasn't thinking about how that affected you. I was thinking about myself."

"So, apart from my concerns, you're happy living out of a hotel room and seeing me on weekends?" It was a cheap shot, she knew, but she said it anyway.

"Liz, I'm meeting you more than half way. And I'm saying that things are going to change. Starting now."

"I miss you, David," she said simply.

"I miss you, too," he said. "And I love you."

The conversation was over. He had not asked about her plans for the day. He did not know that the police would raid the *Ultimate House Makeover* trailers in an hour and a half. He did not know that John Flynn had kissed her a few hours earlier.

And David did not know that she had felt the urge – however momentary and motivated by loneliness – to invite John Flynn back to their home and to their bed.

* * * * *

Flynn awakened in the fire department barracks to the smell of frying bacon. He had not gone home, he did not want to go home.

Nor had he slept much. He had felt this energized in perhaps a dozen cases over the course of his career. *I understand how and why you did it, and I am going to nail you, you son of a bitch.* Except that in this case, he still was not certain of who had wielded the murder weapon, nor did he know what the weapon was.

Most search warrants he had executed over the course of his long career were cut-and-dried affairs. He was looking for a gun, a bloody shirt, or a stack of money. In such cases, the only question was the exact place where, in a given domicile, the evidence being sought was hidden. On rare occasions, the perp had thought himself clever. The gun was under a floorboard, the money was concealed in a bag of dog kibble. But, once those items were found – and most perps did not think far enough ahead to hide such things away from their homes – the case was effectively over. A few days of paperwork and a consultation with a prosecutor working on a plea deal, and he was done.

The stupidity of murderers continually baffled Flynn. They killed with guns and did not take the logical step of throwing the gun off the Martha's Vineyard ferry. They killed with knives, but only rinsed the knives and put them back with the matching set of cutlery. They found themselves doused with the blood of their victim but could not bring themselves to part with their favorite leather jacket, even though it would be the means of sending them to prison for twenty years.

Flynn had been part of many 'headline' cases. He had handcuffed corporate executives and priests. He had collared politicians who found out they were not above the law. He had found the crucial evidence in multiple-homicide investigations. He had been, and was still, a very good detective.

He was confident that, by the end of today, he would have the solution to the murder of Fred Terhune. And, if he did his job well, he would have a confession in hand.

Thinking about all of these things this morning was a way of avoiding things in that swamp that was his personal life.

There had been that kiss.

And there had been that phone call.

He had not planned the kiss. He kept telling himself that. He had only known the elation of the *eureka* moment when he saw Liz, Chip Gilman and Whit Dakota in the pool of light. Even though he had not been the first to make the connection – Liz clearly had done so minutes earlier --Flynn felt the same excitement. When he saw Liz come around the corner, the smile of satisfaction on her face at having re-enacted what Fred Terhune had seen four nights earlier, he was overwhelmed.

He had embraced her out of joy, but in the moment of contact with her skin and her clothing, he had known instinctively that this embrace was, for him, something else. It was the desire to feel this woman in his arms.

He had kissed her, a clumsy, ill-aimed effort. It was on the lips, but everything else about it had been poorly executed. So it *had* to have been unplanned. You could not kiss a woman for the first time and do such a lousy job of it. And as soon as he kissed her he knew this was not the time, and so he pulled away. He had continued to talk to hide his embarrassment, ultimately walking Liz back to her car. She seemed not to hear him. She was likely trying to extricate herself from an uncomfortable situation.

He had sat in his car for several minutes, sorting out the emotions, laying the foundation for the execution of the search warrant.

And, while he was there, in his car, still feeling Liz's warmth against his body and her lips on his, his cell phone had rung. He wanted it to be Liz, he feared it might be Liz.

He looked at the Caller ID: an unfamiliar Hardington number. He answered the call.

"Since I'm no longer a suspect, I thought I'd be so bold as to issue an invitation, Detective Flynn." It was the low, throaty voice of Mary Ann Mandeville.

Flynn did not respond. He only stared at his phone.

"I believe you to be a man of passion, a man who longs to let go," Mary Ann had said with a voice that was almost a purr. "I also believe that passion of yours is frustrated. I believe that, like the very excellent wine I am holding in my hand right now, your emotions have been bottled up for a very long time."

He had listened, entranced, not knowing how to respond. "I would enjoy being the outlet for that passion, and I would return it in kind," she had said. "No commitments, no promises, no strings attached. Just a man, a woman, and a good bottle of wine. If not tonight, then soon. What do you say, Detective Flynn?"

He had not known what to say. He had murmured something like, 'not tonight,' and had been ready to end the call when she said, "Of course, if Liz Phillips is more your cup of tea, I'll understand. I'll be disappointed, but I'll understand."

And with that, she had hung up.

Jesus Christ, he had thought to himself. And he stared at his phone for many minutes.

Now, eight hours later, he showered, dressed, and joined the firemen for breakfast. They welcomed him because he had brought a bag of fruit and box of donuts after his last stay. They did not question why he was there. He made small talk as he waited for the time to come to execute the search. But he did not relax.

* * * * *

At 7:15, Liz was at the Cardozo home. She had been allowed to drive through the roadblock, she had passed buses loading at the elementary school. At the construction site, she could already count the twenty, first-shift volunteers from the garden club. Eva

Morin, on whom she had foisted the responsibility for selecting plants, was supervising the unloading of pallets of trees and shrubs from three nursery trucks.

"I feel redundant," Liz said to Eva. "You've got this under control."

Eva, a short, stocky woman in her 40's, wiped a trickle of sweat from under the brow of her hat. "I figured you still had your hands full with all these other volunteers."

And other things, Liz thought.

"Let me plant something," Liz said. "Otherwise I'll feel I let the club down."

Eva looked at her plot plan and the plant manifest. "All right, Liz, we have three mountain laurels going in over here. You're going to be my 'how to' person."

Eva shouted "Garden Club volunteers!" and waved her arm. Twenty people came immediately.

"We have eight hours to plant everything on this property," Eva shouted. "Some big strong people are going to help me move things to where we're going to plant them. But first, let's talk about how we plant."

She picked up a hydrangea and carried it to the correct corner of the house. From a can of crushed limestone, she made a circle in the topsoil twice the width of the container in which the mountain laurel's roots were encased.

"We dig a saucer. At the saucer's center, it's exactly as deep as the roots, no deeper."

Liz began digging. The topsoil, probably graded in the night before, moved easily.

"Position the plant, then come get me," Eva instructed the group. "We make certain that the plant is facing the proper direction." Eva rotated the plant ninety degrees. "We make certain the hole isn't too shallow and isn't too deep." She placed a yardstick across the undisturbed topsoil. The plant crown was just above the plane of the topsoil. "We don't add fertilizer – this is

August --and then we fill the saucer with the hose. When it soaks in, we refill the saucer with topsoil. Tamp the soil down gently with your hands so there no air pockets, and then soak the soil again."

Liz did as instructed, the crowd watching.

"Don't be afraid to get your hands muddy," Eva said. "Air pockets kill plants."

In twenty minutes, Liz had planted the hydrangea.

"Go," Eva said to the group. "Make this place beautiful."

Liz glanced at her watch. Seven forty.

Whit Dakota's Jeep came down the street, once again trailed by the camera crew. With his bullhorn, Dakota delivered an inspirational speech that this was the final day and that the Cardozo family would be arriving in Hardington at three. He got a rousing cheer.

Dakota made his way slowly into the house, stopping to say hello to people and offer encouragement. He was ebullient, friendly and charismatic. The men whose hands he shook smiled broadly. The old ladies whose cheeks he kissed beamed afterwards.

How do you reconcile the two Whit Dakotas? Liz thought as she watched him organize the people around him. *How can you have a man who is building a house for a family also be a man who forces himself on a teenage girl? How can a man who is famous and presumably wealthy, with access to thousands of eager women, need to do what he did?*

Satisfied that she had done something tangible to get the landscaping underway, Liz drove to the sanitarium and sorted through messages. Despite having worked until nine the previous evening, more requests had accumulated through the night. Dutifully, she began making calls. Just before eight o'clock, Don Elwell walked by the entrance to the trailer. She was on the phone and waved. He nodded and walked on.

Checking up on me, she thought.

Janey Matthews came by a few minutes later.

"Let's go over to the refreshment tent," Liz said.

Liz poured two glasses of lemonade. The tent was deserted. The crime scene tape was now gone. On this, the last day, there was no need for saws or planed wood. Everything was on site.

"I talked with Michelle this morning," Janey said. "The quarterback's wife went to see her, and last night, she went to a hospital."

"We need to know she's OK," Liz said. *And to check for diseases Whit may have passed on, pregnancy, and rape trauma*, she thought.

"The quarterback's wife, as you put it, is a doctor, and that's the way you need to think about her. Did Michelle get along with Doctor Snipes?" Liz asked.

"Michelle really likes the Patriots," Janey said. "Mizzus…. Doctor Snipes said she'd bring Michelle an autographed football today."

"Michelle is counting on you," Liz said. "She's going to need your friendship more than you can know. She also needs for you to not tell anyone."

"Is Whit Dakota going to get into trouble?" Janey asked.

"We're going to find out very soon," Liz said. "Janey, I have messages for you to take to the construction people. I want you to go down to the site, give them the messages, and then stay there. Some things are going to happen here that might make it hard for you to leave later. I promise I'll explain everything to you but, for now, you have to trust me that I'm doing what's best for you."

Janey nodded and took the messages. She drank the last of her lemonade and headed toward her bicycle. Janey looked back and waved as she pedaled down the sanitarium drive.

I remember Sarabeth on her bicycle, Liz thought. *I remember that innocence. But that is the past and you cannot freeze that moment in time. Children grow up and become adults. And when they become adults, they start making their own decisions and some of those decisions inevitably hurt you.*

Go to Cabo San Lucas for Christmas, Sarabeth. Go with my best wishes and build this new life of yours. I, too, have my life to live…

* * * * *

At a few minutes before nine, Flynn led a three-car convoy to the grounds of the former Hardington State Sanitarium. Chief Harding rode beside him, attired in his regulation captain's blues. In the back seat were Joe Lieberant and Karen Bowie, twenty-something computer experts from a data security firm in Cambridge. In the other two cars were five police officers, one of whom was Eddie Frankel.

They parked, and the policemen spread out to selected motor homes according to the diagram marked up days earlier by Frankel. Flynn and Chief Harding walked to Don Elwell's Winnebago. Sam Hirsch answered the knock at the door and looked quizzically at the two men and the other policemen fanning out.

"We need to see Mr. Elwell," Flynn said.

"He's tied up," Hirsch said. "Can I…"

Flynn walked into the trailer and saw Elwell talking on a phone.

"This is a warrant to search each of these motor homes," Flynn said, and handed Elwell the papers.

Elwell glanced at Flynn and then at the warrant. "I'll call you back," he said to the person on the other end of the phone and hung up.

"I need the keys for all trailers," Flynn said. "If I don't have them in thirty seconds, I will use a crowbar to open them."

"Get our lawyers in LA," Elwell said to Hirsch.

"What the hell are you looking for?" Elwell said to Flynn.

"Twenty seconds," Flynn said.

"Tell me what you're looking for and I'll see if we have it," Elwell said. "My God, you can't come in here and…"

"Ten seconds," Flynn said.

"We're wrapping today!" Elwell screamed. "You could destroy everything. We'll never get back on schedule. Who the hell do you think you people…"

Flynn went to the door of the Winnebago. "Use crowbars if the doors aren't open," he shouted. "Video trailer first. All occupants out of the trailers. No exceptions."

"Video trailer?" Hirsch said, and his eyes widened. He took out his flip phone walkie-talkie and pressed a button. "Joel, it's Sam…"

Flynn grabbed the phone from Hirsch's hand, clamped it shut, and put it in his pocket. "Mr. Hirsch, you can consider yourself under arrest for interfering with a police officer. I'm a little too busy to handcuff you but, if you leave the premises, I will add flight to avoid prosecution to the charges against you."

Flynn's radio beeped. "Video trailer secured. One occupant removed." It was Eddie Frankel's voice.

"Please tell our two guests to go to work," Flynn said into his mike.

"Please leave your trailers until we've finished our search," Flynn said to Elwell and Hirsch. "I must caution you, though, that this is going to be a very thorough search and we will likely be quite a while in executing it."

"Where the hell are our lawyers?" Elwell demanded of Hirsch as they walked out of the trailer.

"It's just six o'clock on the coast," Hirsch said. "No one is answering."

"Then call their goddam homes!" Elwell screamed.

Elwell stopped in the trailer entrance. He had been reading the warrant. "Electronically stored images and/or computer disks containing images of women recorded… My God, Whit, what the hell have you done?"

* * * * *

Liz saw the policemen go by. Two minutes later, a policeman she did not know knocked at the trailer door.

"Mrs. Phillips? Detective Flynn sends his regards," the policeman said, smiling. "We're getting everyone out of the Winnebagos, and I'm afraid that includes you. However, Detective

Flynn suggested you might want to join him over in that big trailer behind you. I think it belongs to Whit Dakota."

Liz went across the lawn to Dakota's Vectra. The door was open and she could see Flynn and another policeman inside. Nevertheless, she knocked on the door.

Flynn turned around and grinned. "Kind of close quarters, but you're welcome in here."

Flynn and the policeman were systematically opening drawers and examining their content, looking for disks.

"I'd love to stay, but I'm afraid I'd be in the way," Liz said. She was in the lounge area of the motor home. She remembered being impressed by the statues and awards on the shelves. She walked over to them, three People's Choice, two Emmys. Behind them were photos of Dakota on the day each was given, a wide, happy smile on his face. *Tools of seduction.*

Liz looked again at the awards.

"John, what did the medical examiner say about the murder weapon?" Liz asked.

"What?" Flynn turned to her.

"You described for me the indentation left in Fred's skull. Something metallic, maybe six inches across, an inch thick and tapered in, right?"

Flynn joined her in front of the awards. He looked at, but did not touch the Emmy awards.

Twelve inches high, resting on a round, metallic base, six inches in diameter and an inch high. Beveled in slightly.

Flynn pressed the button on his radio. "Eddie? John. I hope you brought the Luminol, because I think we may have found ourselves a murder weapon."

He turned to Liz and smiled. "Liz, for the sake of the prosecution's case, you were never in this trailer this morning."

* * * * *

It took six hours to thoroughly search the trailers. Alerted by Don Elwell, Whit Dakota and Chip Gilman came back to the site twenty minutes after the search began, Dakota screaming that the warrant was illegal and a product of fascist minds. Flynn assigned one officer to restrain Dakota, further slowing the search.

Chief Harding took the further step of sealing off the grounds, pulling two officers who had manned the roadblocks to prevent anyone from entering the sanitarium site. Anyone who walked in was asked to leave. Anyone already on the grounds was forbidden to leave. The production staff was confined to the food tent, out of sight of the search. Liz kept her distance from Elwell and his staff, remaining in one of the other tents. Policemen occasionally asked her questions about the function of specific motor homes, but her role became peripheral.

Luminol was sprayed on the Emmy awards. One of the awards showed no reaction. The other glowed blue, with traces of blood still visible in crevices.

"We have a murder weapon," Flynn said, quietly, to those in the trailer. "I think we're just about home." Under his breath, he added, "And perps never learn."

It took Lieberant and Bowie, the two computer experts, three hours to break the passwords and encryption key on the editing equipment but, when they did, it revealed several dozen hours of footage, including that of Michelle Spencer. Multiple disks labeled "Whit's Greatest Hits – Hardington" as well as other locales, were found in drawers and DVD players in several of the motor homes. Dakota had freely duplicated DVDs and given them to the production staff for entertainment.

Computers were seized to determine whether any of the DVDs had been copied onto hard drives, or whether any footage had been emailed or otherwise uploaded to the Internet.

Once the raw footage was found, Flynn called Jack Brady at the Norfolk County District Attorney's office. Brady was on site in twenty minutes, examining the disks and footage.

Liz, uncertain of her role, suggested Felicity Snipes be present. Flynn agreed.

"Is that Snipes like in Tom Snipes?" Brady asked. "He lives in Hardington."

"It's Snipes like in Dr. Felicity Snipes, PhD specializing adolescent psychology, with privileges at Newton/Wellesley and Brigham & Women's hospitals," Liz said. "She's treating the girl in the video."

Once Felicity arrived, the door to the trailer was closed and a portion of the unedited video was shown to those inside. There was complete quiet in the trailer, with everyone focused on the screen. In the video, Whit Dakota's coercion and Michelle's innocence were readily apparent to everyone. She was reluctant to be undressed by Dakota, who made occasional, self-conscious glances in the direction of the camera. Only his relentless insistence and flattery got her into bed.

"We've seen enough," Flynn said and asked that the video be stopped. "If this isn't sufficient, nothing is."

"I think it's enough to trade for a confession on the murder," Brady said. "A trade-off of second-degree murder for statutory rape and distribution of pornography."

"Why do you have to trade?" Flynn asked. "Why not go for the whole thing? We have a murder weapon…"

Brady cut him off. "And Dakota will say, 'Of course my fingerprints are on it, it belongs to me. I have no idea who may have come into my motor home and borrowed that award.' With a very good lawyer, we've got reasonable doubt."

"Then let's remove the reasonable doubt," Flynn said.

Brady looked at him, quizzically. "You have a plan?"

"Whoever killed Terhune wiped the blood off of the award, but they left enough for us to get a sample. I think it's a safe assumption that the blood on the award is going to match Terhune's," Flynn said. "Right now, only a handful of us know that we've ID'ed the murder weapon, and no one from the program has been allowed anywhere near these trailers. I say we put the award back where we found it. Then we give everyone access to the trailers for five minutes to 'gather their personal effects'. The killer or his accomplice is going to see that the evidence is still there, and they're going to do something with it – remove it, bury it, whatever. We observe. Whoever tampers with the evidence, we have our killer. No more 'reasonable doubt'."

"And how do we observe?" Brady asked.

"The same way Dakota did." Flynn turned to Lieberant and Bowie. "How fast could you rig one of the cameras in that trailer to keep watch on the area where the awards are kept?"

Lieberant looked at his watch. "Give me three minutes. We'll record the signal onto our own computer."

Flynn turned to Brady. "Do we need a new search warrant?"

Brady shook his head. "Everyone is aware that there are cameras in that motor home, so there's no expectation of privacy. But I'd advise you to go in as soon as there's tampering and get them in the act."

Flynn nodded. "Then this is our story: they're being taken in for questioning on the pornography, we expect to keep them several hours while we take their statements. Before we go to the station, they're welcome to freshen up and change clothes if they like. We tell them we're leaving in five minutes."

Everyone was in agreement. Lieberant and Bowie went to work.

* * * * *

At three o'clock, Chief Harding spoke to Don Elwell, Sam Hirsch, Whit Dakota, Chip Gilman, and Joel Silverstein in the food tent.

"We have gathered certain evidence that leads us to believe that one or more women may have been filmed without their consent in sexual acts, and that your facilities were used to edit and make copies of those films," Chief Harding said. "We believe that there may be additional evidence on the computer hard drives in the video trailer, and we have called in experts to try to help us."

Chief Harding cleared his throat. "We are taking you to the police station for questioning. I understand that several of you may have arranged for legal counsel during our questioning. We will leave here in five minutes. You should expect to be gone for at least three or four hours."

"The walk-through with the Cardozo family is supposed to be starting right now," Dakota said, holding out his watch arm. "Can't this wait two hours?"

"I've got a team of lawyers coming from LA," Elwell added. "They land at five o'clock local time and I'm not talking until they're here."

Chief Harding looked at Jack Brady. "Can we give him two hours?"

"No one else can do this walk-through?" Brady asked Dakota.

"Not and maintain the continuity," Dakota said. "I'll just need to change my shirt," he added.

"We ask you not to touch anything inside the motor homes," Chief Harding said. "Anyone else who needs to… do anything personal, be back here in five minutes or an officer will come in and get you."

The five *Ultimate House Makeover* people walked away briskly, each toward his own trailer.

On the other side of Whit Dakota's Vectra, Flynn squatted with Karen Bacon. Wordlessly, they watched on the laptop as Dakota entered the trailer. Dakota looked outside the front of the motor home to make certain he hadn't been followed. He went inside and locked the door; looked carefully around the lounge area and seemed to hesitate. Then, he hastily grabbed one of the Emmy awards, took it over to the galley sink, and turned on the water spigot.

"That's what I needed," Flynn said. He raced around the trailer to the entrance and opened the door.

"Whit Dakota, you are under arrest for the murder of Fred Terhune. You have the right to remain silent…"

As he did so, Dakota furiously turned the taps on the galley sink, not understanding why no water flowed from the taps. He also wondered how someone was able to enter his Vectra after he had activated the electronic lock.

Ten minutes earlier, Flynn had disconnected the water line and disabled the locks.

Flynn handcuffed Dakota and walked him back out of the trailer. The Emmy award was now in an evidence bag.

"You got a bonus," Bacon said as he came out. "Mr. Silverstein just attempted to erase the hard drives in the computers in the video trailer. Someone is going to have to break the news to him that it didn't work." Silverstein, too, was in handcuffs, being led by Officer Frankel.

* * * * *

The 'reveal' of the new Cardozo home began at three, as planned. Jenny and Mac Cardozo and their two children arrived in a limousine supplied by *Ultimate House Makeover*. When it pulled into the driveway of their home, they were met by Tom Snipes, starting quarterback of the New England Patriots, in full game-day uniform.

Before the Cardozos there stood a miracle. A week earlier, when they had left for Logan Airport, their fire-damaged, five-room Cape house had sagged, forlorn and abandoned. Now, on the same spot there was a magnificent ten-room Colonial. One wing housed a three-car garage with an au pair suite above it for the nurse who would likely be needed for Jackie Cardozo's care. A two-story sunroom was situated off the back of the house and a large deck provided space for outdoor dining.

Colorful flower baskets hung from the front porch and the deck. The landscaping was immaculate. And everything was hardy to Zone 5 or better.

Five hundred cheering Hardington residents were there to watch and to applaud. Liz stood next to Roland Evans-Jones. She had arrived only a few minutes before the Cardozos and so had only a brief opportunity to inspect the work done by the garden club. To her eye, everything was perfect.

"Liz, we've been hearing rumors all day," Roland said. "Whit Dakota disappeared almost as soon as he got here, and he hasn't been back. The sound and camera people have been as nervous as cats, and they don't seem to know what to do. No one is allowed up to the sanitarium and people keep saying there are police all over the place up there. Come on, tell me what's happening!"

Liz was uncertain what to say. "Let's just say that Tom Snipes' standing in for Whit is a good decision, and the last time I saw Whit, he was wearing some interesting wrist accessories."

"I may never speak to you again as long as I live," Roland said.

"Then ask me again in a few hours," Liz said.

* * * * *

Jack Brady put the deal on the table to the 'gang of five' as he called them.

"The first person who gives me all of the details of Fred Terhune's murder gets the charges knocked down to 'accessory after the fact' and gets a walk on the rape and pornography charges."

By the time Don Elwell's Los Angeles attorneys landed, found their way through Boston's rush hour traffic and reached Hardington, Chip Gilman had provided a full statement, with Flynn leading him through the process.

My name is Charles Gilman, Junior and I reside at 4265 Marina City Drive, Marina Del Rey, California. I am an associate producer for Hammer and Saw Productions, LLC of Beverly Hills, California.

On the evening of Sunday, August 12, I attended a reception hosted by my employer on the grounds of the former Hardington State Sanitarium. The reception was given to encourage volunteer participation in a homebuilding project undertaken by my employer. One of my informal duties as associate producer is to scout these receptions for attractive women volunteers on behalf of the program's producer, Whit Dakota. Mr. Dakota is also a senior vice president of Hammer and Saw Productions. I introduce these women to Mr.

Dakota over the course of the evening and it is Mr. Dakota's custom to have me relay to certain of them that Mr. Dakota would like to see them again later in the evening or over the course of the week we will be in a given location.

It is Mr. Dakota's practice to film the sexual encounters he has with these women. It is the production company's usual practice to park a series of motor homes at a locale adjacent to the construction site. In Hardington, the motor homes were parked on the lawn of the Hardington Sanitarium. The motor home provided by Hammer and Saw Productions to Mr. Dakota serves as his office and as sleeping quarters on those evenings when he expects to be at a home construction site either very late or very early.

This particular motor home has three cameras and a microphone in the bedroom, which provide a wireless audio and video feed to a production trailer that is also leased to Hammer and Saw Productions. The cameras were installed in February 2011 by Mr. Dakota and Joel Silverstein. Mr. Silverstein is Principal Video Engineer for Hammer and Saw Productions. To the best of my knowledge, none of Mr. Dakota's sexual partners have ever been aware that they were being filmed.

One of the duties assigned to Mr. Silverstein is to edit the footage obtained from the cameras into a series of erotic videos. While these videos are principally for Mr. Dakota's personal amusement, he also directs that copies be made of them, under the title, 'Whit's Greatest Hits.' I have delivered as many as ten copies of these videos to members of the production staff and have also FedExed or used the U.S. Mails to send copies to certain of Mr. Dakota's friends in California.

On the evening of Sunday, August 12, Mr. Dakota pointed out several women to me and asked that I introduce them to him. At about 10:30 p.m., Mr. Dakota escorted two of them to the motor coach I described earlier. One woman left without entering the motor home; the other went into the trailer with him.

When Mr. Dakota went into the motor coach with the woman, I went to my own motor coach and waited for his call. Mr. Dakota seldom spends the entire night with a woman, rather, he calls me after two to three hours and it is my responsibility to ensure that they get home safely.

I received a call from Mr. Dakota at approximately 12:30 a.m. informing me that the woman with him would require a ride to her home, about a mile away. I then escorted the woman home. At the time I left, I saw no other activity among the various motor coaches.

I returned less than ten minutes later. I found Mr. Dakota kneeling over the body of Fred Terhune. Mr. Terhune was known to me as the volunteer coordinator for the homebuilding project being undertaken by Hammer and Saw Productions in Hardington. Mr. Terhune and Mr. Dakota were at the exterior wall of the motor coach that serves as the office of the volunteer coordinator and another assistant producer. There were sprays of blood on Mr. Dakota's clothing as well as on his face.

I asked Mr. Dakota what had happened and he said that, a minute after I had left, Mr. Terhune had started banging on Mr. Dakota's door. Mr. Dakota told me that Mr. Terhune said to him that he knew both the woman whom Mr. Dakota had taken to his motor coach and the woman's family. Mr. Terhune said he was going to call the police because the woman was only fifteen years old.

Mr. Dakota told me that he attempted to reason with Mr. Terhune, but that Mr. Terhune would not listen. Mr. Terhune started back for the motor coach in which he had been working, which is adjacent to that of Mr. Dakota. Mr. Dakota told me, "I had to stop him."

Mr. Terhune was still alive though unconscious and bleeding heavily when I arrived. Mr. Dakota held an Emmy Award in his right hand, and the award was covered in blood.

Mr. Dakota said, "We need to get him out of here," and I asked if we should call for an ambulance. Mr. Dakota replied, "And tell them what?" He then instructed me to grab Mr. Terhune under his arms, and we dragged Mr. Terhune about 50 feet to a point behind one of the construction foremen's office.

Mr. Dakota then said that we should carry Mr. Terhune to the campus of the sanitarium, which he said were all abandoned buildings. Mr. Dakota said, "He could be there for weeks before anyone finds him." He instructed me to stay with Mr. Terhune while he scouted the path to the sanitarium campus. He was gone about ten minutes. When he returned, he said that a security patrol was parked by the tractor-trailer that contained the power and construction tools that the show carries, and that we could not carry Mr. Terhune to the sanitarium grounds without being observed by the security patrol. He said he was worried that the security patrol likely made an hourly round of the tents and motor homes, and that we had less than ten minutes to do something.

Mr. Dakota then went off for another five minutes looking for a location. During this time, I reached down to feel Mr. Terhune's pulse, and discovered that he had died sometime in the previous few minutes. Upon Mr. Dakota's return, I informed him of this and he said, "Well, that's one less thing we have to worry about."

Mr. Dakota then said that we should drag the body to the refreshment tent nearest to the parking area. He had found a large crate that was brought by the tent rental company, and that Mr. Terhune's body would fit easily inside of it. He said, "It may only buy us a couple of hours, but it will give us time to get our stories straight."

We then dragged Mr. Terhune to the tent and placed his body in the crate. Mr. Dakota wiped the crate in case either of our prints were on it.

We then returned to where I had first found Mr. Dakota with Mr. Terhune. There was blood on the exterior wall of the motor coach and Mr. Dakota instructed me to get a rag and a bucket of water and wipe down the wall, which I did. I then helped Mr. Dakota move several boxes and tarpaulins over the area where I had first seen Mr. Terhune.

We went into Mr. Dakota's trailer, where he placed several items of clothing including a shirt, pants, socks, and a pair of shoes in a black plastic trash bag. I do not know what became of that bag. Mr. Dakota then rinsed his Emmy Award in the sink and wiped it with a cloth, which also went into the trash bag.

Mr. Dakota instructed me to go get Joel Silverstein, who was in the bedroom of the video trailer. When Mr. Silverstein arrived, Mr. Dakota told us that he had "saved us". "I couldn't let Terhune go to the police," he said. "He would have made trouble for all of us." And he looked at both of us and said, "Elwell would fire your asses in a heartbeat the minute Terhune filed a complaint. So, what I did, I did for all of us."

He said Terhune had told him, *"I know this girl. She's barely fifteen. She babysits for my daughters."* Mr. Dakota said he told Mr. Terhune in response that the girl had told him she was nineteen. Mr. Dakota said Mr. Terhune replied that he was a lawyer, but that he would let the police decide whether the charge was aggravated rape or indecent sexual assault of a minor.

Mr. Dakota said, *"Terhune was going back to the trailer to get his phone. I stopped him from calling the only way I could be certain he wouldn't change his mind."*

Mr. Dakota then asked that we keep silent about what had happened. He said, *"This is a small town and small town cops don't know their ass from a hole in the ground. By the time they're gearing up to investigate, we'll be long gone."*

To the best of my knowledge, no other member of the Hammer and Saw Productions staff knew the truth of what had happened to Mr. Terhune. At no time was I ever asked by any senior member of the production staff if I knew what had happened. I stress that Mr. Donald Elwell, in particular had no knowledge of the events of the evening, and he never questioned me about it. I have never distributed one of 'Whit's Greatest Hits' to Mr. Elwell.

This is a truthful account of the events of the evening of August 12 and the early morning hours of August 13. I have given this affidavit of my own free will.

Charles Gilman, Jr.
Hardington, Massachusetts
August 17, 2012

Epilogue

Once the five suspects were brought to the Hardington police station, word quickly spread that something else important was unfolding along with the unveiling of the Cardozo home. By late afternoon, a crowd had gathered at the station, just as it had gathered earlier at the Cardozo residence. At nine o'clock, well in time for the late television news and the home delivery editions of the Boston newspapers, Chief Amos Harding and Norfolk County District Attorney Jack Brady held a press conference outside of the police station.

They announced that Whitney "Whit" Dakota, 37, of Los Angeles, California, had been arrested in connection with the murder of Frederick Terhune, a Hardington town selectman who also served as volunteer coordinator for the *Ultimate House Makeover* program. Also arrested as accessories were Charles Gilman, an assistant producer of the program, and Joel Silverstein, a production engineer. The three would be held at the Norfolk County Jail in Dedham pending arraignment.

Jack Brady added that, in the course of the murder investigation, police and the district attorney's office had uncovered evidence that volunteers working on the construction of the home had been surreptitiously filmed in what he termed, 'sex acts', and that facilities of the production company that owned *Ultimate House Makeover* were used in the filming, editing and duplication of videos. There was evidence, Mr. Brady said, that Fred Terhune's death may have been linked to his discovery of this activity, as he had extensive access to the facility as part of his duties as volunteer coordinator.

Three additional members of the Hammer and Saw Productions staff, including its president, Donald Elwell, were being held pending investigation into the latter matter.

Whit Dakota's 'perp walk' made the front pages of newspapers and was television news across the country. Thus, for the second time in two months, Hardington was the dateline of numerous stories relating to a murder, although this time, the tabloid and celebrity website headlines continued for several months. Large sums were offered for any videos that might exist. While 'Whit's Greatest Hits' from other cities did eventually surface, none that could be authenticated were ever found for Hardington.

The network that aired *Ultimate House Makeover* cancelled the program before the scheduled airing of the first episode of the season, citing violation of multiple clauses of the contract between the network and Hammer and Saw Productions.

Michelle Spencer did not return to Hardington Middle School in September. She was, instead, enrolled in a private academy in Wellesley, Massachusetts, specializing in the treatment of young women who have experienced or dealt with post-traumatic stress disorder. She continues to be under the direct care of Dr. Felicity Snipes, with whom she has formed a close bond.

Liz Phillips, who was known to have been at the Hardington Sanitarium site during the search for evidence and the arrest of members of the Hammer and Saw Productions staff, became an object of press interest. On the morning after Brady's press conference, she and her husband flew to Seattle to be with their daughter. She would not return to Hardington for three weeks, dividing her time between Seattle and Pittsburgh. By that time, the media had moved on to new scandals.

* * * * *

A month after the arrests, Chief Amos Harding assembled all members of the Hardington Police Department in the bullpen of the police station. Also present was Liz Phillips, president of the Hardington Garden Club.

"I guess everyone here has already heard the news that the grand jury up in Dedham indicted Whit Dakota for second-degree murder yesterday morning," Chief Harding began. "You probably also heard that part of the indictment was 'sealed' and part of it was 'unsealed.'"

"What that means is that the grand jury actually handed up a couple of indictments," Chief Harding continued. "The one we know about is the murder charge. That's the 'unsealed' part of the indictment. We don't know specifically what's in the rest of it – the 'sealed' part -- though it probably has something to do with that video business. Unless the judge unseals it, we may never know. And, we don't even know if it's one indictment or a couple of them."

The chief cleared his throat. "This town and this department have taken an awful lot of knocks over the past couple of weeks, courtesy of Mr. Dakota's lawyers. We all know those lawyers proclaimed his innocence, and that his rights were violated fifteen ways from Sunday by us and by the district attorney, Mr. Brady. They said our search warrants were illegal, the statement we got from Mr. Gilman was coerced, and that we engaged in illegal surveillance. Of course, when that happens, all we can do is keep our mouth shut and let the evidence speak for itself. It's a shame that the television stations and the newspapers report that stuff, but I guess that's part of being 'innocent until proved guilty'."

"We know we ran a clean investigation. We know we did everything by the book. I guess we also know that when a suspect is facing the kind of trouble Whit Dakota is facing, you throw up as much smoke and dust as you can and see if you can sneak out the side door. Those lawyers were especially hard on me and on Detective Flynn. I can't speak for John Flynn, but my wife was extremely upset by what was said about me. I think everyone in this room knows the truth."

The chief ran his finger down a sheet of paper. "I called everyone together this afternoon for two reasons. The first one concerns Liz Phillips, which is why she's here. She's asked me to pass along her thanks to all of you; especially those who pulled duty at the end of her driveway when the media feeding frenzy was at its peak even though she wasn't there."

"Well, starting Monday morning, you're going to see a garden get put in here at the station. I think most of you remember that the Snipes family paid for it out of their foundation. Well, the plans are all done and approved, and starting Monday, a backhoe starts pulling out those ratty bushes along the building. If the garden that gets put in is half as nice as the drawings, we're going to have the finest garden of its type anywhere in New England."

Chief Harding looked at his watch. "It's four o'clock, so I can tell you the other piece of the news because it's being released right now by the district attorney over in Dedham."

"When I said that part of that indictment was sealed, that just means that it isn't made public. The people that get indicted certainly get to see it, and they get to ponder what happens to them if the stuff in that sealed part of the indictment gets out into the public, or is discussed at trial."

"Well, whatever was in that sealed part of the indictment must have been something else, because this afternoon, Whit Dakota changed his plea to 'no contest' on a second-degree murder charge and he's struck a deal with the DA. He's going to prison for a couple of years at least. There's some other, lawyer stuff that's being done but the upshot is that no one is going to question but that this department did everything right. In fact, part of the plea deal is that Mr. Dakota specifically recants any statements made since his indictment related to the investigation, and that he now says what we did was 'fair and thorough'."

Chief Harding coughed. "None of that is going to bring back Fred Terhune. I knew Fred from the time he was a boy. He was good people, and he came from a good family. In fact, he was the best kind of people, giving of himself in service to the community. He got killed because he volunteered to help a family in need."

* * * * *

Following the meeting, Liz left the police station to drive home. Before she did, she found and spoke with Flynn in a corner of the squad room. Anyone observing, or even overhearing the conversation would have found it ordinary and would have thought it unmemorable. And, in fact, what was said was not important. What an observer might have remembered was that, as she left, Flynn took her hand and held it with both of his own. The two of them stood that way for several seconds before parting.

Acknowledgements

Writing mysteries is hard. Writing mysteries with all the plot points and facts straight is much harder. *Murder for a Worthy Cause* required expert assistance in a number of areas. First, I need to thank Medfield Selectman Osler (Pete) Peterson for reviewing and commenting on an early draft of this story. I will also emphasize that he is *not* the model for Fred Terhune.

Thanks also go to the staff of Millbrook Homes for explaining the nuts and bolts of modular home construction and the staff of Westchester Modular Homes for allowing me to tour their factory and see first-hand how it's done.

My profound appreciation goes to Dr. Lori Waresmith, who provided the psychology that underlies Michelle Spencer's story. If anything about Felicity Snipes' diagnosis, intervention, or treatment is incorrect, it is only because I failed to completely follow Lori's guidance.

Proofreading is one of my many failings. Fortunately, I know people who have a gift for spotting spelling and syntax errors and one of them is Faith Clunie. My wife, Betty Sanders, has an eye for detail and for how people (and especially women) speak and think. This story bears her strong imprint.

Both this book and *A Murder in the Garden Club* have striking covers that are the work of Lynne Schulte of Georgetown, MA (www.LynneSchulte.com). I sometimes suspect that people buy my books as much for her eye-catching artwork as for the story inside.

The book's dedication is to Dorothy Jasiecki. More than any other individual, I can say she is the reason I am a writer. Through my three years at Miami Springs High School, she was the teacher who inspired us to dream.

'Hardington' is a figment of my imagination, a pastiche of elements from many New England towns. 'Taylor's Department Store', however, is plucked directly from my own Medfield. Like its fictional *doppelganger*, Lord's Department Store is the soul of the community and, this year, Lord's lost its patriarch of seventy-plus years, Bill Kelly. Lord's was one of the first outlets for my writing. His passing is a loss to the town and to everyone who knew him.

* * * * *

A growing number of book clubs, libraries, book stores, senior centers and now garden clubs have had me as their guest. I am honored for the opportunity to tell my stories and meet readers. I am not getting even remotely jaded; it is still a thrill. Please keep the invitations coming.

14338969R00146

Made in the USA
Charleston, SC
06 September 2012